"You through?"

"That's about it."

"Good. You can quit worrying about Reed."

"Oh, he's here? Good. When did he turn up?"

"Just a few minutes ago."

"Where'd he been?"

"In the house." Hen took a deep breath and straightened up, arching his back until it popped. He jerked his head to indicate the man on his knees behind the hydrangea. "Wallace found him."

★

DEATH AND THE EASTER BUNNY

LINDA BERRY

WORLDWIDE.

TORONTO • NEW YORK • LONDON
AMSTERDAM • PARIS • SYDNEY • HAMBURG
STOCKHOLM • ATHENS • TOKYO • MILAN
MADRID • WARSAW • BUDAPEST • AUCKLAND

DEATH AND THE EASTER BUNNY

A Worldwide Mystery/November 1999

First published by Write Way Publishing, Inc.

ISBN 0-373-26326-0

Visit us at www.worldwidemystery.com

Printed in U.S.A.

Acknowledgments

I must thank some of the people who have helped and encouraged me in all of my writing, and life in general: Denver Women's Press Club members Barbara Fleming, Nancy Peterson and Betty Swords; my cousin Johnny Shuman, who's been policin' in south Georgia for quite a while, and inspired (but is not exactly) Henry Huckabee; and, of course, Jerry Berry, without whom I cannot imagine myself, much less the people and events in Ogeechee.

ONE

I WAS RUNNING from a group of drunken deer hunters who had mistaken me for a buck. I was the buck, panicked, bounding for cover, bounding for safety, bounding over a precipice. I woke from the nightmare when the buck's death screams became silent screams I couldn't force through paralyzed lips, became the whoop of sirens, fire sirens cutting through the Georgia night.

It's been six years since my husband, Zach, was killed on that hunting trip and I started having that nightmare. Usually, now, it only comes when I'm upset or worried, not just out of the blue like it used to, and I don't spend nearly as much time as I used to, asleep or awake, dreaming that if I'd been there I'd have been able to make a difference in the way things came out.

Shivering, I focused on the reality of the sirens, letting the dream recede behind the mental exercise of following the whoops through the town. The sound seemed to come nearer, then recede, falling silent on the other side of 280, I guessed, and a little east. I visualized each house in the neighborhood near the elementary school. Naturally, in my mental picture, none of the houses was on fire. I knew I wasn't going to fall asleep again, so I rolled out of bed. The luminous clock on my bedside table said 11:40. Still groggy, half-in and half-out of my dream, I pulled on a pair of jeans and a shirt, and moved quietly down the hall to the kitchen, my sneakers tucked under my arm. It's a habit I formed for Grandma's sake and can't seem to break even with her gone.

I put some coffee powder in a mug, added water, and stuck it in the microwave. While I waited for it to heat, I dialed the phone and sat down on a kitchen chair to put my shoes on.

The calm, deep voice of Brenda Whitson, the night dispatcher, said, "Ogeechee Police Department. What can we do for you?" Brenda's rich, smoky voice has a calming effect on the excited folks who have a reason to call the police in the middle of the night. Some people like her approach so much they call any time they have trouble sleeping. Ogeechee's Chief of Police, Henry Huckabee, my cousin Hen, calls it Brenda's All Night Talk Show.

"Brenda, this is Trudy."

"Trudy, what you doin' up? Aren't you coming off days?" Our day shift is 4:30 a.m. to 4:30 p.m., which is more day than night and puts 11:40 PM right in the middle of sleepytime. It would be death on a social life, if there were such a thing in Ogeechee.

"I did, and I was catching z's trying to get my clock re-organized for a few days of normal life, but the sirens are making too much noise for me to sleep. Where's the fire?" The fire department is all volunteer, so the police dispatcher takes fire calls, forwarding them as necessary.

"Six-seventeen Palm."

"Six-seventeen. Isn't that—"

"Mm-hmm. You've got a good memory. The old CCC."

"Uh-oh." The picture I had now was of a small, squarish frame house in bad need of a coat of paint and some yard work. I didn't have to ask who lived there. A few months earlier Reed Ritter had made a complaint about some vandalism, and I had been the officer in charge of looking into it.

The only thing even mildly dangerous, or mildly interesting, about that investigation had been wondering when or if one of Reed's piles of old newspapers or stacks of used TV dinner trays might fall over on me. Hen likes to save assignments like this for me, rather than putting—or wasting—one of the men on it.

The vandalism had taken the form of the kind of thing boys at a certain age think proves something about how smart they are, or how tough or independent—eggs thrown against the house, porch lights broken out, and the real *pièce de résistance*, piles of dog poop just outside both doors.

Except for the clue that the perpetrator(s) must have owned or had access to several dogs, the investigation hadn't turned up anything. The rest of the police department with great wit and originality referred to it as Trudy's CCC, my Canine Crap Case.

"Yeah. The Chief's gone over," Brenda said.

"Why'd you call him?" The microwave pinged and I took out the boiling coffee.

"He was still here finishing some paperwork when the call came in."

"The man never sleeps. Okay. Thanks, Bren. I'm awake now, so I guess I'll go take a look. You go on back to sleep, now."

Brenda chuckled. "Yes'm. I'll try to fit in a nap between takin' requests from my fans."

I picked up my coffee mug and made my way out, stepping carefully around the cats who had made themselves a living minefield all over the glassed-in porch. I headed for town, enjoying the fresh air, and drove through the stoplight where the east-west highway, 280, goes by the name of Court Street and the north-south highway is Main Street. I turned left past the post office and a few blocks later saw the fire engines. I swung my car across the street half a block from where smoke was pouring from the house at 617 Palm. Sparks and steam and billowing smoke made a hellish pattern against the night sky.

Three men stood near where I stopped, hands in pockets, quietly critiquing the fire and the performance of the firefighters. I waved.

"Hey, Trudy," one of the men greeted me softly, as though speaking out loud might disturb the neighborhood even more.

Nearer the fire, a couple of boys who looked to be about seven or eight years old were crouched behind a lush hydrangea, presumably under the illusion the heavy pink blooms made them invisible. I didn't wave at them. Why spoil it? ·

Directly across the street from the fire, Miss Sarah Kennedy, swaddled in a purple velour housecoat, watched from the comfort of a wicker porch rocker as the volunteer firemen in their yellow bunker suits moved with hurried purpose. The crackle of the flames was punctuated by the hiss of water and the calls of the men who were wrestling hoses into position.

I joined Miss Sarah, sitting on the porch and leaning against the wooden rail at the top of the steps. Her gaze flickered just enough to acknowledge my company, then returned to the scene across the street.

"That old place was doomed from the first spark," she said in the commanding voice I remembered so well from tenth grade American History, when she had been known in my circle as The Terror of Ogeechee High School.

The "old place" was decades younger than Miss Sarah's own, probably built in the early 'fifties. It had even been a reasonably nice place not too long ago, before Reed let it run down.

"I don't see Reed," I said.

"No, I haven't seen him, either," Miss Sarah said.

"Wouldn't he be home this time of night?"

"He usually is, but his car's not here."

As part of the investigation of the CCC, I had talked with Miss Sarah. We had sat in her living room drinking iced tea, our chairs positioned so that we both had a view of Reed's house through the tall windows. I liked the fact that she hadn't bothered to pretend she didn't keep an eye on Reed's house, but of course we didn't get right down to talking about Reed. First we had to talk about how I liked being back in Ogeechee and how my job was working out, working for Hen and all. Those are both topics I try to avoid, since in the first place bad-mouthing somebody's home town, even if it also happens to be your own, is generally considered rude, and in the second place there are a lot of people in Ogeechee who think Henry Huckabee hung the moon, and as far as I know Miss Sarah is one of them.

Childhood training being what it is, I couldn't quite lie to Miss Sarah, but my answers to her questions must have been unenthusiastic enough to give her a hint. She changed the subject on her own.

"Poor boy," she said, meaning Reed. Reed was thirty-five years old but to Miss Sarah he'd always be a high school student with promise, as all her students had been. No matter that his marriage had dissolved messily, he lived in a place a goat couldn't stomach, and he had a job only at the whim of his ex-father-in-law. All that just meant the promise was still to be fulfilled. "Poor boy. He doesn't need all this nonsense."

As if anybody did, but I knew what she meant.

"Do you know who's been messing up his place?" I asked.

"I have a notion."

"Do you want to tell me? I could have a talk with him. Them?"

"It's pretty definitely 'them,' but I'm not sure and I wouldn't want to have the police scaring the daylights out of the wrong boys." I might as well have argued with her over whether she would turn in those high-spirited hooligans who threw the tea into Boston Harbor.

"I'm glad you think I'm scary," I had said. "Hen isn't convinced."

"Oh, I wouldn't worry much about Hen. He's always been tractable."

If I was drawing up a list of words to use to describe Hen, "tractable" would come way down, somewhere after "stubborn," "chauvinistic," "spoiled," "tough," "hard-headed," and, okay, "strong," "smart," and even, when he feels like it, "entertaining." 'Tractable" might not make the list at all, but I decided to remember it and try it out on him sometime.

"So you don't want to tell me?" I asked Miss Sarah then.

"No, not right now. But when I do get ready to tattle, you'll be the one I tell."

And that had been that. The investigation languished and the vandalism, for all I knew, continued to thrive. But, I did know for sure that Reed had quit calling the police about it.

Now, on this April night, sitting with Miss Sarah on her porch and watching the fire, I thought about that earlier talk. "Did you ever find out for sure who was bothering Reed?" I asked.

"Not for sure." But as she spoke her eyes cut over to the hydrangea bushes and she seemed to have a worried, thoughtful look. "You know, Trudy, it's pretty late for boys that young to be out."

I followed her gaze, but couldn't see them clearly. "Who are they? Do they live around here?"

"No."

Hm. I stood up and stretched, very casually. "Excuse me, Miss Sarah. I'll go see about them." I started strolling in the direction of my car, then angled toward the hydrangea.

Hen's voice interrupted my sidelong advance on the more-or-less alleged vandals. "Hey there, Deputy Roundtree." Actually, what he said was more like "Deppity." He can speak English as well as anybody and he has a law degree, but he likes to act like a hick and give people a chance to underestimate him. His blue uniform shirt was a little rumpled, his thinning blond hair was in disarray, and his chin showed a faint shiny stubble, but the long day he'd put in didn't affect his innately irritating manner.

He hitched up his britches and nodded toward my car crosswise in the street. "I suppose the idea is to keep traffic back out of the way?"

The only traffic since I arrived had been a couple of dogs and one slow-moving car that had turned off two blocks away. I hitched up my britches in return and grinned at him. He hates being reminded that his belly is beginning to force his britches into a position where they need to be hitched. "I saw it on *Kojak* when I was at an impressionable age," I told him. "Didn't see what it could hurt."

"Unless some citizen runs into your car, not expecting it. Miz Wolters down at the corner doesn't look where she's going anymore, figures people can look out for her for a change."

"She ought to be in bed asleep by now. Bad fire," I added.

"Uh-huh."

"Where's Reed?"

"No telling. Haven't seen him. His car's not here. Gonna be a blow to him when he does come home. Won't be much worth saving."

"From what I remember, there wasn't much in there worth saving even without a fire," I said. "Beats me how he ever noticed a little vandalism. Hen, I swear he hadn't swept the floor or thrown out a newspaper since Rhett walked out on Scarlett."

Hen watched the fire, rubbing at his throat with the back of his hand as though gauging the length of his whiskers. "Looks like they've about got it under control," he said.

"Maybe I'll cruise a little and see if I can find Reed," I suggested.

"Good idea. Be a shame for him to stumble up on this without any warning. He drives a pre-divorce Chrysler, about a 'ninety-three. Red."

As if I wouldn't know what kind of car Reed drove. But I let it pass. "Okay. I'll go look. And Hen? Can you tell who that is?" I nodded toward the hydrangea.

He squinted in the light of the fire. "Looks like Dawsons. Daniel and David are about that size. What in the world are they doing way over here this late?"

"Slumming?" The Dawsons are the town's rich folks. Just coincidentally, Daniel and David's Aunt Vivi used to be married to Reed Ritter.

Hen snorted and stared thoughtfully at the hydrangea.

"I'll give them a ride home," I said.

"They won't appreciate it much."

"No," I agreed. "But their parents might. See you later."

Hen turned his attention back to the fire and I went to extend my invitation to the boys, but by the time I reached their hiding place they were gone. Well, they'd found their way here, I guessed they could find their way back. I tried to decide where to start looking for Reed. There wouldn't be too many options in Ogeechee this time of night.

When I came back to Ogeechee from Atlanta a couple of years ago I'd taken a fresh look at the town and been surprised to see how little it had changed in my lifetime.

Thirty years in Atlanta had seen suburbs pop up like chigger bites, superhighways writhe around the edges like nightcrawlers, and the construction of a knock-'em-dead airport that Aunt Lulu compares to Disney World, but there'd been no reason for Ogeechee to change much. It's too far from Savannah for the land developers to be after it, and nobody has discovered gold or oil nearby. Ogeechee is in one of the four counties that can grow honest-to-god Vidalia onions, so the economy picked up a little when they got to be popular, but that boom was really more like a rat-a-tat-tat. A dress shop opened up a few years ago, but it didn't thrive since people were already in the habit of driving someplace where they could have some choices. There are still only two grocery stores, if you don't count the four newish mini-markets on the outlying arms of the highways. There are no more than a dozen places to "eat out," and to get up to that you have to include Kathi's Koffee Kup and the Daytime Deli, which is only open for lunch and caters mostly to people who have courthouse business. The same five churches—two Baptist (Missionary and Southern), one United Methodist, one Church of God, and the Abundant Light Pentecostal Holiness—still hold their ground, but the last time one of them (the Southern Baptist) had a Together We Build campaign was when I was in seventh grade.

I decided to cruise the outskirts, so back at Main Street

I turned left, driving south toward the edge of town to look in the parking lots at the Twilight Inn and the Jive Joint, wondering as I drove if Vivi Dawson, the ex-Mrs. Reed Ritter, would have been petty enough to put her nephews up to the vandalism that had been perpetrated on Reed Ritter's property, and if it had gotten out of hand. It sounded a little childish for Vivi, Miss I'm-Rich-and-You-Aren't, but you never know.

Circling around behind the Twilight Inn, I came up on a group of young people huddled around a rusty old Pontiac Catalina that I knew could outrun any horsepower the town owned. I recognized Half Pint Conroy and his big brother Pint. I had been disappointed to learn that the rest of the large Conroy family weren't measurements—say Tablespoon or Liter—but a series of botanical names of which Wisteria was the most ordinary. Mrs. Conroy was apparently an old-fashioned kind of woman with interests that centered around children, canning, and gardening.

The last time I'd seen Pint was over at the courthouse where I watched with interest as Judge Griner tried to explain to him that puncturing people with screwdrivers would almost always irritate them. Pint had seemed to be bored at the time, bearing little resemblance to the smiling young stud he was at the moment.

"Hey there, Fuzz Lady," he called, giving me a friendly wave I figured was designed to show me he held no grudges and to show his friends he was on good terms with the law, which is pretty much true. Except for their occasional lapses from socially approved behavior, I like the Conroys. His brother and the girls inside the car all smiled and waved, too.

"Hey, Pint. Half Pint. Having a party?"

They all laughed. "Yeah. We talking about riding over to Vidalia. Wanna come? Half Pint here ain't got no date.'' Half Pint poked at his brother, and the girls giggled at Pint's nerve.

"That whole carload of women for you, Pint?''

"Oh, yeah. Cain't fight 'em off.''

"Well, thanks anyway. Maybe another time. Right now I'm looking for a red Chrysler four or five years old. Seen it?''

They all looked at each other, faces blank. Then, apparently deciding it couldn't bring unwanted attention to any of their friends, one of the girls spoke up.

"Was one at Billy Watson's a while ago. It'll still be there.'' They all laughed.

"Thanks. Y'all behave yourselves now.'' I eased the car back toward the middle of town and turned left on Court Street, wondering what was so funny. I hate it when I don't get a joke. If Reed wasn't at Billy Watson's, I'd call off my search and go back home to bed. Reed might not even be in town, and I wasn't on duty anyhow.

Billy Watson's Fish Place is one of the few eating places in town where you can sit down and have dinner. This late at night, Billy had turned out the neon beer signs and roadside flashing lights that tell people when it's open. The building is ramshackle and unpainted. Driving past when it's closed, anybody who didn't know better would think it was just sitting there waiting for demolition.

A few cars were parked in front, none of them the one I was looking for. I swung around the building to head back to town, and there it was, parked at the back edge of the shell-and-sand patch that Billy calls a parking lot. All four tires were flat. So now I knew what was so funny. It was too juvenile a stunt for Pint Conroy's Southside Gang to have bothered with, but they weren't too sophisticated to enjoy it.

Pulling back around in front, I parked the car and pushed open the plank door. The smell of grease and fried catfish was strong, but the lights and the noise level were lower than they would have been earlier in the evening. At this hour, without hungry patrons digging into catfish and hushpuppies, and covering up the deficiencies in the decor with their presence, the place looked worn-out and dreary.

Billy called to me from a booth where he was playing cards with three other people. He showed all eight of his teeth in a friendly grin. "What can I do for you? We're closed, just waiting for Idella to finish cleaning up, but we might could find you a leftover hushpuppy."

A clatter of metal on metal from the kitchen punctuating his offer indicated that Idella, Billy's wife and Ogeechee's unchallenged kitchen queen, was listening.

For a restaurateur, Billy is remarkably skinny, as though the constant familiarity with his food has bred contempt. Or maybe the fact that he's dentally challenged slows him down. His work uniform is a pair of denim overalls. In winter he wears flannel shirts with it; in summer, T-shirts. On Sundays, year round, he wears a long-sleeved white dress shirt, which is only slightly paler than Billy himself. He chooses a necktie from a collection he hangs from a nail-studded beam in the dining room. Faithful customers sometimes contribute particularly interesting specimens to the collection and watch to see when they turn up on Billy. Hen has been known to say that Billy Watson's necktie collection is the closest the town can come to a porn shop. In fact, Hen once confiscated a particularly lurid one Billy indiscreetly wore on a Sunday when Hen took Teri and Delcie there for dinner after church. Tonight, a Tuesday night in spring, Billy wore a modest, long-sleeved yellow-and-blue striped T-shirt with his overalls.

Besides Billy, the only people I could see were the three playing cards with him, two rough-looking men I had never seen before and Vivi Dawson Ritter. Coincidence was working overtime on the Ritter-Dawson connection.

Vivi was sitting back in the corner of the booth with one foot on the seat and a denim-clad knee bent up between her and the table in what looked like an extremely uncomfortable position and would have been impossible except that she was so thin, all angles. If I could give her ten pounds we'd both be better off.

Her right hand rested on the table and held her folded cards. A cigarette trailing smoke dangled from between the long, thin fingers of the left hand. What had to be acrylic fingernails were painted the same carmine as her mouth. With her sculptured short black hair, intense black eyes, and pale skin, she looked like she should have been in a cosmetic ad, not killing time with a couple of rednecks in a ramshackle small-town fish joint. That's how she's always been, too dramatic for Ogeechee. Even in jeans, obviously making no effort to be glamorous, she had it. Me, now, I could pull a sequined tank top over my 34Bs, sprinkle glitter in my short brown hair and paint green smudges around my bright blue eyes and all I'd look like was somebody who was trying to look glamorous but had no clue how to go about it.

"I'll come back Sunday for some catfish, Billy," I said. "Right now I'm looking for Reed Ritter. Is that his car around back?"

"What's the matter? Reed stand you up?" Vivi asked, lazily fishing a shred of tobacco from the end of her tongue with her carmine tongs. "I wouldn't have said you were his type." Vivi and her friends laughed at this even though it didn't seem particularly witty to me.

"I didn't think you ever figured out his type," I said. "Anyway, this is business."

"Business?"

They all laughed again and cut their eyes at each other, we-get-the-joke-and-it's-on-you. Ha. Ha. I still didn't see anything funny.

"Police business," I said, determined not to give them a reaction. "Is he here?"

"The police are after ol' Reed? I never thought he had enough imagination to do anything that would interest the police. Or anybody else."

"Is he here?" I yawned. It was a natural yawn that sneaked up on me but I liked the effect so much I did it again on purpose. I was getting a little tired of the question, not to mention the company.

"Nah. Left—what would you say?" Billy appealed to the others. "About nine?"

"About nine, I guess," Vivi volunteered. "Who'd notice?" She dreamily ran one of those fingernails across the back of the neck of the man sitting next to her. It didn't seem to bother him, but it made me shiver.

"How'd he leave? His car's still here."

"With Gordie. Too polluted to drive." Vivi had noticed that much and seemed pleased to report it.

"Gordon Albritton?"

"Uh-huh. But you still didn't tell us why you want Reed." Vivi fanned her cards, glanced at them, and drew one from the deck, which she immediately discarded.

"There's a fire at his place, and I thought he'd like to know about it."

Vivi folded her hand again. All four cardplayers looked up. "Bad fire?"

"Looks pretty bad. Do you know where he and Gordie were going?"

All four shook their heads. "Your turn, Billy," one of the strangers said. Compassionate bunch.

"Thanks for your help."

As the plank door squeaked shut behind me, I heard them laughing again.

I swung back by Reed's in case he'd turned up there and I found an entirely different scene from the one I'd left not so much earlier. The fire was out. The rushing water and shouting men had quieted. Grimy firefighters stood in twos and threes, except for one who was sitting behind the hydrangea where the boys had been, his head hanging between his knees. Dwight Wilkes, the police officer on night duty, had joined the crowd and was standing with Hen and Fire Chief Phil Pittman.

As I came to a stop, I saw Phil walk over to the man behind the hydrangea. Hen made some final comment to Dwight and trudged in my direction, every minute of his long day showing now. Some trick of my tiredness or the night light even made him look smaller.

He leaned against the car, his arms making a frame for his head as he bent and peered down at me through the window. I began to report.

"The Conroy boys are over at the Twilight with some sweet young things, all of them high on something, and I guess it could be spring and romance and being out of jail, but that's probably not all. They sent me to Billy Wilson's."

Hen waggled a hand as though to cut me off, but I went on. "Reed's car's there at Billy's, but they said Reed left with Gordon Albritton. If he hasn't come back here, I could see if he's at Albritton's or I could go home and go to bed. You could, too. Do you ever sleep in a bed, or do you just nap at the office?''

"You through?''

"That's about it.''

"Good. You can quit worrying about finding Reed.''

"Oh, he's here? Good. When did he turn up?''

"Just a few minutes ago.''

"Where'd he been?''

"In the house.'' Hen took a deep breath and straightened up, arching his back until it popped. He jerked his head to indicate the man on his knees behind the hydrangea. "Wallace found him.''

TWO

THERE WAS A LOT to do before we left poor Reed and the remains of 617 Palm and I got back to my bed.

First thing, Hen used Miss Sarah's phone to call Willie over at the mortuary and get him set up for a trip to Atlanta. Since Reed's death was unattended by a physician, the body had to go up there to the medical examiner. As one of the town's two morticians, Willie Calloway doubles as coroner, but that's a political office, not a medical one. We don't run to much of anything high-priced and high-tech in Ogeechee and a medical examiner fits slap into both categories.

"Willie must have been sleeping with the windows shut and the air-conditioner running. Never even heard the sirens," Hen told us when he re-joined Miss Sarah, Dwight, Phil, and me on Miss Sarah's porch. "Thought I never would get it through his head that there'd been a fire, much less that we had"——Hen stopped to clear his throat and dart a glance at Miss Sarah before finishing——"some business for him. He'll be here as soon as he's had time to drink a pot of coffee and wake up a little."

"Think we ought to see if we can find out what started it?" Phil Pittman asked. He's a volunteer like the rest of the firemen, and he takes it very seriously. As far as I know he's never missed a training class, and that's at his own expense. That's how he was in school, too. Serious. Not even Miss Sarah scared him, because he was always prepared. I never liked him much, which he never seemed to notice. To be fair, as an adult I can see that being called

Pee Pee all through grade school might have helped Phil develop indifference to peer approval.

"We'll get around to that, Phil," Hen said, staring across the street. "Right now what I figure we'll do, we'll get Willie on the way with Reed and string us up some of that nice yellow tape that tells people to keep out of the way of the po-lice. Ol' Dwight here can keep an eye on things 'til morning, make sure that fire doesn't come back to life. Okay with you, Dwight?"

Dwight grunted.

"We can come back in the morning," Hen said, "When we'll have some daylight to see by and the place has had time to cool off. That'll be time enough. Sound okay to you, Phil?"

"Yeah, I guess," Phil said. "It'll be a while before it'll be cool enough for us to do much poking around." But from the way he couldn't keep his eyes away from the steaming ruin, I could tell his mind had already moved past the fire and even Reed's death and he was itching to start sifting ashes and putting some of his esoteric fireman knowledge to work on finding an explanation. Putting out fires has to be more interesting than putting out the *Ogeechee Beacon* every week, which is what he does in real life. If he hadn't always been such a goody-goody, I'd suspect him of setting an occasional fire himself, just for the excitement.

Hen's plan sounded reasonable and appropriate. After all, at the time we didn't have any reason to suspect there was anything sinister about the fire. But it irked me that he didn't ask me if it sounded okay to me, like he did Dwight and Phil.

I think Hen keeps hoping if he ignores me, I'll go away and he can quit worrying about me. He should know me better than that. I'll admit our boss/minion status has put a new spin on our relationship, and in the past few months there's been an extra edge that I haven't decided how to deal with, but for now, I tell myself that having to put up with me is probably purifying his soul, sort of a Methodist purgatory. And he does have to put up with me. Grandma and Aunt Lulu made him promise. Bless them both, they were trying to help me over another rough spot.

Not long after Zach died, I went off to the big city to give myself a chance to see and do some things that wouldn't remind me of him. On the strength of my English major at the teacher's college, I got a job with an ad agency and after a while I started going out with Brad Phipps, a man as different from Zach as bacon is from butterbeans. What can I tell you? I finally realized I had no future with a man who still has his mother shop for his clothes, and broke that off. At about the same time, I was "let go" from the agency, which felt a whole lot like being fired. I'm sure there was no connection. Anyway, it seemed like a good time to take a deep breath and go in for some agonizing reappraisal of my options and priorities, or to crawl back into the womb and suck my thumb. For me, that meant going back to Ogeechee.

Grandma made up the bed in my old room and coddled me and cooked for me and sympathized with me and I lapped it up just like I was one of her countless cats.

Most people my age have left Ogeechee for greener pastures, and the others have pretty much settled into the home and motherhood bit, which left me out, so I drifted into a low-stress routine of volunteering at the library once a week, substituting in Grandma's bridge club once in a while, and doing research for the historical society. When I found myself arguing with Caroline Smithfield at the Garden Club one day over the right formula to feed hydroponic tomatoes, I looked around and realized I was leading the life of a 70-year-old and decided I'd be better off back in Atlanta.

I think Grandma hid my suitcases. Anyway, by the time I found them, up on the rafters of the smokehouse behind a rusty lawnmower, she and Aunt Lulu—Hen's mother— had talked him into offering me a job to keep me in Ogeechee. One of his "deppities" had gone on to greener pastures in Statesboro and there was an opening.

I wish I could have heard the uproar when they went head-to-head with Hen. They probably had to threaten to cut off his peach cobbler and pecan pie to get their way. Whatever they did, he folded. He probably felt safe. How could he have known it would appeal to me? I figured it was more like a life than bridge, the library, and the garden club, and would tide me over until I decided what I really wanted to do.

He took note of the self-defense course I'd taken to equip me for living in Atlanta, acknowledged my proficiency with firearms, since I grew up knowing how to hunt, and thought he was calling my bluff by sending me to the eight-week training course at the police academy.

When I came back from that undaunted, he took me down to the station, showed me where the coffee-maker is, and sat me down in his cramped office for a talk.

"I'm not crazy about this idea," he told me, "but it looks like we're gonna do it."

"Looks like," I agreed.

He shook his head at me, "Okay. Ground rules. First off, you've got to remember that Ogeechee ain't Mayberry. There's more to what goes on here than Sheriff Andy and Barney Fife sitting around being folksy and taking turns being in charge of the bullet. We get violent crimes every now and then, mostly when somebody gets over-stimulated and hurts the delicate sensibilities of somebody else who's likewise over-stimulated. It can get right messy. And we do have drugs, even if we are just a little ol' two-stoplight town. Since we're so near the Florida line and the coast highway, we get a bigger share of it than most people think."

"Should I be taking notes?" I asked.

"There won't be a test on this part," he said, and went on with his talk. He must have worked on it some.

"But you don't want to go gettin' the idea that we're *NYPD Blue*, either. Matter of fact, we probably are a whole lot more like Mayberry than the Big Apple, but I don't want you to take the job under false pretenses, thinking we never have anything serious to contend with."

"Right."

"Just so you know. And don't expect to get away with anything because we're cousins."

"Right, Chief. Boss."

"'Chief' is fine, if you can't bring yourself to call me 'Your Reverence.' So you still want to give it a try?"

"Why not?" Even if my only reason at the time was to pass time and get on Hen's nerves, it was more motivation than I had to do anything else.

"Okay, then. There's one more thing we've got to get straight." With that he sighed like a man who was trying to do the right thing but didn't have much hope it was going to work out. "We've got security and ethics and discretion involved here. We don't talk about what anybody's done to get mixed up with the po-lice."

I nodded to show I understood, but it turned out he wasn't making the point I thought he was.

"That's what you owe the community. But family is different. Around home and hearth, you get three choices about how to talk about policin'. You could say that you get a choice of what kind of lies to tell, because all the choices put a little polish on the plain unvarnished truth. In spite of what you might think you know about the ninth commandment, you can't afford to be squeamish about that.'' He re-adjusted his bulk in the chair and explained. ''One choice is to make like you don't ever do anything scarier than watch out for expired parking meters.''

''We don't have parking meters.''

''Right. You're observant. That's gonna be a big help to you in your new career. That brings us to choice number two, which is to make like everybody who might have felonious intent and or the desire to inflict harm upon your body or mine is so inept that we are never in any danger.''

''That's your way,'' I said, realizing it for the first time. Listening to Hen talk about crime in Ogeechee was prime entertainment. He always made it sound like the people he arrested had run south to avoid being put in a cute television series about the zany goings on in some oddball New York police precinct.

He winked at me. He has the Roundtree eyes like I do, and on him that bright blue wink can be devastating. ''That's my way,'' he agreed. ''I drifted into it because I am a natural born ra-con-toor, but it serves the extremely practical purpose of distracting all my nearest and dearest from the fact that these good-for-nothing drug dealers and booze-happy wife-beaters who are my reason for coming to work every day don't all have hearts of gold.''

He sighed and slogged on, trying to be fair. ''Now you might like to go along with that or you might want to try out option three, which is to go to the other extreme and let on that all our local riff-raff are just short of being master criminals. Your audience will naturally discount some of what you say, and being nice people and comparatively naive they will more'n likely discount too much. That's important because it'll keep 'em from worrying too much. If they get hold of the idea that people shoot real bullets at either one of us, we might both have to quit policin' and try to get work washin' squash. I like my job and I'd have trouble forgivin' you for that.''

I was a little surprised to see he really had thought about it, and I did see the sense of what he was telling me. So, not being a natural born *raconteur,* I have taken option three. I never have figured out how Teri and Aunt Lulu and Grandma manage to keep themselves from realizing that policing is a dangerous line of work, even in Ogeechee, but if anybody's noticed a discrepancy between Hen's criminals and mine, they haven't mentioned it.

Anyway, all that accounts for why I was sitting with Hen and Phil and Miss Sarah in the middle of the night waiting for the coroner.

I guess Willie figured there was no hurry about picking up a dead body, so by the time he got there most of the fire equipment was gone and we'd strung the yellow tape around the perimeter. We spent the rest of the time arguing about whether I could go with them into the house for the body. Phil and Hen both tried to object, Phil on the grounds of liability, and Hen because no matter what else is going on he can't forget he's ten years older than I am and he's the only man in the family and therefore is responsible for looking out for me.

"It'll make me a better police officer," I insisted. What could they say to that? They've both known me long enough to know they weren't going to talk me out of it even if it was a bad idea. Phil found me a bunker suit.

The fire had officially been declared out, but the house was still hot. It steamed and creaked, and we sloshed. In spite of my bravado, which had seemed necessary in order to prove something or other, I was not happy to be there.

I'm sure I'll never forget the heavy, stifling air; the overwhelming mingled stench of burnt wood, plastic, rubber, metal, and paper, that seemed to clutch at my stomach and make me gag; the claustrophobic feeling of the hot, rubber bunker suit and heavy boots. Everywhere I looked, some detail etched itself into my mind. A clean, unburned patch where a box had protected the desk underneath; the shattered screen on the television; and worst of all, of course, Reed lying peacefully on his bed under a blanket of fine black ash. Mercifully, it didn't take long to get the body, and I was able to stick it out, but as soon as I was away from the house I wrenched off the boots and the bunker coat. I pushed up the sleeves of my shirt, grateful for the clean air on my arms and in my lungs.

It was a little after 3:00 a.m. when Hen slapped the back fender of Willie's departing ambulance like a farmer encouraging a horse. We said goodbye to Miss Sarah and Hen told Dwight, "Don't you go to sleep now, or some young'un'll be bound to get in there and mess around and get hurt, and the OPD will get sued right down to our Fruit of the Looms. Besides which, it might keep us from finding out how that fire got started."

Sleepy, grumpy Dwight nodded unhappily.

Five minutes later, 3:17 by my bedside clock, I finally got back into bed. I'd been on shift since 4:30 the morning before, with just a little sleep before the sirens woke me, and I fell into sleep like a child falling down a playground slide, totally and quickly, but found I'd traded one nightmare for another.

This time I dreamed of flames, not rifles, and of the pitiful ash-covered thing that had been Reed Ritter. More than once I woke in a sweat because I wasn't able to get to Reed, who beckoned me with filmy gray arms to save him.

When I counted eight bongs on the courthouse clock, I gave up trying to sleep and rolled out of bed. As I smoothed the old chenille spread, I couldn't help but think of the fuzzy, strangely clean imprint left on Reed's bed when his body was taken away.

In an attempt to get my systems to function, I spent a few minutes bending and stretching in front of the full-length mirror behind the bathroom door. My body's okay, but, as usual, when I'm actually looking at myself, I wished I could be either a little taller or a little lighter. Five six and 130 isn't gross, but it isn't svelte, either.

Of course Hen had been inflexible about physical fitness requirements when he hired me.

"You being a police officer don't work out, it's blame sure gonna be your fault and not mine," he had told me. "Ain't nobody gonna be able to say it was because I shouldn'ta hired you in the first place."

Nobody says anything about Dwight's beer gut, or the fact that Hen himself could afford to lose a few pounds, not that he ever will with Teri cooking a big meal for him every night and him slipping over to Aunt Lulu's most noontimes for what he calls a bite, but never fails to include at least four vegetables and some kind of pie. Teri gave him some gym equipment for Christmas one year, and he must use it because he's got muscles that would make me look twice if they were on any other man.

I went to stand in the bathtub and pulled the shower curtain on its oval rod around me. With the hot water pouring over me, I shampooed my hair and smoothed the herb-scented lather over my body, wishing I could wash away the memory of the past evening as easily as I was washing away the scent and smudge.

The real-life nightmare kept sneaking up on me. I reached for a towel and was suddenly back at Reed's. His bathroom, at the back of the house and with the door closed, was the least damaged room in the house. There had been green towels hanging there. I rubbed more vigorously.

I dressed in a tan cotton skirt and soft white shirt, not in uniform. It was supposed to be my day off and after the night before I wanted to do whatever I could to prove I was alive, to feel like a woman, to have something to think about besides Reed. Next: the kitchen, coffee, food.

The kitchen is a big square room, built in the days before built-ins, to accommodate a wood-burning cook stove, which was traded in for electric before I was born. A walk-in pantry is at the back, its shelves filled with jars of peaches, plums, black-eyed peas, zipper peas, green beans, and tomatoes; pints and quarts of summer that glow like jewels when the sun strikes them, the work of Aunt Lulu and Grandma. For some reason we still call it canning.

A round oak table takes up the middle of the floor and in spite of knowing it wouldn't be there, I caught myself looking for the crossword puzzle from *The Savannah Morning News* on the tabletop, where Grandma had left it every morning for as far back as I can remember.

Another flashback: Reed's small kitchen had smooth countertops with stove and sink built in and a breakfast bar along one side. Most of the damage was there, but not a single room had escaped the smoke and flame. Maybe if Reed hadn't been drinking, had been awake—

I made some coffee—brewed, not the instant I make do with when I'm in a hurry—and fried some bacon, trying to force myself to think of nothing but getting the bacon just right. Then I wrapped the bacon in a paper towel and carried my breakfast and a sack of Purina Cat Chow outside, carefully opening the screen door to avoid damaging any cats. Over the years the word has reached all the cats in south Georgia that if you need a place to hang out, Jessie Roundtree in Ogeechee won't turn you away. Wild or tame, they come and go. A few regulars hang around to explain the one rule to the transients: Get along or get gone.

After I filled the cats' dishes, I sat on the top step, nibbling bacon and sipping coffee, running my fingers through my hair every now and then to fluff it up as it dried. When I keep it short that's all I have to do with it to make it presentable. I trim it myself. That suits me fine, but does separate me from the grapevine at the Cut-n-Curl, which puts what passes for police intelligence in Ogeechee to shame.

Sitting there as I have so often, I could almost see Grandma making her early morning yard rounds with an apparently boneless cat draped over her forearm. Spring was in full flower in time for Easter, with azaleas rioting under the pines and the fruit trees well leafed. She'd be pulling down an occasional plum branch to check for fruit moth or brown rot or some such.

A yellow-and-white kitten dodged in and out of the cave made by my skirt. A lazy gray mama cat watched the yard with me. Do the cats miss her, too?

Ghosts. Focus, Trudy.

Forcing myself back to the present, I was struck by the natural elegance of the place that will always be home no matter where I live. Could I ever leave it again? I sometimes think all the good parts of my character are the result of learning to appreciate the old house, unpretentious but solid, naturally beautiful, dependable. Growing up around the place, like Hen did, like his mother and my daddy did, had to have an effect on our value system. I wanted Hen's daughter Delcie to have it, too.

The contrast with the destruction and death at Reed's couldn't have been more vivid.

The wide lawn of coarse grass blends into the pines between my house and the houses on the road behind. I used to think those pines went on forever, that if I got too absorbed in building a lean-to out of downed branches and dried needles and lost sight of the house I'd never find it again.

A dirt driveway circles the house. It was the ideal place to learn to drive a car. With the wheels safely in the ruts, I was free to concentrate on the clutch and the gearshift. It's all lovely, and it's home. There hadn't been much loveliness at Reed's neglected place, even before the fire. His yard had been under-watered, under-trimmed, under-raked, and under-planted.

Among the many beauties of this old house are twelve-foot pressed-tin ceilings, step-through windows (ideal for sneaking out after bedtime), and carved fireplace mantels, a different style in every room. The pantry is larger than the bedrooms at Reed's house. There are no closets, no central heat, no air-conditioning, not even any insulation—things my years in Atlanta taught me to appreciate, along with the pressed-tin ceiling—but in its day it was fine. It is still fine. That morning I was grateful even for the rust stains in the bathroom sink.

Reed's place might have been comfortable; it had never been gracious; it would never be habitable again. Reed's face swimming between me and the pines, taunting me, made me decide not to waste another minute getting over there.

If I could see the place now, with Reed gone, and get my mind onto what I could learn by helping Hen and Phil investigate the fire, surely it would drive that grisly vision away.

I came to my feet suddenly, startling the cats so that they melted through a gap in the brickwork under the house, their departure marked by a single offended "yeowlp."

THREE

As I PULLED my car to a stop in front of Reed's house, I was relieved to see how calm it looked after the confusion of the night before. By now everybody in town would have heard about the fire and driven by for a look, seen the smoke-and-fire blackened carport, known a man had died there, a man they knew. The Police Line—Do Not Cross tape circling the house must have chilled them, kept them quiet. The scene was calm, but grim.

Dwight was gone, but Hen and Phil were there. Hen looked like he was dressed to go hunting instead of policing, but he was there. Phil was carrying a camera. His stocky build and round, freckled face gave him an earnest boyish look that was somehow enhanced by his round, rimless glasses. Boyish, yes, but at least he didn't look fresh and perky. He was wearing slacks and a sports shirt instead of a bunker suit and I was glad to see he looked as tired as I felt.

"Well, look who's up and out already, and it not even the crack of noon," Hen said when I joined them on the sidewalk, just as though I was late for work instead of showing up on my own time after a hard night. I wondered how much sleep he'd gotten.

"You sure you want to go back in there?" Phil asked.

"I'll skip it if you know a better way to learn," I said. "How's Wallace this morning?"

"I hear he called in sick," Phil said.

"And you're so tough you're back on the job. We get the point," Hen threw a grin in my direction, then spoke to Phil. "Okay, let's go. I gotta be somewhere before too long. Now, Phil, you try to use language she'll be able to understand. None of this highly technical fire investigator talk."

I figure every dig I pretend to ignore is a moral victory, so I let that go. We ducked under the tape and went up the two concrete steps and through the door into the house from the carport.

That put us in a room bounded on the right by a wall and door leading to a living/dining room and on the left by the breakfast bar and kitchen. Oh, lordy. Bad as it had looked from the outside, the cheerful, merciless, morning light exposing every detail made it worse inside. I took a deep breath, and was immediately sorry, because the smell hadn't improved. It called to mind the worst elements of a trash fire and a barnyard, with just a tang of burning tires. Overnight the water had seeped out, so it was no longer like wading through a swamp full of mysterious swimming things. I comforted myself with the thought that at least Reed's body was no longer there.

The doorway to Reed's bedroom was straight ahead from where we were standing. To the left, through the kitchen at the back of the house, were two smaller bedrooms and the bathroom.

Phil rounded the breakfast bar and stopped in front of the stove to begin his lecture. He looked pleased at the prospect of showing off some of his expertise. He's a little older than I am but he looked like a kindergartner who has something special for Show & Tell. Hen had a look on his face that said he already knew all this stuff. I tried to adopt the same expression. Nevertheless, Phil mostly looked at me as he talked, so of course I tried not to look at him. I looked at the stove.

"It's pretty obvious this is where the fire started. You

can tell from the fact that there's more damage here, and from this big V burned here on the wall.'' Phil spread his arms in front of the V to make sure I recognized it, then pointed to the open oven door. ''Heat vees out around the source of the heat.'' He slipped his glasses into his breast pocket and took up the camera, which hung from a strap around his neck, then took his time about setting up a series of shots. After clicking off several frames, he replaced his glasses, as though he couldn't see what to say without them, then looked at me again.

''What it looks like is he turned the oven on with the door open and set something flammable on the oven door. Maybe a pizza box. Anyway, whatever it was, it caught fire and it spread to something that was hanging over the edge of the counter. See what looks like paper or cardboard there? And this burn scar up here? Then this skillet on top of the stove caught. Probably full of grease. From there the fire just licked its way around the room from one pile of mess to another. This house was probably as dry as tinder, anyway.'' His gesture took in piles of cinders.

''But why would the oven door be open?'' I objected.

Phil shrugged. ''He'd been drinking. Maybe he took something out and forgot to turn it off and shut the door.''

I had to agree that's what it looked like, at least the way Phil explained it, even if it didn't make much sense.

''Any question about it being an accident?'' Hen asked Phil.

Phil looked like he was thinking about it. ''Not in my mind. I don't see any reason to call it anything else. We'll look around some more, but from what I saw last night I don't think we'll find anything to indicate a heat source anywhere except here at the stove, where you'd expect it, no suspicious hot spots. Are you thinking of arson? No.

It's not like when the mercantile went up because some-body wanted to make sure it burned and they could get the insurance.''

"He didn't have much of a chance, did he?" I asked. Phil blinked and cleared his throat before answering.

"It would depend on how alert he was, and I guess he wasn't alert at all. To tell the truth, if I was setting out to build a fire trap, this is pretty much how I'd lay it out. With a fire here in the kitchen, both outside doors are blocked off from anybody in the bedrooms. It's lucky there wasn't anybody else here. They'd have been trapped, too.''

"But he didn't even try to get out, did he?" I asked. "He was still on the bed, like he was asleep.''

Hen nodded grimly. "Right there in the bed.''

I looked around. Everything in that entry/breakfast room was black. Magazines, newspapers, and soda pop cans were black shapes on the breakfast bar. A pile of beer bottles was surrounded by ashes that might have been what was left of a cardboard six-pack. An easy chair, its outline blurred by the papers and clothing that had been draped across it, sat near the door. Formless shapes here and there could have been anything Reed had put down and never gotten around to putting away. The scorched golf clubs in the corner behind the easy chair were right where they'd been when I was there on the CCC.

"How long would you say it had been burning before you got here?" I was trying to ask intelligent questions to prove I could, even though I really wanted to be out-side, away from the smell and sight of the place.

"It's hard to say. It's a rule of thumb that a fire doubles in size every three minutes. With all the mess in here, this might have spread faster than that. And it might have been going for a good while before Miss Sarah noticed it,'' Phil answered.

''So what would you guess?''

Phil wrinkled and unwrinkled his nose in concentration, making his glasses dance up and down. ''The call came in a little after eleven-thirty. The fire might have been going fifteen or twenty minutes before she saw it. It didn't take us long to get here.''

''Wouldn't you think he'd have woken up?''

The men glanced at each other. ''Depends on how drunk he was,'' Hen finally said.

We went into the bedroom where Reed had died. Everything there was black and sodden, too. Flames hadn't reached it, but heat and smoke had done enough. A mirrored chest across from the foot of the bed held a ruined television set. A pile of fabric at one side of the television might have been clothes. There was nothing on the chest on the other side of the television. Maybe the firefighters had washed it away, or maybe there had been one uncluttered surface in the house after all.

Phil, still lecturing, pointed. ''That window being open fed the fire with oxygen and pulled the heat and smoke this way. That's why there's more smoke damage here than in the little bedroom in back.'' He adjusted his glasses and glanced at Hen, then spoke to me, the eager pupil. ''Reed probably died of smoke inhalation. He wasn't burned. In bad fires, I've seen it where the heat would draw 'em up so hard and fast it'd break their bones.''

I clenched my teeth and nodded, determined not to let them see my reaction, but I was glad he didn't seem to be expecting me to say anything. He led the way to the next room.

The bedroom behind the kitchen clearly belonged to

six-year-old Mark, Reed and Vivi's son. It had one twin bed and a unit with a desk—bookshelves above, drawers below—along the wall that backed on the kitchen. The open drawers held a few tumbled T-shirts, a couple pairs of jeans, and some small underwear. Video games were on one shelf, along with some plastic Power Ranger figures, grotesquely mutated by the heat. There was nothing in the closet except a soccer ball and a pair of sneakers. The lack of clutter in this room was almost as startling as the mess in the rest of the house. Except that it was obviously meant for a child, it was as impersonal as a motel room.

The other back room, past the bathroom, held office furniture—a charred desk, swivel chair, and computer. As in the kitchen, the clutter was conspicuous. Drawers hung open. Boxes, files, and loose paper littered the room like needles under a pine tree, randomly, carelessly.

"Did your men make all this mess?" Hen asked Phil.

"We spread a lot of water around, but you can't blame all that on us."

"I told you a little vandalism would have been hard to notice around here," I contributed.

A closed metal file cabinet had protected its few contents from some of the fire and water damage, but the computer was scorched and the plastic boxes full of disks drooped sadly. If Reed had done much work at home, and it looked like he had, this could mean trouble for his clients. Would a modern accountant keep paper records, or rely on his computer? There'd be more hope of recovering data from the file cabinets than from the computer.

We returned to the living room, where Phil clicked off pictures of each wall, pausing to replace his glasses and choose a vantage spot between each shot. The smell, the situation, and Phil's slow, finicky business with his glasses and the camera, had my stomach tied in knots. Maybe bacon hadn't been such a good idea.

"I guess I'll go over and speak to Miss Sarah," I said, hoping I sounded like a police officer on an investigation and not like a delicate female who desperately needed some fresh air.

"Tell her hey for me," Phil said, reaching for his glasses again.

As I crossed the street, Miss Sarah was opening the screen door. Of course she'd been watching. "Come on in, honey," she said. "I've got to talk to you. This is all my fault."

FOUR

Miss Sarah's large living room felt like a haven after the chaos across the street.

"You sit on down and I'll go get you a glass of tea. Sweet or unsweet?"

"Unsweet," I said, and Miss Sarah disappeared down the hall to the back of the house. Apparently her confession was going to wait on southern hospitality.

The intimidating figures from your childhood are supposed to shrink when you grow up. Miss Sarah never has. She has to be close to eighty since she taught not only me and Hen and Phil and Reed but all our parents, too, but she's still impressive. Her face is creased and this morning the creases of age were deepened by concern and grief, but she was brisk and commanding as ever. Her white hair was pulled into a neat knot at the back of her head. She wore a red shirt and red plaid slacks, brave protests against darkness and death.

I sat in one of the two fat chairs facing the front windows. From there Reed's house looked bigger than it really was because part of the front wall to the left was the front of the carport. The big old oak tree farther to the left, across the gravelled driveway, had blackened leaves where it overhung the house. The rest of the yard looked no worse for the fire. The dispirited boxwood and patchy grass might even have benefitted from the firefighter's water.

Miss Sarah returned with two glasses of iced tea wrapped in white cloth napkins.

"Thank you, ma'am," I said. I'd been wondering how to get back to the subject of her confession. Of course, I needn't have wondered. Miss Sarah was completely in charge.

"Do you know how the fire started?" she asked as she settled herself in the chair beside me.

Pop quiz, I thought. I swallowed some tea before I answered. "Phil says it looks like it started in the oven."

"The oven?"

Another time I might have enjoyed the comical mingling of surprise and relief on Miss Sarah's face. Even when a usually dull student in one of her classes had shown flashes of intelligence, she'd managed to act like that was what she'd expected all along.

"Yes, ma'am."

"The oven. How?"

I sketched out Phil's theory about the cardboard, cloth, and grease.

She thought about it and seemed to relax a little. "I don't mind telling you it's a load off my mind to know it was the oven. I've been in a tither for fear it was those boys, that some of their mischief got out of hand and that if I had told you who I thought it was you'd have put a stop to it and this wouldn't have happened. And I couldn't stand thinking about them, in case they were responsible." She held up a finger to keep me from leaping to a wrong assumption. "I don't mean I ever thought they would have done it on purpose, but boys don't always think about the consequences of what they're doing, you know, and I was afraid they'd done something silly with matches and…" She let the thought hang, as though finishing it would make things worse, then, "Especially when I saw them watching the fire last night."

So it had been the Dawsons.

"It looks like you worried for nothing," I said.

"Yes, thank the Lord. It's no help to Reed, but it's a weight off me to know. Well. None of their mischief—*if* they were the ones," she added, raising the cautionary finger again, "was ever inside the house, and none of it was really destructive, was it?"

"No, not really."

"So they didn't cause the fire. Still..." Her voice trailed off again and she sipped at her tea, looking at the house across the street.

"Hmm?" I followed her gaze and saw Hen and Phil in the yard. Phil was stowing his camera gear in the back of his car and Hen was wiping his hands on a handkerchief. As I watched, Hen clapped Phil on the shoulder and they drove away in their separate cars.

It was quiet, peaceful. If I let my eyelids droop and looked through the screen of my eyelashes, I could imagine there was nothing wrong with the scene. I jerked, momentarily disoriented, when I felt my iced tea glass slip from my fingers. I looked up to see Miss Sarah holding it firmly and shaking her head at me as though I'd tried to convince her one of the cats ate my homework.

"Having trouble sleeping in that big old house by yourself?" she asked. I looked at her suspiciously. If it was a loaded question she didn't seem to be aware of it.

"I've slept there all my life," I said, trying not to sound defensive.

"How long has it been now?" she asked.

"About five months," I said, although she knew that, too. "Right after Thanksgiving."

"That's not such a long time."

"In a way it seems like forever. Everywhere I look I see her, her things, hear her voice."

"She'll always be there in that house," Miss Sarah said.

"Yes."

"We all miss her," she said. "When you've lived as long as I have, you start seeing all your friends go, and it's hard. It's a lonely feeling. Try to be thankful she didn't suffer. Think of that instead of how you miss her."

"I am thankful for that," I said. In fact, I'd thought of it myself after I'd gotten over the shock of losing her so suddenly. When I came home one afternoon, I'd found her peacefully gone, in her sleep. How could Miss Sarah know that wasn't the problem?

"And, my goodness, it isn't like you're all alone in the world," she said, "with Lulu and Hen and his family." She skewered me with a look, but instead of forcing me to bare my innermost secrets, she gave me an out. "That little Delcie is something, isn't she?"

"Yes." I said, and I'm sure I had a fatuous, if wistful, smile on my face. Delcie is Hen and Teri's only child and she's my darling, as well as theirs. She's six now, and we've always had a relationship I think is special, maybe because I think if I had a daughter she'd be a lot like Delcie, which would suit me right down to the ground. But I didn't have Aunt Lulu and Hen and his family anymore, not like it used to be, not like Miss Sarah meant. Instead of a warm net of family, all of us together, now it was me and them. Grandma left that big old house to me, and Hen's wife, Teri, was taking it hard. Why did I get the feeling Miss Sarah knew all that, but didn't feel it was her place to meddle?

"We're all having trouble adjusting," I said.

"I expect so," she said, looking at me.

"We had Christmas at Aunt Lulu's," I said, meaning we didn't have it in the only place any of us had ever had

Christmas, with a tall pine Christmas tree in the bay window at the front of the house, decorated with ornaments as filled with memories as Grandma's fruitcake was with pecans. I felt a wash of self-pity and sipped my tea to hide it.

"Everybody is missing her in different ways," Miss Sarah said. "Jessie was the heart of your family just like she was the heart of the Garden Club. It'll take all of us a while to figure out what to do without her, and we'll be different without her. That doesn't have to be all bad, you know."

"Yes, ma'am." Was she trying to make me see Teri's side?

We sipped tea.

"Will y'all be having Easter dinner at your house?" she asked.

I looked at her. "Where? Oh. My... We haven't talked about it." My house? Yes, I guess it was.

"Well, it's time you talked about it, isn't it?" She prodded. "Here it is Wednesday already."

"Yes, m'am. You're right. Yes. It is my house and we do need to get after those plans. Yes. Thank you."

She nodded and smiled at me and I felt like we'd been having two different conversations that had fetched up with a thump at the same point. We sipped some more.

"It is funny Reed would have been cooking at that time of night," Miss Sarah said after a while. "I didn't think he ever did much cooking any time."

"People get hungry any time," I said. "Phil said it might have been a pizza box." It *was* funny though, that Reed would have decided to heat up a pizza after he got home just after he'd been out to Billy's, especially if he was, as Vivi had said, too polluted to drive.

"I think Reed was lucky to have a neighbor like you to keep an eye on things," I said.

"Not lucky enough. Maybe if I'd been watching closer the firemen could have gotten here before...it was too late."

I shook my head. "I doubt it. Phil says it went up in a hurry." She wasn't listening. Having dealt with her concern about the young boys, Miss Sarah had moved on to the next thing, her dereliction of duty.

"I have my television in here so I can keep a look out for things. When I started to bed last night, I got up to let Lester out for his evening walk and that's when I noticed Reed's house. It took me a while to figure out what was strange about it, then I realized it was because the shades were pulled down. At first I thought that was what got my attention because they're never down, but then I noticed the smoke and realized that it was fire behind the shades that made them show up at all."

"It's a good thing you saw it when you did. The fire could have been much worse. It might have got that tree and the houses on both sides."

"For all the good it did Reed. Poor Reed. He always did have hard going. Don't know what it was—stubbornness maybe, maybe something that grew out of him and his mama having such a hard time after his daddy died. You wouldn't remember that. You're too young. I never could pin it down, but there was something about him that brought out the contrariness in people. Good thing he didn't try to be a salesman. Like everybody else in town, I was flabbergasted when Vivi Dawson decided to marry him." She sighed. "Then when that broke up, he was worse off than ever. But he's always been nice and polite to me."

I nodded. There didn't seem to be anything to say.

"Seeing how hard it's been for him to keep up with things, I've been sending my yard man to do a few things over there when I don't have enough to keep him busy, but it takes more than that to keep a place up. I do it more for myself than for Reed," she added. "I'm the one who has to look at the place, after all."

Heaven forbid I should think she was soft.

"I'm sure he appreciated it."

"I was sitting out on the porch last evening when I saw him going off. He gave me a wicked grin and told me he had a date. I was glad to hear it. He's been by himself too much since the divorce."

I murmured something or other and Miss Sarah went right on.

"When I know he's gone, like last night, I keep a closer eye on things, because of that other trouble, you understand. That's how I know they came back in her car about nine. I tried not to pay attention after that, knowing how young people are these days."

Well, maybe he died happy, I thought. I said, "Who was his date?"

"Oh, I didn't see who it was. He didn't say, but I think it was probably that McCloud girl who works over at the florist."

"Suzanne McCloud? I didn't know that." How in the world does Miss Sarah know things like that? I'm supposed to be the one out in the mainstream of Ogeechee life. I tried not to get sidetracked. "How'd you know they came back?"

"Because I heard the car. I knew it wasn't his."

"You knew it wasn't his because of the sound?"

"Oh, yes. I'm nosy, but I'm too lazy to get up every time somebody goes by. I keep track of the regular traffic by ear."

I must have looked skeptical because Miss Sarah smiled. Then an intent look came into her eye and she said. "Now, there's the cleaners."

"What?"

"Don't you hear it? That's the cleaners' truck that just went by."

"Oh." I looked out in time to see the faded green van turn the corner. "Which cleaners?" I asked. This was a welcome change of topic.

"City Cleaners, of course, and Randall Sikes is driving. He always rushes down the street like something's after him and then has to put on the brakes when he comes to the corner. I think he's trying to run over the Creech's dog and make it look like an accident. That dog sets up a howl every time Randall goes to their door."

She looked so pleased with herself I couldn't help but laugh. "Okay, okay. I'm convinced."

"Whoever it was with Reed didn't stay long. It wasn't more than fifteen minutes before he or she left again. Then Reed came back a few minutes later in his own car, but it was gone again just a little while later. All that comin' and goin' couldn't have left much time for romance, unless…" She smiled, and though years had added wrinkles to her face and silver to her hair, Miss Sarah exhibited the same insight that had served her so well at Ogeechee High School. "She might have come back later and parked around back where a nosy neighbor wouldn't see."

That could account for the drawn shades, all right.

I left Miss Sarah's thinking Hen ought to put her on the payroll. She seemed to know more about what was going on in Ogeechee—even more about me—than I did.

FIVE

I WENT HOME and started going through Grandma's room, a chore I'd been putting off all this time, telling myself it wasn't hurting a thing for her belongings to stay right where they'd been for years. Miss Sarah was right when she said Grandma would always be all through the house, whether her shoes and hats and underclothes stayed or not. That shouldn't be a bad thing. So what was the bad thing, the thing that was making me want to sleep all the time, but giving me nightmares when I did?

I had gotten around to emptying the dresser drawers onto the bed when the telephone rang. Dawn, the day dispatcher, was so agitated I could hardly understand her.

"Trudy! I'm about to lose my mind! I can't get hold of the Chief or anybody, and I don't know what to do! He said he'd call in because I shouldn't try to reach him on the radio, but he hasn't and I've got to tell somebody."

Dawn has been working for the police department since last spring, two weeks after graduation from Ogeechee High School and one week after her wedding. It hadn't been much of a honeymoon because her husband, who graduated with her and works on his daddy's farm, couldn't take much time off. She's a thin, nervous, conscientious girl and she worries a lot. One of her big worries is that Hen will be able to find fault with her job performance, which he never has. Since I've outgrown hero worship, I'm usually amused. No telling what this might be about.

"Okay, Dawn, I'm somebody. Calm down. What it is?"

"I just got a call from the medical examiner in Atlanta, about Reed."

"That was quick. Must be having a slow week up there."

"Trudy, this isn't funny." She thinks Hen is God and doesn't think I'm funny. No accounting for taste. "He's going to send down a full written report, but he thought we ought to know right now."

"Know what?"

"Reed didn't die in the fire like everybody thought. I mean, he was dead like everybody thought, but it wasn't the fire."

"Get a grip, Dawn."

"Okay. I wrote it down. The ME said he died of trauma to the trachea. He says a pipe or something hit him across the throat and crushed his windpipe. There's no—something I can't make out—in his lungs and what that means is that Reed was dead before the fire got there."

Good lord. My ears took in the words all right, but for a minute my brain couldn't handle the information. The idea of Reed dying a horrible death in the fire took a sickeningly more horrible turn.

"Trudy?"

"I'm here. Did you say Hen doesn't know yet?"

"No. I mean yes. I mean the Chief's out in the woods somewhere meeting with the guy from the DEA. Remember?"

A Drug Enforcement Agency rendezvous down toward Waycross. That explained the hunting outfit he'd been wearing. With everything else that was going on, I'd forgotten about it. I was impressed that Hen had remembered, even though I knew he'd been looking forward to it. He likes working with the other agencies. About half the time he comes back all cranked up about some new technique or material or gadget he thinks we need. The other half, he entertains anybody who'll listen to him with stories about how the bigger the agency the more they depend on technology instead of common sense. Like the "idjit" over in Columbus who has so many play-pretties he spends more time deciding whether to use the tape that says Caution or the one that says Crime Scene—Do Not Enter than Hen spends on most investigations. (Ogeechee uses the all-purpose Police Line—Do Not Cross for all occasions requiring tape.)

Hen never has come right out and said so, but I figure he likes these cooperative cases because they remind him of what police work is supposed to be about. Even Ogeechee's most interesting cases aren't usually all that demanding, and before he had me he had to investigate things like the CCC himself.

This meeting was with a DEA agent and somebody he called "Winston the 'Gator." Winston was supposed to tell them about a drug route that might be moving in our direction since they've been cracking down over on Highway 95.

I had recovered a little from Dawn's news and was thinking as fast as I could. "When's Hen supposed to be back?" I asked.

"He didn't say exactly, but sometime tonight, I think. Maybe in the morning."

"And you haven't told anybody else about this?"

"That's right. I told you, there isn't anybody here! They're all gone."

Right. I remembered Hen's briefing.

"I'm not going to put you out on this," he had told me, leading the way to the file room where he rolled the typewriter stand out of the way so he could reach the wall-mounted map. With a pencil he pointed to some roads so small they aren't on most maps. "But you need to know what's going on. I'll brief Dwight and Freddie when they come in and then we'll all sit back under the blackberry bushes and see what crawls down the path."

"Come again?"

"Which part didn't you get?"

"That part about not putting me out on this. It happens to be the most interesting thing that's come along since I've been on the force and a great chance to broaden my experience. Why wouldn't you put me out on it?"

"Somebody's got to keep crime under control here in town."

"It couldn't have anything to do with the fact that you don't want me out there in the blackberry bushes with the rest of the boys, could it?"

"Where's your upbringing? What you want to be out in the blackberry bushes with the boys for anyhow? You want to help the DEA, you memorize these faces." He tapped the mug shots he'd thumbtacked next to the map. "One of 'em drops by the Mini-Mart, you detain him so we can have a chat."

I'd stared at the photos and drawn breath to tell him what I thought of the plan, but I didn't have to tell him what I thought of the plan. He already knew. He was gone before I turned around.

So that's where everybody else was. Hen would break out in hives when he found out we had a murder and he didn't know about it because he was off sitting in some cone of radio silence under the blackberry bushes with the rest of the boys. There didn't seem to be any way around the fact that we had a murderer in Ogeechee, somebody who deliberately schemed to kill Reed and cover it up, and was almost certainly somebody we knew. Regardless of how the fire started, it was a cinch Reed hadn't crushed his own windpipe and then gone peacefully back to bed.

Dawn interrupted my thoughts.

"What should I do?"

"Dawn, listen. You don't need to do another thing right now. You've done just what you should have done. You've passed the word along to somebody else. I'll take care of it."

"You're sure?"

"Hen's out of pocket anyway, isn't he? So I'll get things rolling. There is one thing."

"What?"

"I think it would be a good idea for you not to go out of your way to tell anybody else about the ME's report. When we start talking to people, it could help our investigation if we don't let on right away that we know it wasn't an accident."

"I don't know—"

"It's what Hen would want. Don't disappoint him, now."

That did the trick. She agreed, which bought me a few hours. Hen would have hives on top of hives when he got back and found out I had an investigation underway.

Where would I start? Vivi had said Reed left Billy's with Gordon Albritton. Miss Sarah thought he had a date with Suzanne McCloud. That made one of them a good bet for being the last to see him alive, if not the one who whomped him across the windpipe and set fire to the place. I'd work on motive later. I decided to start with Suzanne.

SIX

SUZANNE MCCLOUD HAD heard about Reed, and she had
cared about him. That much was obvious to me as soon
as I laid eyes on her through the glass door of the cooler
at City Floral, where she was culling out faded flowers
and throwing them with entirely unnecessary force into a
pile on the floor.

Judging from the blotches on her face and an occasional
angry swipe at her nose with a crumpled handkerchief,
she hadn't killed him, or if she had she was already sorry.

She caught sight of me and came out of the cooler. Her
lips jerked and I guessed it was supposed to be a business
smile. "Hey, Trudy. What can I do for you?"

I hadn't worked out a plan beyond trying to find out if
she had any idea how the fire could have started. "I don't
need anything, Suzanne, thanks. I just came to see if
you'd heard about Reed Ritter."

She nodded and swiped at her nose. I couldn't imagine
a greater contrast to the glamorous Vivi Dawson Ritter
than drab, quiet, tentative Suzanne McCloud. They were
both thin, but in Vivi it looked like nervous energy; in
Suzanne it looked more like ill-health. Even given that I
wasn't catching Suzanne at her best, it seemed like Reed
had learned enough from his marriage to Vivi to look for
a different kind of woman.

"I'm sorry," I said.

She closed her eyes and leaned back against the cooler.
I thought she was about to faint. She looked so watery I
wouldn't have been surprised to see her slide down the

door and seep through the floor, but she just leaned. "I can't get over it. I just can't get over it."

"Did you see him last night?" I asked, noticing how much a sympathetic friend, which I was, sounds like a nosy police officer, which I also was.

"No. I wish I had. Then maybe it wouldn't have happened." She looked at me and frowned. "Whatever happened. Do you know how it happened?"

"No, not really. I hoped maybe you could help us piece it together."

"Oh. No."

"A fire like that, and somebody dying," I explained apologetically, and truthfully, as far as it went, "we need to see if we can find out what caused it."

She nodded as though she understood. "I didn't see him last night. He said he had some business with Gordie Albritton." She swiped at her nose again and looked pitifully at me. "You know, we were talking about getting married. We were going to go somewhere else and start a new life, as soon as we got a few things worked out."

"What kind of things?"

"Mostly to do with money. And Mark. If we left Ogeechee both of us would be leaving our jobs." Her eyes lit up briefly as she looked at her dream, momentarily forgetting that the dream had died.

"That could be a problem, all right."

"Yes, but lately Reed was all excited. He'd been working on something that was going to take care of that."

"You mean he had a job lined up somewhere?"

"Maybe. He wouldn't tell me. He didn't want me to be disappointed if it didn't work out, I guess. He was so good to me, Trudy." Reality set back in. She looked away and dabbed at her eyes.

"Was it something to do with Gordie?"

Suzanne looked back at me.

"This thing he was working on," I prompted.

"Oh. I don't know. Maybe."

"What about Mark? What was there to work out about him?"

"Well, Reed was all revved up, convinced we were going to take Mark with us, but I think he was kidding himself about that. Can you imagine Vivi, not to mention her daddy, letting Reed take Mark to live anywhere but Ogeechee? It's all they can do to let him sleep over at Reed's once in a while." Her eyes widened and she came upright, away from the cooler. "Thank God he wasn't there last night; I thought Reed said he was supposed to be." She sank back. "I'm sorry, Trudy, I guess I'm not making sense. I know I'm not functioning very well. I sent a funeral arrangement to Mindy Shoeman's new baby and the baby arrangement to old Miz Fillmore at the hospital. Miz Fillmore thought it was funny, but Mindy didn't."

She was rambling, but she'd stopped swiping at her nose, which I took as a sign of progress, so I just listened.

"It was so good to see Reed excited, you know, like he used to be, before Vivi sank her fangs into him. She never did care about him, just married him to spite B.L., sure as God made tadpoles. You remember him from school, don't you, Trudy? Even if you are younger? He was so smart and hardworking. You know, he was supporting his mama even when he was in high school. That's why he couldn't play sports like most of the guys. I had such a crush on him! But Vivi blinded him, like a flashbulb going off in your face, and he couldn't see me at all."

Smart and hardworking? The stuff crushes are made of? That wasn't how I remembered Reed. It seemed to me that, like Miss Sarah, Suzanne hadn't taken a good look at him in fifteen years or so. Too bad there wasn't somebody out there wearing my senior picture in his ID bracelet. I was thinner then and maybe a little less prickly. I'd give a pretty penny to know what Miss Sarah sees when she looks at me.

In a last effort to learn something useful, I asked, "Did you ever know Reed to have trouble with his stove?"

She shook her head and swiped at her nose again.

The bell over the door announced a customer, so I said again, "I'm sorry, Suzanne," and left.

SEVEN

I FOUND Gordie Albritton at his office in the old bank building, which faces the courthouse across Court Street just a block west of the stop light at Court and Main.

The old bank building is one of the few buildings in downtown Ogeechee that ever had any pretensions. Now years past its prime, it still has style. It was abandoned by the bank, partly on the grounds of security, which makes one of Hen's favorite stories the one about how the town's first bank robbery took place two months after the grand opening of the new bank. When apprehended down near Brunswick, still driving the car with the plates Hen had told the State Patrol to keep an eye out for, the two felons confessed that the open house and tour of the new bank had inspired the crime. One of them even explained how they drew a map of the layout on the napkins provided with the pecan sandies and banana punch, using the free pens that were part of the promotion. The pens and napkins were still in the car along with the loot.

I have pleasant memories of coming to the old bank with Daddy when I was little. The stained glass panels in geometric pinks and greens at the top of each outside window fascinated me. I liked the cool, quiet, serious, solid atmosphere and the red lollipop the tellers always gave me. The pervasive scent of old paper and that oily red sawdust they used to clean the floors with still make me think of money.

These days the main floor is occupied by an insurance agency. Albritton Real Estate has offices on the second floor. I climbed a narrow flight of stairs, leaving behind marble floors and finding oak. I don't remember being upstairs before.

When I opened the door beside the plastic plaque announcing Albritton Real Estate, I looked into a room about twenty feet square, furnished with tweedy shag carpet and a metal-and-Formica secretary's desk, a coffee table, a chrome-and-tweed client chair, and a matching chrome-and-tweed sofa.

The door opened quietly and did not disturb Gordie Albritton, who was sitting at the typewriter, frowning in concentration as he slowly hunted and pecked.

Gordie is a lanky man in his early forties who fancies short-sleeved shirts and dark ties. He looks serious most of the time, even when he isn't intent on error-free typing. When he had safely negotiated his way to the end of the letter and removed it from the machine, I knocked on the door frame to get his attention.

He jerked around, slapping the letter face down on the desk. "Oh, hi! Come in. I didn't hear you. Come to list your house?"

That's one solution to my problem with Teri that had never occurred to me. "Do you think there'd be a market for it?" I asked.

"Could be. We could list it and find out. It's got a lot of character. Might be able to sell it to somebody for a bed and breakfast. They're getting to be a big thing. Probably need a lot of fixing up, though."

I was immediately defensive. I tried to remember if he'd ever been in my back bathroom. Could he know about the roof?

"No offense, Trudy," he said, as though reading my thoughts, or maybe my face. "Most places need new carpet and paint, even fairly new ones, if they're going to show well. Updated appliances, stuff like that."

"I'll give it some thought, Gordie," I said. "Actually, I came to talk to you about Reed. You've heard about Reed?"

Gordie sank back into the chair, shaking his head. "Yeah. I got the news with my first cup of coffee over at Kathi's this morning." He ran a hand through his dark hair, which could have used a trim. "Bad way to die."

I nodded agreement. "Yes. I'm sorry. It must have been a bad shock for you. I heard you were with him not long before it all happened."

"Sure was. I still can't believe it. I mean, I believe it, but—"

"I know. I apologize for bothering you, but we're trying to find out what might have caused it. I'm hoping you can help."

Gordie quit shaking his head and clucking and looked at me blankly. Then he shrugged his shoulders. "I don't see how I can tell you anything useful. The place wasn't on fire when I left." He offered an uneasy smile. "But I'll do whatever I can, of course. Come on back here where it's more comfortable and have a seat."

He led the way into the adjoining office, about the same size as the reception room. "Let me get this going," he said, turning to the air-conditioner. "The sun really beats in here in the afternoons."

While he fiddled with the knobs and vents, I looked around. The furniture could have come from the same sale as that in the reception room, but in addition to a desk, Gordie's office had three four-drawer metal filing cabinets along one wall and a brown Naugahyde sofa with matching chairs in what was surely called a conversational grouping around a wood-framed, glass-topped coffee table.

An enlarged aerial photo of the town covered most of one wall. Using the courthouse as a landmark, I found the Roundtree house and was surprised at how small the center of my world looked beneath the spreading trees. It also surprised me to see what a short distance it is from there to the edge of town. To the west, just beyond the pines, is the highway. To the north, after a couple of rows of houses, farm land dotted with ponds and pecan orchards takes over. Going around there by road makes it seem farther away than it looked on the map.

When Gordie had the air-conditioner humming to suit him, he came to stand by me in front of the photo and began pointing out landmarks as though I were an out-of-town customer and not a native.

"People sometimes have a hard time getting oriented looking at things from this angle," he said. "Now, here we are, and here's the courthouse." He slid his finger along Court Street a few blocks, "And the city building."

As he slid his hand along the road some more, I wondered if he ever gave into a wild and crazy impulse to entertain himself on slow afternoons by running a little toy car along, negotiating turns and stopping at stop signs. Gordie? No, not serious, boring, Gordie. Still, I was so taken with the notion that I was a little surprised when he said, "This is the city limit," instead of "Varoom, varoom."

"What are the red flags?" I asked. One was near my house, another out in the direction of Billy Watson's, a third east of town.

"They're the parcels the county is considering for the new park and sports complex."

"You don't mean after only three years of talk they're

finally down to actually thinking about property! Why, at that rate it probably won't be more than three or four more before ground-breaking.''

"Don't be so cynical," he said. "Once they make a decision on the land, we could see some development within months.''

"What's holding them up?"

"You know the kind of thing," he said, sounding pretty cynical himself. "They have a lot to consider. Suitability. Price. Whether the present owner will be grateful for the sale."

"I get it. And whose land values will go up afterwards?''

"Um-hmm.''

"Speaking of land, was it real estate business you and Reed had to talk about last night?''

Gordie looked surprised. "Why'd you ask that?''

"Well, real estate is your business. And I heard he was trying to raise money to leave town.''

"No kidding?''

Was he surprised to hear it, or was he surprised to know I'd heard?

"Was he looking to sell some real estate?" I asked.

Gordie looked disgusted. "He told me he had some financial prospects, but he wasn't selling property." He started shaking his head again. He indicated a chair for me and took his seat behind the desk, leaving behind the animation he had shown earlier and assuming the unctuous manner that seems to come naturally to professional salespeople, from evangelists to used car salesmen. Well, if he was making a living selling real estate in Ogeechee, he'd have to have plenty of unction.

"Real shame about Reed. You knew he was my cousin? I guess I'll be the one to bury him, too, since me and the Dawsons are all the family he had and I doubt they'll fight me for the privilege. Never saw anybody attract bad luck like that boy. Of course," he continued, "the fire itself wasn't necessarily a bad thing. That place was so run down it wasn't worth as much as the land it's on, so he could have come out okay on insurance. If he hadn't been in it."

That was an interesting line of thought. Did Reed set the fire after all, for the get-out-of-town money the insurance would have meant?

"Did he have a lot of insurance?" I asked.

"Oh, not that I know of. It was just a thought. A man in my line of work has to be thinking about property values all the time."

"We're trying to figure out how the fire could have started. Hen and I have been over the place with Phil, but there are still some things to piece together. It's too much to hope that you went to his house and smelled smoke, but why don't you start there."

"How'd you know I was at his house?"

"The people out at Billy Watson's told me. I went looking for Reed to let him know about the fire and saw his car in Billy's lot."

Gordie nodded and squinched his eyes, the picture of a man deep in thought, before he spoke again.

"Well, that's right. I drove him home from Billy's."

"Because the tires on his car were flat?"

"Were they? That's funny. They must have been okay when he drove it over there. No, we didn't even look for his car. He'd been drinking a lot more than he was used to, and didn't have any business driving."

"When he was leaving home a little before seven he told Miss Sarah he had a date. Do you know anything about that?"

Gordie laughed. "That would have been his date with me, I guess. We had some things to talk about and we decided to do it over a mess of Billy's catfish."

"And Reed had been drinking a lot?"

"A lot for him. He didn't drink near as much as some people wanted to let on. Of course, some people act like you're a drunk if you drink at all. A good Baptist like me is taking his reputation in his hands to sit at a table with somebody who's drinking. Somebody might get the wrong idea. You know what they say. 'Baptists don't drink—in front of each other.'" He brought out the old joke as though he'd just made it up. "But up 'til Vivi started in on him last night he'd been nursing one beer. After she got through with him he started slurping up that Colorado Koolaid like it was water."

"Was Vivi having catfish with you?"

His answer was a derisive snort. "She came in after we'd been there a while and it took her about five seconds to decide Billy's place wasn't big enough to hold the two of them and Reed was the one who needed to go."

"Why?"

"Vivi has never spent much time huntin' a why for what she wants to do. She just needs a who—and Reed was it last night. That's when our dinner time started deteriorating."

"You mean the sight of her upset him that much?"

"Not the sight of her so much as the sound of her. The woman has a mean tongue. I'm glad I've never been on the wrong side of it."

"What did she say?"

"Oh, it was something about how he wasn't a fit father because he'd promised the kid to take him fishing or something and then didn't do it. Reed told her he'd had to work, and all she said to that was that it proved his kid wasn't as important to him as his job. Then, it was wasn't the kid supposed to be staying at Reed's?, and he'd better not be over there by himself, or else. That kind of thing. From there she went on to what a wimp Reed was and how she was looking for a man to give the kid a healthy male role model—I swear that's what she said—a healthy male role model!—so he wouldn't take after Reed. Like the kid needs to be able to kill alligators with his teeth. And she laughed a lot. I think it was the laughing that bothered Reed the most.''

I could understand that.

"She went back over to those friends of hers from the sawmill and they sat talking and drinking, and every once in a while they'd look over our direction and laugh. They might not have been talking about him at all. It would have been just like Vivi to tell her gang to look over at him and laugh whenever they thought about it.

"I tried to talk him into leaving, going somewhere else to talk, but he wouldn't. He didn't want to give her the satisfaction of running him off. It was like he was a seventh grade girl—I've got one of them so I know what I'm talking about. 'Daddy, she was looking at me!' You know. Vivi's spent her whole life working on being hard to ignore and she's good at it. Gets it from her daddy.''

"Did Reed still care so much about Vivi that she could upset him that much?''

"I didn't think he cared about her at all, anymore. I guess you weren't around at the time, but Reed divorced Vivi, not the other way around, and last night he was telling me about some plans with another woman. No, I don't think he was eating his heart out over her. Last night, it was just that he wasn't gonna let her run him out. I kept trying to tell him nobody would think we were leaving because of her, but every time I thought I was getting somewhere, Vivi or one of her buddies would laugh and he'd be sure they were laughing at him and he just got more and more stubborn—and more and more drunk.''

"So drunk you had to take him home."

He grinned. "That's one thing a Baptist is good for—designated driver."

"What time was that?"

"Right around nine, I guess."

"So you didn't stay at Reed's long?"

"Not long at all. I dumped him on the bed and thought maybe I'd make him some coffee. I hunted around through the mess in the kitchen a little, looking for some coffee and a coffee-maker, and finally I gave up and decided he'd be better off sleeping it off anyway."

"What about the stove? Did you leave it on?"

"I never got around to turning it on."

"Phil says the fire started at the stove."

"I guess Phil knows his business, but I didn't turn it on."

"And it wasn't already on for some reason?"

"No, ma'am."

"Was the oven door open or closed?"

"Closed. Have you seen that kitchen? There's no way I could have moved around in there at all with the oven door open."

"Did Reed smoke?"

"No."

"Maybe he decided to do some cooking?"

"After eatin' at Billy's? You know how much Idella piles on those plates. Anyway, I'd bet he didn't move a muscle after I tucked him in—but Baptists don't gamble, either."

"Did you notice anything out of the ordinary about the house?"

"The mess, you mean? That was ordinary for Reed."

"I meant anything that could explain the fire. Any odd smells, like a gas leak or anything?"

"No, nothing like that. What about spontaneous combustion? Or, I've heard about mice getting into matches and starting fires that way. The place was such a mess it could have been something like that, I guess. It wasn't cool enough for him to have a heater going, but maybe it was something to do with the furnace. Sorry. Spontaneous combustion is the best I can do."

"I'll see what Phil thinks about that suggestion. Okay, I guess that's all, Gordie. Thanks for your time."

As I made my way back down the stairs I was thinking that the real estate business must be pretty slow. The phone hadn't rung once while I was there and it looked like Gordie either couldn't afford a typist or didn't need one.

EIGHT

I WAS SITTING in my cruiser trying to decide on my next
step when I was interrupted by the cackle of Dawn's voice
on the radio.

"Trudy? You there? Havin' a nice day off? You want
to go see Ramona Edmunds? She's had aliens again."

I didn't exactly want to go see Ramona Edmunds, but
that wasn't the point. The good news and the bad news
was that I was pretty much the entire police presence in
Ogeechee at the moment. While that meant I could con-
tinue to investigate Reed's murder to suit myself, it also
meant I had to take all calls, even if the duty roster did
show that I was technically "off."

At least Mrs. Edmunds had solved my problem about
what to do next. I headed to the south end of town and
Cabana Place. You can tell by the street name that it's
one of the newer sections of town, lacking the gentility,
shabby or otherwise, of the older section. Cabana, for
goodness sake.

I took a zigzag path past the town's late afternoon hot
spots, slowing to a crawl as I passed the mini-marts and
liquor outlets (to create a police presence in the minds of
those aimless youth whose boredom might have led them
into the paths of unrighteousness).

I knew there was no hurry about getting to Ramona
Edmunds. She calls in periodically. I've never been able
to make up my mind whether it's because she's lonely or,
as Hen would put it, her pull rope's come loose. Whyever

it is, when she says she's had aliens, she doesn't mean Cubans or Puerto Ricans or Mexicans.

Mrs. Edmunds is a wispy little thing, the kind of woman you'd expect to be living out her last years in her own little drafty tin-roof house in the country somewhere, with a few chickens scratching around in the yard until she'd decide to wring one's neck and have chicken and dumplings. Maybe it was trading in such a place for half of a tiny brick duplex on Cabana Place that had made her a little strange.

One of the points in Hen's orientation speech to me had been the importance of the police force's service calls. "Don't kid yourself that we're gonna stamp out crime, 'cause it ain't gonna happen. There's a certain kind of mind that wants to know what the law is just so they can make sure they don't accidentally get on the right side of it, and I reckon we got as many of them per capita as New York City or Chicago. What we can do is make sure the citizens know which side we're on and be helpful whenever we can. It will help fill the time between crimes. Besides, it'll help keep the non-criminal element on our side." We all try to be polite on calls like this.

Today, in spite of the warmth, Mrs. Edmunds was wearing a sweater and heavy support hose with her cotton print dress. She was waiting for me on the tiny concrete slab that passed for her front porch, darting nervous glances from me to whatever she could see through the screen door.

"It's the aliens again," she called to me as I came up the walk.

"Are they still here? Inside?" I found myself hoping I'd find somebody, something, but she dashed my hopes.

"No. They're gone."

"You want me to make sure?" I'd learned not to take anything for granted with her.

"No. I know they're gone."

"Why don't we go inside then? Can I call somebody over to keep you company?" I know you're not supposed to ask more than one question at a time, but I didn't think those two would throw her.

"Oh, no! They took my phone!"

By now I was between her and the screen door and I could see inside. I could see nothing out of the ordinary. And I could see a telephone on the little bar that separated her kitchen from the rest of the buffet apartment.

"Let's go in, then," I encouraged. "It's safe."

Somewhat to my surprise, she led the way in as I held the door for her. Then I said, trying to sound surprised. "Well, look! Here's your phone!"

She crouched back. "No, that's not mine. It looks just like mine, but it isn't. They took mine and left this one. It's an alien phone."

"Did you see them this time?"

"No. They came while I was taking my garbage out."

The police academy doesn't really help you a lot with cases like this. You have to feel your way. Mrs. Edmunds and I both studied the phone. I don't know what was going on in her mind, but I was trying to figure out what to do next. Finally, I decided to try asking her.

"What would you like for me to do for you, Miz Edmunds?"

"Take it away. Take that alien telephone out of my house. It's got x-rays in it."

Thinking as I talked, I suggested, "How about if I take it down to the station and...fingerprint it...and sterilize it...and de-alienize it...and bring it back?"

"No, I don't want it. It's evil."

"Okay." I thought some more. "How about if I take it and bring you a different one?"

She smiled, and I wished her children and grandchildren and great-grandchildren could have seen the utter sweetness of it. "That would be so nice," she said softly.

Then I had what seemed like a bright idea. "And I'll see if we can't find some alien repellant down at the station."

The smile disappeared and she looked wary again. "I won't have anything with x-rays in my house."

"No, ma'am. Our alien repellants don't have x-rays." Was I really saying all this? It sounded weird even to me, but she bought it. Under Mrs. Edmunds' watchful eye I put the telephone into a produce bag from Grinstead's Market and stashed it in my trunk. In my notebook where I'd made notes on the call, I made a note to myself to come back later with a different phone and a non-x-ray alien repellant. Hen and Dwight were going to love this.

My visit with Mrs. Edmunds had taken my mind off the murder investigation and as I drove away I still hadn't worked out what my next step should be. I was passing the elementary school when an obvious opportunity presented itself.

Two familiar figures, familiar because I had seen them the night before hiding under a hydrangea, were moving down the road away from the school in a strange, erratic dance.

Both were dressed in T-shirts, shorts, and sneakers. When I got closer, I could see a soccer ball rolling back and forth between them as they danced along, seven or eight yards apart.

Genetics had played a trick on the Dawson brothers. I knew they were a couple of years apart in age, eight and ten, but I wasn't sure which was which. Would the slightly taller, thinner one be David, the older one, or Daniel, the younger one? The shorter, sturdier one seemed to move more smoothly and purposefully. Would that extra coordination come with age?

I gave the siren half a wail and the blue lights half a flash and pulled the car to a stop under an oak tree half a block ahead of the boys. I got out and leaned against the car as I watched them come. They seemed not to notice me. As they neared the car, the trailing boy, the shorter, sturdier one, kicked the ball into the street and the taller boy darted after it.

"Hold on a minute, there," I said.

He adroitly kicked the ball into the air and caught it. He glanced at the shorter boy and tucked the ball between his hip and his arm. He looked questioningly at me, but it was the shorter boy, approaching aggressively, who spoke.

"Heck," he said. "We were gonna see if we could dribble all the way home."

Dribble? Wasn't that basketball? Shows how much you don't know.

"Maybe I can make it up to you, give you a lift home or something," I said. "That is, if you can help me out."

"We don't ride with strangers," said the taller boy.

"Or talk to 'em," the shorter one added.

"Good for you. But I'm not a stranger. You know who I am. I'm Trudy Roundtree and I'm a police officer."

"Policemen are men and wear uniforms and carry guns." The shorter one. He stopped short of accusing me of stealing the car.

"Plainclothes division," I said, deciding a lie would be more practical than trying to explain why I was wearing a civilian skirt and blouse and working on my day off. "And you're wrong about police being men. I'm a woman

and I'm police. Here." I fished in the glove compartment
and came out with my ID and my gun. The boys studied
them with avid eyes.

"Okay. What do you want with us?" asked the shorter
boy.

"For one thing, you ought to stop dribbling down the
road. I can see why it would be more fun than just walk-
ing along, but it's dangerous."

"Are you gonna give us a ticket?" The taller boy finally spoke.

"For what? Driving a soccer ball without a license?"
The shorter, cynical one.

I looked from one to the other. "I could probably write
you a ticket for recklessness or obstructing traffic—"

"What traffic?" The cynic.

"—or being a nuisance, but I'd rather just talk to you
for a minute."

The taller boy looked nervous. The shorter one looked
smug. I wanted to see if I could erase the smugness.

"The last time I saw you two, you were crouching under a bush watching a house burn down."

The taller boy paled. The shorter one looked wary.
"Who says?"

"I say. You are"—I reached into the car for my notebook, flipped it open to the notes I'd made at Mrs. Edmunds', and pretended to read—"David and Daniel Dawson," watching them as I spoke the names to see which
responded to which. Evidently, the shorter, heavier, more
aggressive one was Daniel, the younger. He had the same
strong coloring that his Aunt Vivi had. By comparison,
David looked a little faded. Neither looked like a hard-
bitten hooligan, but who can tell by looks? Their features
were similar. Both boys were handsome, but David looked
softer, gentler. Maybe he'd been sick.

"You were seen at midnight last night on the premises of Six-seventeen Palm Street. I have a witness."

"So?" Daniel, of course.

"So since you were there, I thought you might be able to help me with my investigation."

"Investigation of what?" David asked at the same time his brother said, "We don't know anything about it."

Not much of a team.

"We didn't have anything to do with the fire," David added.

"And we don't have to talk to you." This Daniel would have been at home in any lion's den. "You can't give us a ticket and if you did it wouldn't matter because our granddaddy would make you sorry you did. Our granddaddy is very important."

"Yes, everybody knows B.L. Dawson is a very important man. Don't you think he'd want you to cooperate with the police?"

That stumped Daniel. Neither of the obvious answers seemed to appeal to him.

"What do you want to know?" David asked.

"We don't have to talk to her," Daniel repeated, sure of that much.

"I hoped we could have a friendly talk and you could give me some help, but if you want me to treat you like criminals, I can do that. You do have the right to remain silent. If you choose to give up that right, anything you say can be used against you in a court of law. You have a right to have a lawyer present while you are being questioned and if you can't afford a lawyer, one will be appointed for you."

"That's the Miranda warning. We've been Mirandized, Danny." David seemed pleased at the idea. Surprisingly, so did Danny. He relaxed and looked a little less tough.

"If you understand that warning and want to talk to me, you could sit in the police car while we talk." That clinched it. They climbed into the back.

David put the soccer ball on the seat between them and they both looked expectant. Danny no doubt was braced for intense interrogation, maybe even hoping for some police brutality.

"Okay, first tell me what y'all were doing out at midnight last night."

"Is there a law against that?" It sounded like simple curiosity coming from David. From Danny it would have sounded like a challenge.

"There's a curfew," I told him. "That means people younger than sixteen—you are both younger than sixteen, aren't you?—aren't supposed to be out alone after midnight. We don't make a big deal about it unless we're forced to." I tried to sound menacing, like they were forcing me to arrest them.

"Who're you going to tell?" David again.

"It depends. If what you have to tell me is important to what I'm investigating, I'll tell the chief of police. If it doesn't have anything to do with police matters, I don't have to tell even him."

I watched them out of the corner of my eye as I reached for the radio and reported to Dawn. "I'm parked on Southside Drive, near the school, talking to a couple of suspicious characters. No. No need for backup." The boys nudged each other.

"What was the question again?" Danny asked.

"What were you doing out so late?"

He gave a so-what kind of shrug. "We sneak out a lot at night."

"Why?"

The shrug again. "To see if we can."

"What do you do when you sneak out?"

They both shrugged and David fielded this one. "Most of the time we just go down to the lake. We have a gang."

"You're not supposed to tell about the gang, stupid." Danny hit his brother angrily with a fist.

"Was there a gang meeting last night?" I addressed the question to David since Danny had folded his arms and was looking out the window in disgust.

"No."

"Is Mark Ritter part of your gang?"

"That baby?" The voice was Danny's, but even David looked offended by the suggestion. Their poor cousin was only a couple of years younger.

"Were you at Reed's when the fire truck got there?"

"No. We heard the sirens and thought it would be rad to see if we could follow it."

"Where were you when you heard the sirens?"

"In bed."

And their parents thought they were safely tucked in for the night. I resolved never to have children.

"How did you get out without anybody knowing?"

The desire to brag outweighed Danny's determination not to cooperate with the cops. "Mama always turns up the television so loud she can't hear anything, and she never checks on us once she tucks us in." His sneer indicated his opinion of being tucked in, or maybe his mother's stupidity.

"And Mark always goes to sleep in the family room because he likes the noise. Mama won't let us do that." So even David had a grievance.

"Does he sleep at your house a lot?" Both shrugged, not much interested in Mark. Okay, then. "How did you know where the fire truck was going?"

"We didn't. I told you. We followed it." Danny gave

me a look that made it obvious he had no patience with people who don't pay attention.

I tried a little unction. "Wow! Wasn't that hard? How did you keep up?"

"We didn't keep up." That look again. "We followed it."

"How?"

"Easy as pie," Danny said. "We could tell which direction it started off."

"But we lost it when we had to hide from Granddaddy," David admitted.

"Was he out looking for you?"

"He was just coming home from work. He works late a lot, like Daddy." They seemed to take it for granted, but then it sounded like they'd grown up with it. To me, it sounded like pretty late hours to be putting in at a car dealership.

"And you recognized his car and hid from him?"

"When you're sneaking, you hide from everybody." Even David had contempt for my ignorance of something so basic.

Danny added, "But we could tell which way the fire truck went by following the lights."

"What lights?"

"When the sirens woke people up they'd get up and turn on their lights. So every time we came to a corner and didn't know which way to go, we went whichever direction had the most lights."

"That's very smart." My admiration was genuine. The story even sounded convincing. Still, I made a mental note to ask Miss Sarah and Phil when they had first noticed the boys at the fire.

"How long did you stay at the fire?"

They looked at each other again. Both shrugged.

I persisted. "You've heard about Reed, haven't you? Were you there when they found him?"

Both boys looked uncomfortable—not sad, just uncomfortable. Both nodded.

Finally, Danny said, "We didn't stay very long. Chicken gizzard''—he nodded in his brother's direction—"thought we ought to get home before we got in trouble, so we left. Not long after you did." He grinned wickedly. This was Danny Dawson at age nine. God help the world when he was grown.

I tried a finesse, a do-you-still-beat-your-wife. "What does your gang do besides pick on people like Reed?"

"You mean he called in the police? All right!"

Danny was so pleased at hitting Ogeechee's most wanted list he didn't seem to realize he'd confessed. One crime wave solved.

"Why pick on Reed?"

"He was a wimp."

"And it's okay to pick on wimps?"

"He was mean to Aunt Vivi." David needed to justify it.

"What did he do to her?" I'd really have liked an answer to this one.

"He divorced her," Danny said.

Oh.

"I don't know exactly," David admitted, "but everybody knows he was mean to her."

Maybe everybody in the Dawson family.

"Let me tell you about a stupid trick some friends of mine pulled once. Really stupid. Even stupider than the kind of things your gang was doing to Reed."

The boys perked up, alert for pointers.

"There was somebody they didn't like, and they'd been playing tricks on her. They put some dog doo in a paper bag and set it outside her door. Then they set fire to the bag and rang the doorbell. What they had in mind was that she would stomp out the fire and get the mess all over herself and they'd have a good laugh.''

These two were giggling at the very thought of such a great new trick with dog doo to add to their repertoire. I hastened to get to the cautionary part of my tale.

"Trouble was, the fire got out of hand. It wound up burning down her porch, and it was a wonder the whole house didn't go." They had stopped giggling, but I pulled out all the stops. It was fiction anyway, so what did it matter? "The mama dog and puppies under the porch didn't make it out. Sometimes things don't work out like you think they will. So you can see why I'm interested in the kind of thing your gang might think was funny." The dogs were a last-minute inspiration, based on their access to plenty of CC.

"We know better than to play with matches," David said.

"Yeah, that's stupid baby stuff." Danny spat that at me then turned to his brother. "See! I told you we'd get in trouble! The gang was a secret!" he said, hitting David with the soccer ball.

"It was kind of fun to do that stuff, to prove we could get away with it," David said, flinching away from the ball as he spoke. He looked sad as he said it, possibly identifying with the wimps of the world. "We didn't know he was going to die."

"Everybody dies," Daniel said. "And we didn't set fire to anything."

I decided I'd done pretty well, but wasn't likely to learn any more from them.

"I'd better get y'all home before your mama starts worrying about you getting run over for playing soccer in the street.''

I wound my way back to the highway and turned left, a route that took us past Billy Watson's Fish Place. ''Y'all were pretty busy last night. When did you find time to let the air out of Reed's tires? Before or after the fire?''

''Before,'' said David.

''We didn't,'' said Daniel.

There wasn't much conversation after that since the boys were busy pummeling each other. I swung off the highway onto Lake Loop. Most of the land on both sides of the road was still undeveloped, conspicuously including the twenty acres right around the lake that had been identified by one of Gordie's little red flags.

In the hope of minimizing the mayhem going on in the back seat, I said, ''It'll be handy for y'all if they put the new soccer field over here.''

''They won't,'' Danny panted between blows to his brother.

''They might. They haven't decided yet,'' I said.

''Granddaddy doesn't want to have a big old public park right in his front yard,'' Danny said, sneering the word ''public.''

It was just that simple for Danny. If I ever wanted to know what was cooking in Ogeechee in the future, crime-wise or politics-wise, I'd skip the city council meetings and go straight to Danny Dawson.

I pulled the car to a stop where two long, paved driveways met at the road. A short brick column between the driveways supported a pole and electric lantern. Wrought-iron signs in quaint ante-bellum designs stuck out on both sides of the lantern post. The one on the left featured a horse-drawn carriage. From it hung the words B.L. Dawson. The one on the right, under a lady's spreading skirts, read R.L. Dawson.

B.L.'s house was three-story pink brick, big enough that the six white columns supporting the porch roof didn't look out of scale. It stood well back from Lake Loop, among high-branched pines. The driveway forked near the house. One part led to the back, where I imagined a multi-car garage housing an assortment of brand new Chryslers and Plymouths. The other branch circled a raised flower bed and came back to join the main drive.

R.L.'s house, on the right, was a sprawling ranch of a darker pink brick. White wrought-iron curliques framed the porch and formed a rail across the front. Straight-back rockers painted white posed at one end of the porch. A swimming pool was visible in the back.

"Don't we even get to do the siren?" Danny asked.

"Or the lights?" David added.

"Do you want everybody to think you've been arrested?"

"Yes," said Danny.

"No," said David.

"Maybe next time."

The boys got out and started dribbling up the drive to the house with the pool. I called after them, "And lay off the stupid tricks. Your gang can find something better to do than hassle people, even if they are wimps. If I see any more of your brand of nonsense, I'll come after you, and all you midnight marauders will find yourselves swimming in such deep yogurt not even B.L. Dawson will be able to save you."

"Oh yeah?"

"Yeah."

And my daddy's bigger than your daddy.

As I watched, a pair of golden retrievers loped across

the yard to meet the boys. The final piece of the mystery of the Canine Crap fell into place.

That night, for a change, I dreamt of small boys running around setting fire to dogs.

NINE

EARLY NEXT MORNING I put on my uniform, figuring I ought to look official if I was going to be investigating—and I was definitely going to be investigating even if I was technically off duty—and headed for the small red brick building that houses the Ogeechee Police Department and the city offices.

People with city business go to the front door and enter a room dressed up with panelling and carpet the same color as the dirt they track in from the parking lot. People looking for the police go to the back, into the vestibule with the divided door that allows the dispatchers, who double as clerks, to open only the top half and deal with the public without having to invite them right into the dispatch room.

Dawn was transcribing a tape when I opened the half-door and came in.

"Heard from Hen yet?" I asked. At the interruption, Dawn punched the tape off and swiveled away from her typewriter.

"He called in a while ago. I told him about Reed. He said he'd be here as soon as he could and I'm supposed to have you here when he gets here."

"No kidding? Have me here, just like that? Who does he think he is?" It irritated me, but Dawn would never understand why.

"He thinks he's the boss," she said, matter-of-factly.

"As a matter of fact, I came in to type up reports from yesterday, but maybe I'll go out for coffee instead."

She smiled at me. My bravado impressed her about as much as it did the Dawson brothers.

I settled down at the typewriter in the file room and began typing reports from my notes of the day before. The other officers mutter into tape recorders and depend on Dawn and Brenda to make sense out of them and type the reports during their slow times, but I like to write my own. Working at that ad agency, I'd learned how much difference it makes how you say something, and I think forcing myself to say exactly what I mean is a good exercise. Sometimes it even helps clarify my thinking.

Sensible though it is, I'm considering giving it up. It's one more thing that sets me apart from the other officers. It's one more piece of evidence that I'm not quite on their par. Typing, after all, is woman's work, like dispatching and clerking, not man's work, like driving a cruiser and sitting under the blackberry bushes.

When I finished the reports, I went back to the dispatch room and started reading the reports from the other officers that Dawn had finished typing. It's a way of keeping up with the Ogeechee crime scene.

"What's he saying?" Dawn asked with a frown. "I wish the old bullfrog would take his chaw out when he's dictating."

"Let me hear."

I adjusted the earphones and Dawn ran the tape back.

"Maybe it isn't English," she suggested.

Hen came in while we were giggling over possible interpretations of Freddie Stinson's garbled sounds. Dawn was insisting it had to be "He sweared at Miss Possum," even though she didn't know any Miss Possum, and I was holding out for "He sweetened up his Postum."

Hen listened for a few seconds then enunciated carefully, "He swerved to miss a 'possum." Then he turned to me. "I'm getting myself a cup of coffee. I want you in my office when I get there."

"Yes, Your Reverence."

Dawn hastily returned to her typing. I fetched my reports from the file room, thinking it might improve his grumpy mood to hear some of the best parts of my interview with the Dawson boys. What's the point in polishing your prose if nobody else gets to appreciate it?

Hen's office is almost completely filled by a desk which nobody has seen the top of since maybe a week after he became chief of police ten years ago. The walls are covered with diplomas and certificates proving he takes advantage of in-service training opportunities offered by the Federal Bureau of Investigation, the Georgia Bureau of Investigation, the Georgia Police Association, and the Law Enforcement Assistance Administration. The certificates testify to his successful completion of courses ranging from firearms and explosives seminars to fingerprinting, to arson investigation and detection, to kinesiology. When I asked him if he was so insecure he needed those pieces of paper to bolster his ego, he told me they intimidate the opposition. He didn't define the opposition.

There's a swivel chair for Hen and a wooden client chair in the cramped space between the desk and a bookcase. I wedged myself into the client chair and waited. When he came back with his coffee, I noticed that he looked hot and uncomfortable. His face was puffy and splotched with red.

"What's wrong with your face?"

Instead of answering, he scratched at his neck. "I want to tell you how I've spent the last several hours." He leaned back in the chair and closed his eyes. "Yesterday afternoon, secure in the knowledge that nothing in Ogeechee was demanding my urgent attention, I joined up with a DEA reception party for a group of undesirables. This was at the cost of some discomfort to my person since it involved spending a number of exceedingly long hours with the snakes and chiggers and other little woodland creatures, keeping an eye on a homemade landing strip."

I nodded to indicate intelligent appreciation and sympathy. It didn't seem like the moment to interrupt.

"Up in the wee hours of the morning, it was made plain that the guests of honor were not coming, so we called the party off and I hauled my disappointed self back to civilization, looking forward to a hot shower and a warm bed."

I smiled at him.

He didn't return the smile, being intent on rubbing his eyes and continuing his story. "It was a serious disappointment to me to learn, when I checked in here, that one of the citizenry that I have sworn to serve and protect, one who had died a grisly but apparently accidental death, had been murdered, and that my well-trained and loyal staff had not managed to convey that information to me."

"The word came late yesterday afternoon," I offered, not stretching the truth too much. "Real late. Were you within radio range? Besides, didn't you tell Dawn not to use the radio? Anyway, no harm. I knew you'd want somebody to get after it and all we had was little ol' me, so I—"

Hen's right hand was waving at me to hush and his left was rubbing his eyes. I hushed.

"Then this mornin', just when I had my grits and eggs the way I like 'em, mixed up together with the yellow running through it, but not set hard, Mr. B.L. Dawson took the time out of his busy morning to call me at home and register a complaint about the conduct of the police department. Well, I don't ever want to hear anything like that, and if I did it wouldn't be after a miserable, nearly sleepless night, during which it looks like I got tangled up with the Poison Itchy Weed. By the time B.L. was through, my grits and eggs were cold and I have never learned to appreciate cold grits and eggs. So, what with this, that, and the other, you'll have to excuse me if I ain't my usual lovable self this morning.''

"You're excused," I said. "B.L. Dawson. That's a co-incidence.'' I waved my report at him, "I—''

"No, Officer Roundtree, that is not what you would call a coincidence. It is more what you'd call a cause and effect. You had a talk with Danny and David Dawson yesterday.''

I nodded. Even through my growing sense of unease, I noticed that Hen, and presumably B.L., mentioned the younger boy first.

"Well, ol' B.L. tells me he doesn't much like the idea of one of my police officers harassin' his grandkids and he wants to be sure it doesn't happen again. I'm supposed to make sure it doesn't happen again. Now, Trudy, even you ought to know you don't interrogate minors without a guardian somewhere around. It violates their civil rights or something. And you don't ever, ever, harass 'em. Why don't you tell me about this police harassment.''

"Glad to. If there was any police harassment bein' done, the police officer was on the receiving end.''

"Uh-huh.''

"I did talk to them. I didn't harass them and I'll bet they didn't say I did.'' But Danny might have. And I could easily imagine both boys bragging about being Mir-andized. "Could I hear the complete charges against me so I'll know how to conduct my defense?''

"You've heard the charges. B.L. says you questioned

his grandkids without proper supervision and he wants you officially reprimanded. This is an official reprimand.''

''If I was so far out of line, why isn't Ronnie the one who called? He's their daddy, isn't he? You'd better quit rubbing your eyes. I think they're swelling.''

He looked at me in surprise, but quit rubbing his eyes. ''It's just a wild guess, but it could be they decided the legal ground might not carry as much weight as ol' B.L. Or maybe Ronnie didn't see anything to get upset about even if he is a lawyer.''

''Can I talk now? Put on the defense?''

Hen nodded permission and scratched his neck.

''I'm sorry about Mr. Dawson getting uptight and ruining your breakfast.''

''That ain't much of a defense.''

It wasn't true, either. I don't give a hoot about B.L. Dawson, and Hen's description of his breakfast turned my stomach.

''How well do you know those kids?'' I asked him.

''Well enough to recognize them hidin' behind a bush at night.''

''You remember pointing them out to me at the fire? Well, that and what Miss Sarah said made me think they were the ones behind the vandalism at Reed's and I wondered if maybe one of their stunts got out of hand and started the fire.''

''Don't tell me you were actually harassing those young'uns in the legitimate pursuit of your assigned duties!'' His amazement was as false as his mother's hair color, Tequila Sunrise the last time I saw her.

He had stressed ''assigned duties,'' so I decided to stress the CCC connection. ''I wish you'd quit using that H word. I wasn't harassing anybody. But yes, Your Reverence, I was in the pursuit of my duties. I thought if I talked to them more or less casually I'd find out more than if I made a big official deal out of it, scaring them and having so many guardians of their rights around that they wouldn't tell me anything. I took for granted that if I was right, the boys wouldn't want the guardians to find out, either. And I wanted to know, not necessarily have something that would stand up in court. With Reed dead, that case is closed. They aren't going to bother him anymore and he isn't going to press charges against them."

"Okay, I almost follow your twisted logic. Except that the fire is not a dead issue. Did you learn enough to make it worth an official reprimand?"

"Actually, yes, I think so." I considered. "Unless there's a lot more to the reprimand."

"That's it unless you want to take B.L. and Ronnie to court to clear your good name."

"I think I'll let that go. But here's what I did learn from the boys: We can close that vandalism file; it was them and maybe some of their friends. They're also the ones who let the air out of the tires on Reed's car Tuesday night. But they didn't have anything to do with the fire. I believed them when they said they haven't been playing with matches. Not that I'd necessarily believe anything the little boogers *said*. It was their body language—kinesiology." I gestured in the direction of Hen's framed certificates. "I think I did a pretty good job of clearing up a bunch of unsolved mysteries. That about the fire is negative information, but once we find out all the things that couldn't have started it, we'll be left with whatever did start it, right?"

Hen snorted.

"And I'm giving notice right now that I'm going into another line of work when Danny Dawson turns into a teenager. Actually, Hen, B.L. should thank me for the way

I went about it. It was a way of protecting them and getting at the truth, too. If I *had* found out they were the ones who started the fire, I wouldn't have been able to use it, since I didn't do it by the book, but at least we'd know. I threw in Miranda for flash."

"You're telling me that instead of wanting an apology from you, B.L. should thank you?"

"He wants an apology? After I gave the little hoodlums the thrill of a ride home in a police car?"

"Calm down." Hen came to an upright position and put his feet on the floor. "He also reminded me about how my budget is coming up for review in a couple of months. The old turd."

"If he's half as impressed with himself as Danny is with him, you ought to be worried."

"There's probably no harm done." He was scratching again.

"Thanks."

"You're welcome." The man is impervious to sarcasm. "Seeing's how we've got a murder case on our hands, as well as what begins to smell like arson, no matter what Phil thinks, we need to be on our toes here." He eyed the papers in my hand and sighed. "Maybe you'd better tell me what else you've been doing."

"Gladly." I waved the Dawson report again. "Besides clearing up that earlier crime wave, I think it's interesting that the boys said their granddaddy, your very own best friend, B.L. Dawson, was out Tuesday night, about the time the fire started."

He stared gloomily at the papers in my hand. "So you did start on the murder case."

"Of course I did, as soon as I found out that's what it was. I've talked to a few people trying to see if anybody has an idea how the fire could have started. I didn't let on we think it's murder."

"Who've you talked to?"

"Suzanne McCloud."

"Why?"

"She'd been dating Reed. Miss Sarah thought maybe they were together that night."

"She kill him?"

"No."

"And?"

"And what?"

"And who else have you talked to?"

"Gordon Albritton. He took Reed home from Billy Watson's."

"Find out anything?"

"No."

"Talk to anybody else?"

"No."

"Write up reports?"

"Just finished." I squinted at him and judged that his eyes were just a shade less open. I decided not to mention the ideas my talks with Suzanne and Gordon had generated. Why bother an ailing man?

"Okay," he said. "Give me the reports. Here's what you do now: You go talk to Phil, tell him we need more pictures of the place. If you want to, you can go over it with him again, looking for anything suspicious. I'll take over after I've read your reports."

"You don't want me to keep on talking to people? Why can't I keep on?"

"Because I want you to work with Phil."

"Phil doesn't need my help."

"Maybe you'll learn something. We need to be thorough. Leave your reports here for me." He brushed the air like a farm wife shooing chickens. As I left, I noticed his hands were red and blotchy, too.

It occurred to me that it would be an act of charity for me to liberate Dawn from her unhealthy idealization of Hen. I was describing his breakfast, and Dawn was making retching noises, when he emerged from his office.

Dawn, face crimson, pounded her chest with a fist and said, "It's gone. Don't know what I could have choked on." The girl has possibilities.

"Dawn, honey, the next time you don't have anything better to do than sit around and make fun of the eating habits of your superiors, why don't you let me know and I'll find you something."

"Yes, sir." She turned red again.

Hen closed his eyes and went on talking, making plans. "Trudy, while you and Phil are over at Reed's, look around for something that could have been used to cause fatal trauma to his trachea. And we've still got to know how that fire got started. It might have been an accident of some kind, but—"

"But it might have been that somebody killed him and set the fire to cover up the murder," I said. After all, I'd had more time to think about it than he had.

"Right," he said. "Now, most of the time, it's somebody in the family of the dear departed that gets aggravated enough to kill 'em, so I'll start by talking to Ritters and Dawsons."

"I don't think there are any more Ritters, except Mark," I told him, based on what I'd learned from Miss Sarah and Gordon Albritton.

He shook his head like someone hoping to chase off gnats. Then he shook it again. Beneath his blotchiness he paled. But he was still the Chief. "Trudy, I think maybe you better take me by to see Doc Cummings on your way to Phil's.''

Dawn and I were looking at each other in puzzlement when he explained. "I can't get my eyes open."

"I told you not to keep rubbing them," I said unsympathetically as I took him by the arm and led him to my car.

As it turned out, Doc Cummings was expecting Hen, since everybody else who'd been on the DEA gig had already checked in. Hen was a little behind the others because he'd stopped off to give me my reprimand. The others were already bedded down and I looked in on them.

"Now don't you worry," I told each one in the perkiest, most irritating voice I could muster. "I've got everything under control!''

Nobody seemed to feel well enough to chat, so I found my way back to the doctor.

"Is there anything else I can do?" I asked Doc.

"You could see about filling out the paperwork to put 'em all on sick leave for a day or two," he told me.

"Right," I said. "I'll get Dawn right on it. But why are you putting them in the hospital?''

"It's pretty severe poisoning. Could be poison elder. Whatever it was, it looks like it was building up strength all winter. We'll keep 'em here to make sure we don't get a bad reaction.''

"What I've seen so far isn't a bad reaction?''

"Could be worse. Excuse me, now, Trudy.''

So. I didn't want to be glad Hen and the rest of the boys were suffering from maybe poison elder, but my concern for them quickly faded under a rising sense of excitement. By default, I was in charge of the murder investigation.

Hen wanted thorough police work? Okay. I'd give him

thorough police work. I'd talk to Phil first, since Hen had
been so clear about that. But I had some other ideas, too,
as soon as I was through with Phil.

How had Hen begun outlining the investigation? He'd
made it clear that talking to family members was a pri-
ority. In all the excitement, he'd forgotten to order me to
apologize to B.L. Dawson, surely just an oversight, so I'd
work on something that sounded like a reasonable facsim-
ile of an apology, to launch a conversation with him. Besides, Reed had worked for B.L. Further besides, I thought
it would be interesting to find out, if B.L. had nothing to
hide, why he had such a hissy when he found out I'd been
talking to his grandsons.

TEN

PITTMAN PRESS, with "Home of The *Ogeechee Beacon* for More Than Sixty Years" in uneven gold leaf on the window, is a couple of blocks south of the old bank building, on Milford Street. As I pulled to a stop at the curb in front, I could see Phil, through the picture window that makes up the front of the shop, fiddling with a pile of printing catalogs. He waved when he saw me.

"Well, hey," he said, as soon as the jangling bell on the door subsided. "You doin' okay? That was pretty rough stuff at Reed's yesterday." As far as I could tell, he seemed sincere. He wasn't trying to needle me. "What can I do for you?"

"I'm doing okay, thanks. I need to talk to you. There've been developments."

"What do you mean 'developments'?" He patted the catalogs one more time, then gave me his full attention.

"Our fire has turned into a murder case."

"Murder?" He looked blank. "What? How? Why? You mean Reed? Reed was murdered?"

"Do newspaper people do that who-what-where-when-why thing automatically? Yes, it looks like Reed was murdered. But, Phil, it's the fire chief I came to talk to, not *The Beacon.*"

"Well, sure. I didn't mean to sound like—" He shook himself. "You know, Trudy, I'm still in shock. All day long I've been trying to put Reed out of my mind. And now you tell me he was murdered. Are you sure? How do you know? Who—" He stopped in mid-question and stared at the neat pile of catalogs before he met my eye. "What do you want to see the fire chief about?"

"I want you to go back over there with me."

"We were pretty thorough yesterday. Why go back?"

"Yesterday we were looking at a fire scene, maybe an accident scene. Now we need to look at a murder scene. I don't mean to say we missed anything, but if we go over it again we might see something we overlooked when we had nothing to be suspicious about. For one thing, you said it didn't look like arson to you. You might want to reconsider."

"I see what you mean, but I don't see how I could have been wrong about that. All the indications are that the fire started at the stove, in the oven. Somebody could have turned it on and piled the stuff there to catch, but even if they did, I don't know what kind of evidence there would be. It's the kind of accident that happens all the time."

"You may be absolutely right, but this is one accidental fire that deserves another look, just in case there is something. Can you get loose?"

"Sure I can. That's one of the few benefits to balance all the headaches of being the boss." He disappeared through the door in the wall behind the counter, calling "Molly!" as he went. I could hear his voice and his sister's. Almost immediately he reappeared, pinning his fire chief's badge to his shirt. A camera bag was slung over his shoulder.

"That was quick."

"Quick is one of the things they teach us in our basic firefighter's course."

He followed me to my car. It wasn't until he had his seat belt fastened that he looked around and asked, "Is Hen meeting us there?"

"What makes you ask?"

That seemed to take him aback. "Well, uh, he is the chief of police. It seems like a natural assumption."

"No. He won't be meeting us there. Don't you think I can handle this?"

"Never said you couldn't, did I?"

"For your information, Hen is over at Cowart Memorial with a bad case of poison something-or-other."

"No kidding." Phil's eyes bulged and it took me a minute to realize he was stifling a laugh.

"Care to share your little joke? Surely you aren't laughing at Hen's misfortune. And surely you aren't laughing at the idea that I'm conducting the investigation."

He is quick, I had to give him that. Either that or sincere. "No, ma'am. Neither one. I'm kind of struck by the fact that here's a murder case, probably the most important police business in this town since—well, ever—something that would justify all the time and preparation Hen has put into the job, and he's out of commission. He must be one sick puppy."

"Good comparison, Phil. When I left him, he couldn't even get his eyes open. So I figure I have a couple of days to solve this case before he puts me back on alien patrol."

"More power to you," he said. Again, I couldn't find any sarcasm.

"Okay, then. I have a few answers to some of those who-what-where-when-why questions you started to ask. It looks like somebody whacked Reed across the windpipe and killed him. Then whoever it was set fire to the house hoping we'd think Reed died in the fire—just like w~~~~d think. If Miss Sarah hadn't had to let her dog out, the fire might have done enough damage for it to work."

"But arson?"

"He could have set the fire just the way you say it happened, and then left."

"Or she. She could have set the fire."

I knew he was pulling my chain this time, but I let it pass. "How long did you say the fire had been burning before you got there?" I asked. "That will make it easier for us to find out who it was—somebody without an alibi."

"Couldn't have been much more than half an hour. Probably less."

"We don't have the full report yet from the medical examiner. When we get that, we might be able to pin it down even more."

I parked in Reed's driveway and we went into the house, stopping just inside the door as we had the morning before. The house had been grim enough before, the scene of a fire and a death. Now, the smells had become less pungent, but somehow more pervasive, as though they'd settled down and planned to stay. The overlay of dampness made it seem ghostly, and knowing it was the scene of a murder made it seem somehow colder and the smell more nauseating. Death had crept up and stolen a lot of people from me, but usually in a peaceful way, often as a release from pain. I wasn't a stranger to death. Even Zach's violent death was not like this. I had never seen murder. I shivered and hoped Phil hadn't noticed.

"We need to stay together, so if we have to we can testify that neither one of us planted any evidence, or removed any," I told him.

"Good idea. Did you learn that at police academy, or are you just naturally smart?"

"Both. Don't try to butter me up. You might as well know you're on my wrong side."

Phil looked woebegone, a kindergartner who knew he

was out of favor with the teacher. "I tend to grow on people. Slowly. Like moss." I resisted the impulse to pat his head. He sighed. "Okay, let's get to work. What do we do?"

"I think we should go over everything we did before, see if anything new strikes us. Anything we weren't looking for before. For instance, maybe we'll find something that could have been used as a murder weapon."

"Okay. Sure. What kind of a weapon?"

"Something like a small pipe, Dawn said, something strong enough to do the job." I swallowed and cleared my throat, which felt extremely vulnerable. "Maybe it's just knowing this is a murder scene, but it already looks different to me. Does it to you?"

Phil looked around. "I can't say it does. But I don't trust my eyes anyway. I trust my camera. The light's different now. That's probably what you're noticing."

It was as good an explanation as any.

Phil began to commune with his camera and I tried to commune with the house, trying not to be irritated with the compulsive way he kept taking his glasses off, folding them, and sticking them in his pocket, while he clicked the camera, then replacing them while he planned his next shot. Good lord, now he was practically on the nasty floor, focusing the camera on patterns in the muck. It occurred to me that he could be humoring me, merely trying to look productive, which was pretty decent of him since I don't believe there's a laundry detergent on the market that could salvage those slacks. In spite of myself, I got interested in watching him.

"Those footprints really stand out, don't they?"

"Some of 'em." He sounded like he had to come back from a distance.

"Do you think you're going to get a picture that will show them?"

"I'm trying to."

"Hey, Phil?"

"Hm?"

I'd lost him. I let him click his camera while I stood still and took mental pictures, trying to draw information out of every detail.

We moved on to Reed's bedroom. I studied the bed. Except for the cleaner place where Reed had been, there was nothing to catch my attention. I saw no pole or rod, nor the remnant of a pole or rod, on which he could have clothes-lined himself and fallen to the bed, dead or dying, and stretched out so peacefully.

The curtain rods were hollow, flimsy metal that would have bent instead of inflicting fatal trauma to Reed's trachea.

I opened the closet door. The wooden rod inside was supported at the ends in half-rounds scooped from a facing board. I pushed the clothes to one end and pulled up on the rod. Unattached, it rose easily, but it didn't seem likely that someone would remove the clothes from the rod and the rod from the closet in order to whack Reed with it, even if he was out cold and causing no commotion, and then hang things back on the rod, especially if whoever it was expected the house to burn down. Surely there'd have been something handier. Maybe in an empty closet. Or, if it was premeditated, the killer brought the weapon with him. Her?

"Find anything?" Phil asked.

"Not really. What about you?"

"I found a lot of ashes. I've decided you're right. It could be just the light, but there is something different about the place now."

"Do you believe in ghosts?"

He looked at me hard and didn't answer at once. "Do you?" he finally asked.

"I have to. My Aunt Pet Butterworth lives in a haunted house."

"I've heard about the Butterworth house. Who haunts it?"

"Family ghosts. It's an old house, built by one of my great-great-great-greats. One of the ghosts is a boy who ran off when he was just fourteen, to join the Army of the Confederacy, and was wounded at Fredericksburg and came back home to die. Aunt Pet says he plays marbles on the back porch and sometimes borrows her fishing pole."

"You're kidding."

"She believes it," I assured him. "I think she likes the idea that some of the family still hangs around."

He seemed to think it over before he asked, "Do you think Reed's ghost is here?"

I had to admit I didn't. "I wish it were. I wouldn't mind some help—besides yours, I mean. No. Not a ghost. But there's something."

"Um-hmm." Phil shivered.

I was feeling better, though, and even felt a little warmer toward Phil since he was affected by the place, too. "Have you got enough pictures?"

"You can never have enough pictures," he said, following me into the boy's bedroom.

"Aha! I thought I remembered this closet was almost empty."

Phil put his glasses in his pocket and began jockeying around for a good angle.

This rod didn't have anything hanging on it, but it was nailed in place. Old nails. "Oh, shoot!"

"I'm not ready to shoot."

"Not you, Phil. A theory shot. Let's try the office."

"Be right with you." He was much more interested in the light than in whatever theory I might have had shot down.

"Oh. Phil, there were a couple of smallish boys watching the fire last night, Danny and David Dawson. Did you happen to notice them, notice whether they were there when you got here?"

He shook his head. "Sorry. All I was noticing was the fire."

"That's what I figured."

The rod from the closet in the office was missing entirely, its space having been taken by tall filing cabinets.

The files seemed to be the kind anybody might have to help keep their finances in order. Maybe more of them, since Reed had been an accountant. Car expense? Who'd really keep a file for car expense?

"You about finished?" Phil's voice startled me. Okay, so I could be singleminded, too. And I hadn't really expected to find a file labeled Motive For Murder, had I?

"If you can tear yourself away from all these photo opportunities, I can tear myself away from the files," I told him. "I haven't really found anything. Anyplace that started out as messy as this one did and had a fire on top of that would be a mess, but this looks worse than I'd expect—drawers open, papers hanging out, things like that. This goes beyond run-of-the-mill slovenly. Does it look to you like somebody tore the place apart? Like they were looking for something?"

"I don't know. You'd think a burglar would pick a place that looked more like it would be worthwhile."

"That's a drawback to the theory, all right. But maybe somebody knew there was something here."

"But didn't know where it was?"

"That's weak, I'll admit, but there's got to be some explanation. Did it look this bad yesterday? This messy?"

He frowned. "I'd hate to say. But when we compare these pictures to the ones I took yesterday, we'll know."

"How soon do you think you can have the pictures?" He looked at his wristwatch and seemed to consider. "The sooner, the better. This is a murder case," I reminded him.

"How soon do you want them? I do have some other things I need to get to."

"I have a few other things, too. Later today?"

"How about this evening? It's best if I can do it after hours, when I'm not so likely to be interrupted."

"You develop them yourself?"

"It's the only way to get what you want."

"Okay. What time?"

"Seven or eight should be good."

"Okay. I quit." I looked around hopelessly. "I'm ready to go if you are."

We started back through the house. Whatever I'd hoped to accomplish, I hadn't done it, and now I was impatient to leave. It exasperated me when Phil paused at the door and pointed his camera back into the room. "Just a couple more on this roll. Might as well finish it."

That's when I saw it, right there by the door, and it was so obvious I felt like I must have had a neon sign on my forehead flashing the words Molasses Brain.

Phil, being totally occupied with his camera, didn't seem to notice the sign, so all I said was, "Golf clubs would be about the right size, wouldn't they?"

He looked at me in surprise, then a smile slowly spread across his face. "Of course! Why didn't I see that?"

"You're doing your job; I'm doing mine," I told him modestly.

Conscious of the possibilities of fingerprints, I got a jack handle and a couple of plastic bags from my car and we wrestled the golf bag to over to it, where we placed it in the trunk alongside Mrs. Edmunds' phone.

I was so excited about the possibilities, I could hardly wait to get rid of Phil and get on to the next thing. When I pulled the car to a stop in front of *The Beacon,* I left the motor running.

"See you after a while," I said. Then, "The sooner the better."

Phil took the hint and got out. I headed for Dawson Motors.

ELEVEN

DAWSON MOTORS, the only Chrysler-Plymouth dealership in the county, stretches over several acres along the highway east of town. Neither of the salesmen lounging in the air-conditioned showroom was B.L., but one of them allowed as how B.L. was "back in the office" and pointed.

I made my way past the obligatory isolation chambers for salesmen to use while practicing their craft on potential customers. B.L.'s office at the end of the passageway was easy to identify by a brass plaque on the closed door. I knocked.

"Come on in," B.L. called in a come-on voice, and I opened the door into an office that looked so much like Gordie Albritton's real estate office that it took me by surprise, considering that everybody knows the Dawsons are the richest people in town, and also considering the palatial Dawson home. Maybe B.L. was afraid if his office looked too ritzy, customers would get the idea that he ought to be able to make them better deals.

B.L.'s in his late fifties, early sixties. His plentiful wavy hair is still mostly dark and well-trimmed. I could see Vivi and Danny in the strong coloring, but where Vivi was thin and Danny was sturdy, B.L. was pudgy and red-faced, apoplectic, as though years of prosperity and getting his own way about everything had backed up on him.

"Mornin', Mr. Dawson."

"Morning." He stood and made a sweeping gesture toward the client chair on my side of the desk. As we both sat, he spoke again. "I already told Hen I'd do the cookin' at the Cow Patty Bingo barbecue again this year. How much did that raise last year?''

The anonymous soul who'd invented this fund-raiser would have been called a marketing genius up in Atlanta. It's all profit. The school lets you use the football field, some farmer lets you use his cow, you make a grid dividing the field into sections of one square foot each (about the size of a cow pie) and you sell chances on which square the cow pie, or the major portion of it, will land in. On the day of the event, you put the cow on the field and appoint someone to watch her and call the surveyor when she performs so you'll know who wins the prize, part of the proceeds or something donated by a local business. We usually have a barbecue to entertain people while they wait for the outcome, and Dawson Motors usually springs for the meat.

"It brought in nearly three thousand dollars last year," I answered, just as though I didn't know he already knew and didn't think he was reminding me of what a selfless public servant he was. I figured it wouldn't cost me to use a little unction at this point. "That's a lot of community participation. Sure beats raising taxes to pay for a fire truck and supplies for the women's shelter. But the fund-raiser isn't what I came about.''

B.L. smiled complacently. "No. I didn't figure it was. But you didn't really have to come all the way out here to apologize.''

I stuck my tongue in my cheek and instead of saying anything I gave him what I hoped was a cool, enigmatic Mona Lisa smile. Actually, I was more pleased than not at his assumption of the apology. I'd been working on a carefully worded non-apology. Maybe wouldn't even have to use that.

"Since the grapevine around Ogeechee moves faster

than kudzu, you probably know we've got the medical report back on Reed," I told him to distract him from noticing I hadn't really apologized.

"No, I hadn't heard. That was a terrible thing, that fire."

"It's worse than that. The medical examiner in Atlanta tells us Reed was dead before the fire. That makes it look like it must have been murder. Do you mind if I ask you a few questions?"

B.L. devoted a few seconds to shaking his head and tsk-tsking. Then his eyes narrowed. "Reed was murdered and you want to question me? Where's Huckabee?"

"I left him over at the hospital, being treated for poison elder or whatever's in season."

"That's too bad," B.L. said. "When'll he be back on the job?"

Everybody seemed to be concerned about Hen's health. I was sure he'd be touched. I was more than a little bit peeved, but tried to swallow that for the sake of finding out a few things. "I'm not sure," I said. "I'm trying to help out by getting a little of the underbrush out of the way." I didn't actually gag on that, so I continued. "Now, I know Reed's death has been a shock, with him being an employee and a former family member, so I'll get out of the way of your grief as soon as I can." My sarcasm apparently slid right by him. That's what unction will do for you; it's as good as castor oil.

"I need to ask you a couple of things, so I can get a complete report together. You know I haven't been on the force very long, so you'll understand that I'd better be careful and thorough if I don't want my boss to get after me." I tried to look eager and harmless and, of course, apologetic, as I pulled out my notebook.

B.L. leaned back in his chair and clasped his hands over

his pudgy middle. He gave me a small, civic-minded smile. Not as big as a hot-customer smile, but passable.

"Can you think of any reason for somebody to want to kill Reed?" When B.L. didn't answer, I added, trying to sound like I needed guidance, "Anybody at all you think I ought to talk to besides the Dawsons?"

His smile slipped a little and he gave me a look that convinced me I'd never be able to get a good deal on a used Chrysler from him. He'd have to learn better control if he was going into state politics, as the local kudzu vine had it.

"Besides the Dawsons?" he asked.

I shrugged. "I figure y'all know him best. If he had some trait that would make somebody want to kill him, you'd be likely to know what it was."

"Now wait a minute!"

"Oh, I don't think you should take it personally. Family members—or ex-family members—are a logical place to start inquiries. It wasn't an accidental death," I reminded him. "And it wasn't a bar fight, where he might have just happened to be in the wrong place."

"Don't look at me. I always liked the boy."

I smiled at him, a genteel way of calling somebody a liar. He recognized it and repositioned his own smile and spoke in a frank, fatherly way I didn't believe for a second.

"I always figured Reed for a climber—not somebody who could pull himself up, but somebody who would try to climb up by holding on to somebody else. You know his family?"

"No."

"White trash dirt farmers."

I kept still and he apparently took it for encouragement. "And when he saw that Vivi was interested in him he saw his way up and out. I tried to tell her she could do better than that, but nobody ever could tell her anything. You know Vivi."

I nodded, and my sincerity must have shown through. He sounded a little friendlier when he said, "Well, take my advice and don't ever try to tell her anything."

"I'll remember that. But back to Reed: If you felt like that about him, why did you give him a job?"

"In the first place, Vivi and her ma got after me about it. Said the young folks needed some help and how would it look if I wouldn't help 'em. So I let him keep my books."

"But you kept him even after they divorced."

He studied the cuticle on his left pinkie. "I was used to him by then. There'd have been the trouble of training somebody else. Besides, there aren't that many people in town who can do bookkeeping. Sure I kept him on."

"I heard he was planning to leave town."

B.L. shook his head. "He hadn't mentioned it to me."

"What would you have thought about it, him leaving town?"

"Hmph. I wouldn't have minded seeing the last of him." He didn't seem to notice how that sounded under the present circumstances or even seem worried about finding another bookkeeper.

"What was he going to do about Mark? Just leave him?"

"He'd have had to. His grandma dotes on that boy—on all her grandkids."

"I can see why. Danny and David are great kids. It looks like they're really into soccer. Is that why you're taking such an interest in the new park and sports complex?"

"Who said I was?"

"Danny and David."

"Well. Kids. Matter of fact, I'm keeping clear of that."

"They seemed to think it would go wherever you wanted it to go."

His smile passed smirk on its way to grimace and he made what I thought might be an unaccustomed attempt to look modest. "Well, they do think a lot of their grand-dad. And I will admit I do favor one particular parcel, but it wouldn't be fair to say I exercise undue influence on things around here. The Commissioners will decide."

"It could be pretty important to whoever is trying to sell the land to the town."

"Oh, yes m'am, it sure could. And it's important to Ogeechee for us to get it, instead of letting it go to some other town. Glennville wants it, you know. It makes sense for it to be here at the county seat, and it'll be good for business, too, bring in people from all over the place. We're ready to pay top dollar for worn-out farm land. There's a lot of people would like to get a pretty good price for land that hasn't been doing them any good at all."

"What kind of money are we talking about?"

"It wouldn't be right for me to mention figures, since the town wants to make the best deal possible. Naturally the people who have land to sell are keeping an eye on the proceedings to make sure things are on the up and up. But I don't see any harm in telling you that it will look like a whole lot of money to the people who get it."

"And you could swing the vote?"

He smiled again. Looking modest was something else he'd need to practice, besides self-control. "I probably could."

"You don't happen to own any of those parcels, do you?"

"Me? No. What makes you ask that?"

"Nothing. Just wondered." I believed his denial, but there was something about the look in his eye, something that just darted past like a minnow in shallow water, that made me think I hadn't asked exactly the right question.

I stood. "Well, I appreciate your time, Mr. Dawson. I guess I'll get on."

He had started on a genuine smile when I turned to another page in my notebook. "Oh! Just so I can tell Hen I didn't let any details get by me, let me get down where you were between nine and eleven-thirty Tuesday night."

His smile quit growing and took on a forced look. I tried smiling back, pen poised.

"As far as I remember, I was at home the whole time."

I nodded and started to write, then stopped. "Somebody told me they saw you out pretty late that night."

He sucked a tooth. "Come to think of it," he finally said, "I guess I was working late that night. I do it so much I don't even think about it. It might have been after ten when I got home."

I wrote "after ten" and put a question mark after it.

"Let me see you out." He walked to the door and opened it for me and closed it firmly behind me.

I stopped on the way out to ask which of the salesmen would have been working late with B.L. on Tuesday. They didn't seem to know what I was talking about.

TWELVE

THERE'S A PROVERB that says fine words butter no parsnips, but as Thackeray so sensibly observed in *Vanity Fair,* half the parsnips in society are served up with no other sauce (or words to that effect). With that in mind, and also mindful that blood is thicker than water and chains of command are thicker still, I decided to check in with Hen at Cowart Memorial and butter a few parsnips.

I counted on having to give him a run-down on what I'd been doing on Reed's case, so I was prepared for that. I hadn't counted on, and was not prepared for, finding Aunt Lulu, Teri, and Delcie in his room when I got there.

Aunt Lulu, as always, looked completely put together and elegant. She might have come straight from the Cut-n-Curl where she'd had them pick exactly the right shade of apricot hair to set off the lavender slacks, sweater, and sandals she was wearing. Much as I love her, I blame her inexorable femininity for a lot of what's wrong with Hen's attitudes toward women.

Teri reminds me of a bird. Before she went in for a color analysis and decided she ought to quit wearing autumnal russets and browns, she was a partridge. In the bright clear colors she wears now, she's still a motherly bird of a woman—mothering both Hen and Delcie half to death—but now it's a parakeet or a parrot, definitely something more exotic than a partridge.

I took them in at a glance and drank in Delcie, a three-and-a-half foot bundle of pure charm who combines all the best genes the Roundtrees and Huckabees and Teri

Elkins could put into the pool. Her shiny white-blonde hair and electric blue eyes signal her high voltage. Even her personality is the best mix, combining the easy-going nature Teri always displayed until this house business, with the insatiable curiosity and need-to-know that characterizes the Roundtrees. Hen, Delcie and I are all alike in that. Once any of us gets hold of a problem we're going to keep after it until it makes sense to us, and we're hard to live with until it does. It's as if we all got stuck at that age where no matter what answer you give them, children keep asking why. Why does Mr. Brown walk like that? Because he had a disease that kept his legs from growing straight. Why? Because when he was a little boy, doctors didn't know how to keep people from getting it. Why? Because the right medicine was hard to find. Why? And on back to original sin, if you have the patience.

Delcie and I have been missing each other since Teri decided to hold it against me that Grandma didn't leave the house to Hen. They used to be in and out of the house all the time, but now we're stuck in notions of ownership that are new to all of us. I think Teri's waiting for me to see the light about how much worse they need the house than I do (which is true but beside the point) and give it to them (which isn't going to happen). Until I see the light, Teri's shadow keeps coming between me and the light of my life.

"How're you doing, sweetheart?" I asked, catching Delcie in mid-jump and hugging her to me.

"I'm sad," she said.

Me, too, I thought, holding onto her. "Why is that?"

"We were talking about Reed," Aunt Lulu explained.

"Mark Ritter wasn't at school today," Delcie told me. "Because his daddy died. That's a sad thing."

"Yes, honey, it sure is."

"I'd cry if my daddy died." She looked at Hen.

"Of course you would, honeybunch, we all would, but don't you worry about it, hear?" From Lulu.

"Yessum," but she kept on looking at Hen.

I could see why Delcie was worried. I'd known her daddy a lot longer than she had and I'd never seen him look so vulnerable. He looked even worse than he had the last time I'd seen him. In the few places his skin was visible it was blotchy red and yellowish white, but mostly he was swaddled in bandages, designed no doubt to keep ointment in and scratching fingers out. Except for his size and strong voice, he might have been an extra from *Night of the Living Dead*.

"Delcie, darlin'," Hen said, "Your daddy's going to be out of here and out of these rags before you know it. You'd better be saving up your sugar for me! Are you?"

Delcie clutched her throat and giggled. It took all the grip I had to keep from dropping her as she wiggled in anticipation. "No!" she said.

"No?" Hen yelled in outrage.

"No!" She giggled again.

"Well, then, I'll just have to come and get you!" Hen blindly waved his mummy arms in our direction and Delcie shrieked.

A redheaded nurse struck her head in the doorway. "Y'all keep the noise down, now. We've got some sick people here." She smiled and disappeared.

"You'd better watch out, Betty Jean, or I'll send Dwight over to get your sugar," Hen yelled after her.

"Police brutality," she yelled back.

"I guess we'd better be going," Teri said. "Come on, Delcie." Delcie tightened her arms around my neck and I didn't move to put her down. "Come on, now. Trudy and your daddy probably have police business to discuss.''

"Before you go, we need to talk about Easter," I said.

"We've been talking about that," Aunt Lulu said. "We want you to make that congealed salad of yours with the raspberries.''

I don't know what makes it my recipe except that I made it once before, but that wasn't the fight I wanted to pick.

"Sure," I said.

"And I'm making a pie out of some of those onions I put in the freezer. There was a recipe in *The Beacon* I want to try." That was still Aunt Lulu. "And banana pudding. Hen has to have his banana pudding.''

If Aunt Lulu and Teri have any bone of contention, it's over whose business it is to spoil Hen. He's never seen fit to settle the question.

By now Teri was trying to pry Delcie loose from me. "I'm doing some vegetables and the ham," she said.

"Let me do the ham." I held on and poked Delcie so she'd squirm.

"Come on now, Delcie. Trudy, it makes sense for me to do the ham. There's no point in you bringing something hot and messy.''

"But I want you to come to my house." Thanks to Miss Sarah I was able to say "my house" almost without feeling apologetic. No point in ignoring the fact.

"Come *on,* Delcie," Teri said.

"Holidays aren't the same anywhere else," I insisted. "Easter dinner at my house.''

Teri fixed me with a stare like a bird after a worm, then she blinked. "We'll see," she said. "We'll talk about it later.''

"When? It's already Thursday." No point in backing down now.

"I'll call you. Come on, Delcie."

She'd call me? Uh-huh. But I could call her, and I would, and we would get this settled.

Delcie had been out of the spotlight too long. "I feel sorry for Mark, even if he is a wierdo," she said, out of nowhere.

"Delcie!" From her mother.

"Well, he is."

"Be still."

"He is. Nobody likes him. He gets in trouble all the time."

"What kind of trouble?" Siding with Delcie against Teri is one of my favorite pastimes anytime, and as far as I could tell I didn't have anything to lose by egging her on.

"Well, he started a fire in Miss Wiggins' wastebasket once." Delcie offered this convincing evidence of Mark's wierdo-ness.

"You shouldn't tell tales about people, Delcie," Teri said.

"It's not a tale. It's true."

"We'll talk about it on the way home. Come on now."

Teri was piling up quite a list of people to talk to. I relaxed my hold on Delcie and let her slip to the ground. "See you later, sweetie."

"Okay. 'Bye, Trudy. 'Bye, Daddy."

"'Bye, darlin'. You hold on to that sugar, now."

"Okay." She giggled in anticipation.

"Teri, get me some clothes over here as soon as you can, will you?" Hen said.

Teri made a face at him, but nodded agreement.

"You're breaking out?" I asked.

"If I have to do it buck naked," Hen said.

"I'm glad you're feeling better," I said.

"I'll get you some clothes as soon as I can," Teri told him, but her lack of enthusiasm made me suspect she wasn't going to put it at the top of her list—maybe ahead of calling me, but not right at the top.

When they'd gone, I took the chair Aunt Lulu had occupied. "You're no help," I told Hen.

"About what?"

"About this house stuff."

"I'm a sick man," he said.

"You're a coward," I told him.

"A wise man," he said. "And you're about to make me wiser. Tell me what you've been doing." Sick, wise, and shifty.

"Sure, Chief. I can't tell you how grateful I am for this acknowledgement—even in private—that I might know something you don't."

"Could you get to it, Trudy? I'm not sure I'm up to handling your back talk today. Did you and Phil go back over Reed's place?"

"Right. Yes, we did. It was pretty obvious he went along just to humor me, but he made the most of it by taking a lot of pictures."

"Find anything?"

I tried to sound casual when I said, "I may have the murder weapon in my car."

"Well, now. What is it?"

"One of Reed's golf clubs."

"Where was it?"

"Right there by the door, just like always."

"Why would the killer have left it there?"

Hen naturally takes the adversarial position, so I was prepared to argue my case. "It would have been safer than taking it away. Miss Sarah or somebody else might have seen it. Anyway, the killer didn't expect us to be looking for a murder weapon. We were supposed to think it was an accident, and the fire was supposed to have been worse. Right?''

''Right. So tell me why this possible murder weapon is in your car instead of at the lab in Statesboro where they could be looking for fingerprints.''

''Yessir. Glad to explain, sir. It may have slipped your mind, sir, that except for me the entire Ogeechee police force is taking it easy, being waited on hand and foot by starchy nurses. I've been having to spread myself kind of thin. And I just knew, somehow, that you'd want me to check with you instead of showing any initiative.''

''Okay,'' he said. ''But I want you over there with it first thing in the morning.''

''You want me to go now and spend the night on their doorstep?''

He actually seemed to be thinking it over, but said, ''No, as long as you're there bright and early. Anything else?''

''Phil said he'd have the pictures we took at Reed's ready this evening. Whenever you get your eyes open I can bring them for you to look at. Be a good thing for you to amuse yourself with while you're laid up.''

He snorted. ''Don't get your hopes up. I'll be back at work tomorrow. Did you say ol' Phil's got you coming to look at his photos this evenin'?''

''What's that supposed to mean?''

''Isn't that what you said?'' he asked innocently.

''It sounded different when I said it.''

''Well, just take my advice and watch out if he starts talking about going to out-of-town photography shows.''

''What are you talking about? Phil?'' My surprise

couldn't have been greater if Hen had told me Big Bird moonlights as a tight end for the Atlanta Falcons.

"Just a word to the wise."

"I think whatever antihistamines or antibiotics or anti-coagulants or anti-nuclear devices they've been giving you have affected more than your itch."

"Somebody's got to look out for you, Trudy."

"You're looking out for me by warning me about Phil For-Heaven's-Sake Pittman? I can look out for myself, thank you very much. You'd think you were my father and I was fourteen years old."

"Well, I'm not and you're not, praise be."

I glared at him for a while and I'm sure he'd have glared back if his eyes had been in any condition for it. As it was, he just lay there. He really did look pitiful. After a while, mainly to irritate him so he'd fuss at me so I'd stop feeling sorry for him, I said, "I also went to see B.L."

I couldn't see much of him, thanks to the bandages, but everything I could see registered amazement. "You apologized to B.L.?"

"He probably thinks so. I verified that he didn't have much use for Reed and that nobody at Dawson Motors knows anything about him working late Wednesday night."

"You're saying he could have gone over there and done the awful deed?"

"Why not?"

"Why? Why would B.L. want to kill Reed?"

"I don't know. He didn't like him. It's a place to start. Maybe he thought Reed was going to leave town and take Mark and he was afraid Bonnie would make his life miserable if he let him."

Hen snorted. "The last time B.L. listened to Bonnie, if

then, was when she said 'I do' thirty-five or forty years ago. So you've moved on from hasslin' kids to hasslin' politicians.''

"I've told you how I feel about that H word."

"Whatever. Well, you can lay off. I'll be back on it tomorrow."

"I have a couple of leads I can be following up in the meantime." I didn't, but I'm not too proud to take advantage of a man when he's down. Or try to.

"What leads?"

I thought fast. The only thing that came to mind, because everywhere I went people were talking about it, was the land for the park and sports complex. "Everybody's interested in this park," I said. "I thought I'd find out who owns the land and the surrounding land. Whoever it is might make some money, and maybe Reed was in a position to blow it for somebody."

It sounded farfetched even to me, which is probably why Hen liked the idea. If I was at the county clerk's office I wouldn't be bothering people and getting into trouble.

"Good idea," he said. "You check that out, and don't do anything else without checking with me."

"Hen, didn't you hear? Lincoln freed the slaves in eighteen sixty-five and the United States Supreme Court tried to do it again in nineteen fifty-five."

"But ain't nobody freed the women yet. Yeah, I think you've mentioned it a time or two. See you later, Trudy."

"Have a nice nap," I said. I left, fairly well pleased with myself, and decided I would actually go check on the land. I'd have to hurry to get there before they closed for the day, if they hadn't already. I didn't have any better ideas.

THIRTEEN

THE TWO WOMEN in the County Clerk's office weren't glad to see me coming in so late in the afternoon, just when they'd been considering closing up a little early since they didn't have any business, but they were nice about it. The upshot was they helped me out more than usual, to speed me on my way. I told them what I was after and one of them found the appropriate black ledger while the other reached for a notepad so I wouldn't waste any of their time losing track of whatever information they helped me turn up.

So, not twenty minutes after I walked into the court-house to find out who owned the three parcels of land that were being considered for the park and sports complex, I walked back out with what I wanted. Hen would be so proud.

The parcel near my house, the least attractive in my unbiased view because it was off the main highway, belonged to my neighbor, who kept part of it in pecans and had been selling pieces of it for house lots every now and then for the past twenty years.

The parcel on Lake Loop belonged to a Grady Huggins, who, I thought, owned a lot of land here and there around the county. It would be easy to research that if I decided I cared. If Hen or Aunt Lulu didn't know, Miss Sarah would. Or I could go back to the County Clerk's office near closing time.

The parcel out near Dawson Motors actually adjoined B.L.'s land. All that extra traffic wouldn't hurt his car business any, but I couldn't see any sinister significance in that. It was easy to see why he'd rather have the park there than across the road from his house, anyway.

But the really interesting thing about that particular parcel was that it was jointly owned by Gordie Albritton and Reed Ritter, and the most interesting thing about that, since my conversation with Gordie had covered both Reed and the park land, was that Gordie hadn't mentioned it to me. Gordie was on record as the last one to see Reed alive, and it didn't take much imagination to make this begin to look like a motive.

I was feeling so lucky I decided to stop by Grinstead's Market and buy an Easter ham before I let Hen in on the news that we might have the beginnings of a suspect.

I had picked up my other groceries and taken a detour down the pet supplies aisle and was waiting for Cy Hooker, the meat man, to bring me a Bland Farms ham from the back when I looked up and saw Bonnie and Nita Dawson coming at me. Bonnie is Mrs. B.L. and Nita's her daughter-in-law, the mother of Danny and David. They didn't make a mad dash away from me, so I decided to hone my investigative skills right there in front of the pickled okra.

Nita made it easy. "Thanks for bringing my boys home yesterday, Trudy. They told me you arrested them for practicing their dribbling."

"Danny told you that, right?"

"Right. Danny tends to dramatize things. Anyway, I told them I wouldn't come bail them out if you locked 'em up. I keep telling them not to play in the street like that, but you know kids. It never occurs to them they could get hurt." Nita's a motherly, cheerful woman, a lot like Teri. I know she buys expensive clothes, but it's a waste of money. She always looks like she reaches into her closet with one hand while she's holding on to a young'un with the other, and puts on whatever her hand lights on. Today it was a baggy, striped-cotton knit shirt, probably from Liz Claiborne or somebody else who'd have paid Nita not to wear it, teamed with a pair of gray corduroy slacks that at least didn't clash with the shirt.

"I don't think I scared 'em much," I said. "Y'all doing okay?"

They both looked blank. Apparently Reed's death hadn't upset any of the Dawsons much. I'd never had anything against Bonnie or Nita, but that irritated me, so I decided to try to irritate them. "Everybody handling Reed's death okay? Nobody grieving too much?"

Nita had the grace to look ashamed of herself. Bonnie's attention appeared to be focused on the list of ingredients on the back of a Texas Pete bottle. Bonnie was completely beige and completely L.L. Bean. Teri would have been happy to tell Bonnie that beige wasn't a good color for her. It made her disappear. Maybe that was the idea. There's something about Bonnie that has always reminded me of my Aunt Sue on my mother's side, the one who was a secret drinker. I had the wild idea that Nita might be her custodian.

"Beats me who might have wanted to kill Reed," I said in Nita's direction.

"You're looking for somebody to blame?" Bonnie shifted her gaze from "peppers, vinegar, salt and xanthan gum" to me.

"That's one way of putting it. See, the fact is that somebody did kill him. Somebody is to blame. From the way it looks, it couldn't have been an accident. Somebody killed him and then set the fire, hoping to cover it up."

"Well, it was probably a robber, or a dope addict, or an escaped convict."

I didn't see any point in pretending to take her suggestion seriously, so I addressed Nita. "Can you think of anybody with a grudge against Reed, or anybody he was threatening or hurting in some way? Somebody who would have wanted him out of the way? Somebody who'd be better off with him dead?"

"Well, none of us ever warmed up to him much," Nita admitted, "but I don't see how—"

"B.L. always said Reed married Vivi for her money, trying to move up. That's why he cut her off," Bonnie contributed.

Maybe she wasn't as far out in Never Never Land as I'd thought. Since she'd entered the conversation, I addressed her directly, smiling, just making conversation. "What about you? Did you like him?"

She puckered up her lips. Nita selected a jar of pickles and put it in her basket. "He made Vivi and Mark very unhappy," Bonnie said finally. "I hated that. We've never had divorce in our family." She puckered more tightly. "And it was really hard on Mark. He was just three."

"Did you blame it on Reed?"

She raised her eyebrows. "Of course. Who else would I blame?"

"So you were probably glad he was planning on leaving town." Still smiling, still just making conversation.

"Oh, no!" Bonnie said. "He wasn't going to leave town."

"I heard he was."

"Well, he wasn't." She picked up Nita's pickles and studied the label, a queen signaling the end of the audience.

Okay, okay. Whatever Reed had planned or whatever anybody thought he'd planned, as a matter of fact, he had not left town. No point in arguing about that. Risking another official reprimand, I asked, "Were you home Tuesday night?"

Bonnie didn't seem to be looking to take offense. "Oh, I'm home every night. I go to bed early. I was probably asleep by nine or nine-thirty."

"Was B.L. there, too?"

Bonnie looked thoughtful. "Not 'til later. B.L. worked that night. I don't know what time he came in, but I guess he could vouch for the fact that I was asleep in bed whenever that was."

"But you can't vouch for him, can you?" I don't know why I was persecuting the poor woman. She looked to her daughter-in-law for help, and Nita, looking halfway amused, weighed in.

"Checkin' alibis, Trudy? To save you asking," Nita said, "I spent the whole night putting the boys to bed. I mean to tell you, practically the whole time, starting about eight-thirty, the first time, since it was a school night. Then again about nine, and again about nine-thirty. It was more disorganized than usual because Mark was there and we hadn't expected him to be. He's a little younger and a lot more immature than Danny and David and sometimes they use the excuse to sink down to his level."

I couldn't imagine what it would be like to deal with three of them, but I didn't have to. Nita started filling in the picture.

"As soon as I'd get my two settled down, Mark would be up, saying he was too stressed to go to sleep. Stressed! That's something he picked up from Dr. Whittaker."

"Dr. Whittaker?"

"His psychiatrist," Bonnie explained.

"Over in Statesboro," Nita amplified before going on with her tale. "Then when I'd get Mark down, the other two'd be up, all rested and rarin' to go. If it wasn't one thing, it was another. It's like juggling plates, Trudy, only here the idea is to get them all *down* at one time. Danny had to have a drink and David needed a blanket, and then when I thought it was all over, it turned out Mark didn't have his bed buddy.''

"What's a bed buddy?"

"Sounds pretty stupid, doesn't it? It's this stuffed animal he sleeps with. He was upset—stressed." By Nita's expression when she said the word, she might have crunched into an extra-sour pickle. "Because he thought he'd left it at Reed's. He wanted me to take him over there to get it, but I finally put my foot down and told him he'd have to get along without it."

"Kids really hang on to their routines," I said sympathetically, thinking of Delcie's bedtimes whenever she'd sleep at my house: brush teeth, put on pajamas, say prayers, read story, brush hair, tuck in, read another story, get a glass of water, go to the bathroom, tuck in—

"Oh, yes, and they get pretty elaborate," Nita said, as though reading my thoughts. "I'm fairly tolerant, but you've got to draw a line somewhere. And it turned out the thing was at our house all the time. So, anyway, back to the subject. After about nine-thirty, I was just watching television."

"I know Lieutenant Colombo would ask what you watched." I smiled. I like Nita. I was surprised to get a serious answer in return.

"Oh, that's easy. It was the night of the country music awards. I watched that as much as I could between interruptions. Don't you love Brooks and Dunn? Then the news."

"Does Ron help you with the boys, or was he just watching TV?"

"Oh, he was working late at his office. He has to do

that a lot. You know, there really aren't many good law-yers around here. Seems like he just works all the time."

"The boy always did take after his daddy," Bonnie offered.

"Do you remember what time he got home?"

"Well, I'd already watched the news. Must have been close to eleven," Nita said.

So they could vouch for each other then. Okay.

"It's great for Mark that he has your kids to play with."

"Yeah. He has a hard time making friends, and we're the only family he has, you know. Reed was an only child, and his parents are already gone. It helps that we've al-ways been here to fill in, but the fact is that Mark doesn't need cousins and grandparents and aunts and uncles nearly as much as he needs a mama and a daddy. Vivi makes fun of me for being such a mother hen. Goodness knows *she* isn't. A mother lion maybe—nobody better mess with *her* cub, you know—but not a hen. And now the poor thing doesn't have a daddy at all."

"Does Mark spend the night at your house a lot?"

Nita nodded. "One way or another, it seems like he does, our house or Mama Dawson's. I ought to fix up a better bed for him instead of putting him on the couch, but he likes it there and seems to settle down better if he can be in the room with somebody. It's not always as wild as it was Tuesday night. But that night Vivi came by and stirred things up. She raised a ruckus when she found out Mark was there. I guess he was supposed to be with Reed."

"Why wasn't he? Did something happen?"

"Not that I know of. It wasn't a big deal to anybody but Vivi, and that's just because nothing Reed ever did suited her. It made her mad when Mark spent any time

with him, but she'd have a fit—like she did that night—
if Reed didn't do whatever he said he would with Mark.
Reed brought him over when they got back from Statesboro. It was Mark's day for Dr. Whittaker. Must have
been close to five when they came, and Reed said he'd
pick Mark up later. But he never came back. So between
Vivi throwing a fit and him waiting for his daddy, Mark
just couldn't settle down. That's the kind of thing that has
the kid so messed up. Stressed."

"Just how messed up is Mark? I heard somewhere he
likes to play with matches. Does he set fires?"

Bonnie took her attention from a mustard jar long
enough to flash me a look, and Nita was adamant. "No.
And it's a shame people have gotten so smart they have
to have ugly names for everything. He's just a little boy
and he's no worse than a lot of these grown up know-it-
alls were when they were children. People don't have to
act like he's crazy or something."

"Just boyish hi-jinks?" I suggested.

Nita nodded. "He doesn't understand why he's so unhappy or how to deal with it. Much as I don't like the
idea of a little boy going to a psychiatrist, I'll admit Dr.
Whittaker is helping him. Anyway, it's not Mark's fault
if he's a little confused." She lowered her voice as though
that would keep her mother-in-law, now studying a jar of
pickled peppers, from hearing. "Even if she is Ronnie's
sister, I have to say I blame Vivi for some of it. Hearing
his mama bad-mouth his daddy all the time can't be good
for Mark. He was really attached to Reed. I know a divorce can't help but be hard on a child, but it doesn't
have to be as hard as this one."

At this point I noticed Cy standing there with my ham,
ears flapping, so I put my investigation on hold and said
goodbye to the two Mrs. Dawsons. I was in the check-

out line when the squeal of brakes and the screech of tires from the parking lot got my attention. Bonnie's big gray Chrysler was stopped very close to, but apparently not in actual contact with, a shiny new pickup truck. If Nita was the custodian, why in the world was Bonnie the driver?

Nita and the driver of the pickup were talking while Bonnie watched. Since there'd been no actual collision, I judged there was no call for police interference, so I finished paying for the ham for Easter dinner. At my house.

FOURTEEN

WHEN I GOT BACK to *The Beacon* office, now with an Easter ham and some cat treats in the trunk along with the telephone and the scorched bag of golf clubs, I found Phil arranging printing catalogs just as he had been the day before. He gave them a final pat as I came inside.

"Come on back. The pictures are in the office." He lifted a section of the counter for me to pass through and led the way through the door in the back wall.

The room we entered with its array of machines and shelves of supplies was where the paper was born again week after week, but the two women there were showing no signs of labor pains late on this Thursday afternoon.

The woman at the desk with a ledger open in front of her and a pen in one hand seemed to be studying scraps of paper. She held a crumpled tissue in one hand. Except that her curly carroty hair was longer than Phil's and she wasn't wearing glasses, she might have been Phil's twin. She was a few years older, in her late thirties, but today her swollen eyes and red nose made her look much older.

"Hey, Molly. Got one of those nasty colds?"

Molly nodded vaguely and took a swipe at her nose with the tissue, a gesture that reminded me of Suzanne McCloud.

Phil adjusted his glasses and waved toward the other woman, perhaps in her teens, who was stationed at a computer keyboard. Her short curly hair made a dark halo around a face dominated by sparkling brown eyes and a generous, smiling mouth. "You know Japonica Conroy?" Phil asked.

"Japonica? Glad to meet you. Trudy Roundtree."

"You the fuzz lady," Japonica said, in a voice that would rival Brenda's for smoky richness. "Hi."

"Japonica's on a work-study program from the high school, just been helping us this semester. We're teaching her to set type," Phil explained.

"Are you interested in the newspaper business?" I asked, not thinking it might be tactless to ask her in front of her boss. It didn't seem to inhibit her.

"Maybe," she said. "I'll have to see. I'm getting school credit for this and it sure does beat sitting in a class listening to Old Man Gargle Gut."

"That's Fred Megargel, the journalism teacher, in case you didn't recognize the name," Phil said. "Japonica claims he has a chronic digestive problem. The girl never has learned to respect authority."

Japonica smiled broadly. "I respect authority when I see it, but I don't just hand it out. A person got to earn my respect."

Something clicked. Japonica *Conroy*. "Japonica, are you kin to Pint and Half Pint?"

She grinned. "My brothers."

"There's a definite family resemblance."

"Yeah. We all take after our daddy. He's a mess."

"You see what I mean about authority?" Phil asked me. "Learning that it doesn't do any good to argue with the computer is going to be real good for this girl." He turned to Molly. "Trudy and I will be in my office. Y'all get back to the salt mines, now."

Japonica ostentatiously consulted her wristwatch and shook her head regretfully at Phil.

Molly said, "It's late, Phil. We're closing down."

Phil, the voice of authority, grimaced and gestured for me to lead the way into a small, square office which had been walled-off in a corner of the larger room.

The upper half of the two office walls facing the workroom was glass, but the desk was positioned so that anyone sitting at it saw not the activity (or lack of it) in the workroom, but the other walls in the office. All the wall space not devoted to glass or hidden by furniture was covered with photographs. A close-up study of an intricately painted clay pot was next to one of a herd of water buffalo along a river bank. Many of the pictures must have come from fires he'd worked on, showing awful devastation. I'd known he was a fireman but somehow never thought he might be interested in fires. I had to admit it was a good subject for dramatic black-and-white photography.

A computer screen on the desk glowed with the beginnings of a news story about our latest fire, an orange blip vainly urging the writer to move along, move along. Phil hit some keys and it dissolved. "That story's in for some big-time revision," he said. "I started it yesterday when we thought it was just a tragic fire; we know it was murder."

"Fast-breaking news," I said, only half paying attention to him since I was arrested by a photograph of an old man sitting in a rocker. It took me a minute of getting past the pain in his face to realize it was a picture of Phil's daddy.

"How old is this picture?" I asked.

"Took it last fall."

"I didn't realize he was so bad."

"It's worse now. Have you seen him lately? Hardly ever gets out of his wheelchair."

"Arthritis?"

"Mainly."

"That's tough," I said, thinking gratefully of how active and pain-free Grandma had been right up to the end. I was torn between probing a painful subject or not asking, seeming not to care. Finally I wimped out and asked, "Did you take all these pictures?"

Phil approached the change of subject with alacrity. "Yes, and about a zillion more I don't have wall space for. I got interested in photography when I was off at school. Some of 'em came from the great event of my young life, a photographic safari in Kenya three years ago." He pointed to a zebra herd.

"I didn't know you were a photographer."

"I don't put in credit lines, but I thought everybody knew I take the pictures for *The Beacon*."

"Oh. Well. That. Of course I knew you were the paper's photographer, but I didn't know you were a *photographer*."

"Uh-huh," Phil said.

"That made more sense in my head than it did in words," I admitted.

"I do know what you mean," he said. "It's a stretch from these to the line-'em-up-and-shoot-'em pictures we usually run in *The Beacon*."

He reached for two manila envelopes and spilled photos onto the desk. "Here's what I got at Reed's. This pile is from yesterday morning, and this pile is from today."

I started through them.

"This is this," Phil said, leaning over to point at two prints, showing where a close-up fit into a larger picture.

"You didn't miss much, did you?"

"Tried not to," Phil said.

"There sure are a lot of pictures. The fire department must have a big film budget." I don't know why I said that. I don't care what the fire department's film budget is, and I didn't mean to sound critical, but anyway Phil didn't take it wrong.

"Well, I do bill them for some of the supplies, the film and paper and stuff. But what the fire department—or even the police department—needs, and what I want to do, aren't always exactly the same thing. I don't think they need to pay for four shots like this, for instance." The four shots were studies of footprints in the ashes. "Or this." It was a view along a wall, with the intensity of the burn damage diminishing as it went away from the camera.

"Wow." I was looking at the result of Phil's wallowing around on the floor at Reed's. The footprints were clear and stark. I bent over to look at the bottom of my shoe. "Let me see your shoe," I demanded.

Phil obligingly crossed his ankle over his leg and we both studied the pattern on the bottom.

"Hm. No." I was puzzled, but intrigued. Then the light went on. "Oh! We were all wearing those rubber boots—you, Hen, and me. But the other one—look at that!—isn't any of us. And it overlays some of yours and mine and Hen's."

It took a second for the implication to hit me. "Phil, there wasn't supposed to be anybody in the house after the three of us were in there, but somebody was there."

"Well, if it isn't Sherlock Roundtree." He gave me that smile that made him look like a kindergartner. "You don't suppose it's the footprint of a ghost?"

"Aunt Pet's ghosts are the only ones I know much about, and they don't leave footprints, so I'd guess not. This could be important. Whoever was in there had to know they shouldn't have been, so there must have been a strong reason."

"Unless it was kids," he said.

"Not kids. The prints are bigger than mine. Phil, this is an important clue. Can you make some more copies of this picture?"

"Sure." He didn't look convinced, but he did set it aside.

We went back to the pictures. I stopped at one of the inside of the boy's closet.

"All I saw when I looked in that closet was that the rod was nailed down. You've made that soccer ball and the shoes look sad. It makes me want to weep. You're terrific!"

"Thank you," he said, and I'd have sworn he blushed, which irrationally reminded me of Hen's heavy-handed hints about Phil as a lady-killer, so naturally I blushed, too. What a pair.

"Have you ever thought of being a photographer?" I asked to keep Phil from noticing my blush and getting the wrong idea. "I mean a real, big-time professional photographer?"

"Sure. I used to daydream about it."

"But?"

"But, to be realistic, I get a lot of satisfaction out of what I'm able to do with it right here. And there's the paper. I couldn't just walk off from the family business."

"Couldn't Molly carry on?"

"She might, but it would be hard for her. We both put a lot into it."

He stopped to polish his glasses. "About Molly." He put the glasses back on and turned so that he could see into the workroom. I followed his glance. Japonica was gone, but in spite of what she had said about closing down, Molly was still sitting there, her elbows on the desk and her chin resting on both hands.

"She sure does look miserable," I prompted when Phil didn't go on.

"Yes. She is. But I don't think she has a cold." He swiveled away from the window.

"Sinuses?" I asked. I didn't know where he was headed, but saw no reason to make it easy for him.

He tightened his lips. "I think it's Reed. She's been acting strange lately. Hard as it would be to have any private business in this town, I'm pretty sure she's been seeing somebody, and I think it could have been Reed, but she won't talk about it."

I turned in my chair for a better look into the workroom. Molly's head rested in one hand now. The hand holding the pen was resting on the ledger. Good thing this wasn't supposed to be a busy day at the paper.

"Did you ask her? If she was seeing Reed?"

"Yeah. Well, not exactly. I asked her if something was bothering her and she said no."

"You'd have made a great investigative reporter."

"I'm not naturally nosy," he admitted.

"Nosy or not, there must have been something that made you decide your sister is—was—romantically involved with Reed. What was it?"

He fiddled with his glasses again, a mannerism I was learning to read as a stalling device, something to buy him a few seconds to decide what to do or say.

"Have you been a little nosy, Phil?"

He darted me a look and did the glasses thing again before he answered. "Not on purpose."

"But?"

"It's a little thing. I could be wrong."

"But?"

"Well, for one thing, she's been gone a lot lately."

"Gone?"

"Not home. Not accounted for. You know there aren't all that many places to go around here, not for somebody like Molly. She's not going to hang out at a juke joint or anything."

"No." I couldn't imagine it.

"And the other day—our phones have this button you can program for numbers you call a lot—and the other day I was using her phone and punched the one I thought was Daddy's. And I got Dawson Motors. Why would she be calling Dawson Motors enough to put it on her automatic dial? Their advertising is pretty routine and whoever B.L. sends over with it talks to Japonica anyway. But Reed worked there, you know."

"Yes, I know, but so do a lot of other people. Good grief, even B.L. works there. Is that all you've got?"

"All besides her acting strange."

"Phil, as evidence goes, what you've got here is pretty good bridge table conversation. I think you're smart to stay away from investigative journalism. Face it. Molly probably has a cold."

Phil looked relieved. "I hope so. I don't know much about women."

"It's not a woman thing, it's a sense thing. Reed was eligible. Molly's eligible. If she was seeing him, why would they sneak around? You'd think she'd be glowing with happiness at finding somebody to carry on with in Ogeechee."

I must have put more into the comment that I'd intended, because Phil started to blush again and said, "That's true. You know, I was glad when you came back to town, but..." He seemed to lose track of whatever he'd been going to say. He cleared his throat and resumed on his original tack. "But you're right about Molly. Of course Daddy and I wouldn't think anybody would be good enough for her, but there wasn't anything especially wrong with Reed. Not that we knew of, anyway.''

"Phil, whatever's bothering her doesn't have to have anything to do with Reed. As a matter of fact, unless he was more of a stud than I'd give him credit for, he was already spoken for.''

He brightened a little. "Really? Who?''

"Suzanne McCloud.''

"Huh.''

"Maybe Molly's more tender-hearted than you're giving her credit for. A lot of people are upset about the way he died. Whatever's wrong with her—no matter how bad it is—whether it is Reed or just a cold—she'll get over it. Some, anyway.''

"I guess you know what you're talking about.''

"I do. If you remember when I came back to town, you should remember the coma I was in for about a year. You see before you living proof that people get over things." I pasted on a big smile intended to be a carefree testimonial to the healing powers of time, and to deflect his concern with humor, but he persisted.

"Yeah. I know Zach's accident hit you hard. Then I heard there was somebody in Atlanta?''

"Brad.''

"A big romance?''

"Not much of a romance at all, actually. The main thing he had going for him was that nothing about him reminded me of Zach.''

"Would that have been bad?''

"Very bad. I was trying not to miss Zach." I wasn't enjoying this conversation very much. "Are you practicing up to become an investigative journalist after all?''

"No. I didn't mean to sound nosy. I'm sorry. But if he

let you get away, the jerk must not have had the sense God gave swamp water."

Even if Phil didn't have a clue about what went on between me and Brad, I had to admit his impulses seemed to be right. "I appreciate your support, Phil, but we've wandered quite a distance from Molly's runny nose." Even that topic was more appealing to me than the one we'd strayed to. "You're probably just imagining that she's been acting strange."

"I don't think so, but you've convinced me it wasn't Reed." He got business-like again. "Is there anything else around here I can do to help you?"

"Yes. Gossip. Even if you aren't naturally nosy— which strikes me as a serious drawback in your line of work—you must know a lot of this and that about most people."

"I'll tell you anything I can."

"Okay. Start with Vivi Dawson Ritter."

Phil removed his glasses and polished them as he spoke. "Only daughter, older child, of B.L. Dawson and Bonnie Dawson, who was a Coulter. Graduated from Ogeechee High School in, let's see—it would have been 'seventy-eight. Married Reed Ritter, gave birth to a son, Mark, five or six years ago. She and Reed divorced about three years ago. That's the facts, m'am."

"I asked for gossip, not facts. What's she like? Why did they divorce? What's she been doing since the divorce?"

"And could she have killed Reed? Let's see. What's she like? She was queen of the world when she was in high school. She was a senior the year I was a sophomore. You were a freshman? You'd remember all this. She was Homecoming Queen and I thought she was gorgeous and I was scared to death of her. Even then everybody knew that what she could think of and B.L. could pay for was gonna leave everybody else in the shade. Always did get away with murder.'' He stopped and flushed. ''Figuratively. I mean, nobody ever stood up to her.''

''But Reed divorced her.''

Phil smiled. ''He did. That must have been a real blow to her, but if you're looking for a motive for murder, I don't see it. Vivi didn't have to kill Reed to get rid of him or to get custody of Mark, and she was the one who came from a family with money.''

''Why the divorce?'' A thought came to me. ''Could Reed have had another romance then? Reed and Molly? Is that what you're thinking?''

Phil didn't seem to be offended. ''Whatever this is with Molly is recent. The divorce was two or three years ago. And I never heard anything like that about Reed, anyway. That kind of thing sounds more like Vivi, to tell the truth. Your reporter has heard rumors that B.L. and Ronald— that chip off the old engine block—do what they call working late a lot. Maybe it runs in the family.''

''Do you know anything about the grounds for the divorce?''

''Uh-uh. You'll have to ask her. *The Beacon* doesn't know.''

''She didn't go back to live with her mama and daddy, did she?''

''I don't think she's lived with them since high school. She has a trailer somewhere. If you want to talk to her, maybe you could find her at work. The last time I took Randy—that's Daddy's dog, William Randolph Hearst— in for his shots, she was working at the veterinary clinic out by the hospital. I'll bet it gives B.L. fits, having her living in a trailer and working out there, especially right now.''

"Why especially right now?" I asked.

"Well, he's thinking about a run for the state Senate and you know how political campaigns are. He'd be interested in cleaning up his act, presenting a charming, glossy picture of traditional heart-warming family life. You've got to admit it would take some explaining why anybody would rather live in a trailer than in that place of B.L.'s."

"Is there some particular reason she doesn't live there?"

"Doesn't like B.L., is my guess."

"I can understand that." I remembered how slick he looked behind his desk and tried to remember if I'd seen his feet, his shoes.

"Do you know of anything B.L.'s political opponents could get any mileage out of?"

Phil hesitated long enough I thought he had something, but he shook his head. "Not really."

"Come on, Phil. What?"

"Gossip?"

"Yes. Off the record."

"Off the record—that's funny from the police to the newspaper, isn't it? Well, for instance, I've heard that Bonnie's trip to Europe, summer before last, didn't take her any farther than an alcohol rehabilitation clinic in New Orleans."

I thought of my Aunt Sue and gave myself points for being observant. "Could that hurt B.L.?"

"Might. Wouldn't help."

"What else?"

He cautioned me again, "I don't have any evidence. He's a wheeler-dealer, and there's been talk of him cutting corners here and there. I dislike him on general principles, enough that I don't want *The Beacon* to endorse him."

"He'd need *The Beacon*," I said.

"Yep. Without *The Beacon*'s support in Ogeechee he wouldn't have a chance, and he knows it, too. He may get it. I'm against. Daddy's for. Molly's been a mugwump." Phil smiled. "Daddy dredged up that old word—mug on one side of the fence, wump on the other. It fits Molly, and I'm afraid it shows how up-to-date Daddy is on politics, which explains why he could believe in B.L."

"So it comes down to Molly?"

"That's how we've always handled editorial decisions. You can't have a tie if you have three votes."

"That's a lot to fall on her. Especially if she's love-lorn."

"Uh-huh."

"Well, Phil, you may not be naturally nosy, but you make a pretty good gossip."

"All the news that's not fit to print." He grinned.

We turned away from the window and our view of Molly.

"Phil, can you make a half dozen copies of the pictures of those footprints and get them over to the station? Charge it to Hen's film budget."

"I'll get right at it."

We made our way back through the workroom. In spite of my pooh-poohing Phil's ideas about Molly and Reed, as I said goodbye to her, I found myself trying to get a look at her feet when I went by. I wouldn't have wanted to mention it to Phil just yet, but there are less common motives for murder than love gone bad.

FIFTEEN

THE FIRST VOICE I heard Friday morning was Teri's and I wasn't even out of bed yet. Her call had nothing whatever to do with her promise to talk and everything to do with Hen's determination to get back to work.

"He's got his eyes partway open and swears he can see, so unless you know somebody who'd be willing to arrest the chief of police for drivin' blind, you'd better come get him."

I'm not at my most sociable before I've had my shower and coffee, so, "I didn't think you really meant to call, Teri," I said, lying back in bed and closing my eyes.

"What?"

"When you said you'd call and we could talk about Easter, I didn't think you meant it."

"Didn't you hear me?" Her voice rose. "Hen's determined to drive to the station, and he can't see!"

"That's a shame, Teri. Now about Easter…"

"Later, Trudy."

"Now, Teri."

I could hear Hen's growl in the background.

"You just be quiet and eat your breakfast, Henry Huckabee, and I'll see about you in a minute. Delcie, help him with his grits," Teri said. She sounded frazzled, which was fine with me. "Well? What?"

"Are you talking to me now?" I asked.

"Yes. Are you going to come get him?"

"After we've talked," I said. And maybe after I've had a few minutes to wake up, I thought.

"I'm listening," she said. I could almost hear her gritting her teeth. I plunged in. "Teri, you can't punish the whole family, yourself included, because Grandma gave the house to me. I mean, I know you can, but what's the point? It's not doing anybody any good. This house has always been the gathering place for our family, and there's no reason for that to change just because the title changed hands."

"If you're determined to hash this out," she said, "I'll just tell you straight. You're right about it being the family gathering place. Now that Hen's the head of the family, it ought to be his. Giving it to you was an insult to Hen."

If I hadn't already been lying down and fairly groggy, that statement might have taken me, as they say, aback. As it was, I had trouble understanding what I'd heard. "That doesn't make any sense, Teri. I know you don't believe Grandma meant to insult Hen. You know she loved him."

Her voice was low, intense, as though coming out through the escape valve in a pressure cooker. And as though she didn't want Hen to hear her. "We need it. We have a family, and we're cramped here. There's just you."

"You're dern tootin'," I said. I grew up believing that the use of profanity was as least as much a sign of a limited vocabulary as it was of moral decay, so I'm seriously handicapped at times. This was one of those times. Teri had put her finger on it, and it brought the whole thing into focus for me so perfectly I wanted to burst out with something that would really get her attention. The best I could do, under the double handicap of my upbringing and this epiphany, was to repeat myself. "You're dern tootin! There's just me! Does that mean I don't need a home?"

"You left," she accused. "You left Ogeechee and that house. You left your home."

"But I came back. Remember?"

"And what if you go off again? What about the house then?"

She'd only married into it, not grown up in it like Hen and I had, but she definitely loves this house. Background noises increased at her end, so I pressed my case, more emotionally, less logically and sensibly, than I'd intended. "You could go on and deprive Delcie of this place, but it would be a hateful, hateful thing to do and you're not a hateful person, Teri. Please don't keep this boycott up."

"Teri!" It was Hen in the background. "Are you talking to Trudy?"

"Yes," she said to him. "She'll drive you to the station. You eat your breakfast."

In other circumstances I might have had compassion for poor Teri, caught between me and Hen. As it was, I pressed my advantage.

"Anyway, I already bought a ham," I said.

I waited.

"Teri?"

"Okay, Trudy. Just come get him," she said.

"Okay, what?" I asked.

"Okay, we'll come eat your ham."

I had been imagining hours and hours of heart-to-heart before we got this far and although I didn't really believe the trouble was completely over, I was glad to stop for the time being. "Okay. Give me half an hour. I'm still in bed and I have an errand to take care of on the way."

I showered and dressed in a hurry and on my way to the car I scooped up two of the more passive cats.

Mrs. Edmunds must have been watching the sidewalk for more aliens. Before I was halfway up the walk, carrying her telephone which now sported a smiley face sticker I'd found in a junk drawer in the kitchen, she had the door open and was looking hopefully out at me.

"I didn't call the police again, did I?" she asked.

"No, ma'am, not as far as I know," I assured her. "I'm just following up on my visit the other day. I have another telephone for you." I pointed at the smiley face. "That's the inspector's seal to show that this telephone is alien free."

I held my breath, but she bought it.

"Thank you, officer," she said. "I've been missing my telephone."

"Let me plug it in for you," I suggested. She nodded.

When I had that done, I moved on to my other objective, even chancier than the first.

"Miz Edmunds, I have something else for you."

She looked around in confusion.

"It's in the car," I told her. "But I want to tell you about it first."

She nodded and frowned, ready to concentrate.

"Have you heard about those dogs they have who can sniff out drugs?"

She nodded, her eyes focused intently on me so as not to miss a word.

"Well, I brought a team of special alien repellant cats."

I let that hang there a minute to give her time to take it in before I added, "There's a gray one who's trained in detection. Her name is Alien Detector, we call her A.D. for short, and there's a yellow-and-white one trained in repelling x-rays. She's called Noex. They're out in the car. Come look at them with me."

I was half afraid she'd decide I'd been invaded by aliens after that nonsense, but she followed me to the car and the cats did the rest. The one I had moments before christened A.D. chose to do stretching exercises with her front paws near the window just as we walked up, and Noex (for "no x-rays") was placidly involved in washing her ears. I could tell Mrs. Edmunds was taken with them, so I closed the deal.

"If it's all right with you, I'd like to leave these two, uh, agents here with you. You shouldn't have any more trouble with aliens. What do you think?"

"I like cats," she said.

She took one cat in each arm and headed back to her apartment. I followed with the cat toys and a bag of food. When I caught up with them, A.D. was sniffing around under the sofa and Noex had taken possession of a window sill and resumed her toilette. Mrs. Edmunds could hardly take her eyes off them to say goodbye to me as I left.

I figured the worst thing that could happen would be that the cats would get bored and find their way back to my house. There was no telling how good the best thing might be, beginning with ridding Mrs. Edmunds of mice, which, when I thought of it, might have been the inspiration for the aliens in the first place.

Hen was standing at the curb in front of his house when I got there, feeling extremely pleased with myself. Teri and Aunt Lulu were standing at his sides, obviously ready to catch him when he fell, and hoping he would so they could haul him back inside where he belonged. He was wearing dark glasses. Every inch of exposed skin looked tight and shiny. Teri handed me a cup of coffee through the car window.

I smiled at her as I took it. "Thanks. Good lord," I said to Hen, "I've seen roadkill I'd rather have in my car."

Hen was not amused. "Aren't you supposed to be in Statesboro with those golf clubs?"

"I just got up. Haven't had time yet. You can ride over there with me."

"I got better things to do. I told Teri not to call you."

"You must not have her trained as well as you thought," I said, and I think I heard both Teri and Aunt Lulu snigger. "Look at it this way, Hen. If anybody sees you with me they'll think you're in custody and not part of *The Invasion of the Tomato People*. Get in quick, before you scare somebody."

For once in his life, Hen did what he was told without a smart comeback. He must have been feeling as bad as he looked.

"If he passes out, I'll bring him back," I assured the two women. They stood watching as we drove away, looking not at all reassured.

"Okay, Chief, where'd you want to go?"

"You tell me what you've been up to first. Then I'll know." I stopped the car and pulled Phil's envelope from under the seat. "Can you see?"

Hen nodded, but didn't take off his dark glasses.

"Okay. If you can see, look at these two pictures. Phil took this one Wednesday morning when the three of us first went into Reed's after the fire, and this one when he and I went back yesterday. Look at the footprints."

"The footprints."

"In this picture. See, there are our three pairs of rubber boots. Then there's this shoe with a diagonal pattern across the heel on top of ours. That means there was somebody in there after we left, looking for something I guess."

"Whose shoes are they?"

He knew perfectly well I hadn't seen those pictures

until the night before. When would I have found out whose shoes they were? He didn't wait for my answer, which meant he wasn't expecting one.

"Anything else?" he asked.

I summarized my talk with Bonnie and Nita Dawson. "I guess all it really got me was a couple of shaky alibis," I concluded.

"You mean you're not willing to take the word of Ogeechee's leading citizens that they didn't do it?"

"Well actually, I don't remember asking that particular question, in so many words."

"Good thinking. Wouldn't want to force anybody into lying to you."

"Especially when it looks like they're all perfectly willing to do that without coercion. Here's what we've got: B.L., knowing Bonnie would be asleep and couldn't verify what time he got home, told me he was working 'til about ten on Tuesday night. The trouble is that Danny and David told me they saw him coming home around eleven-thirty. I'd back the boys on that, since I doubt they'd have any reason to lie. About that, anyway."

"Um-hmm." He nodded agreement. "The rule I go by is to trust your sources in inverse proportion to their degree of self-interest."

"That sounds like math."

"It's also good investigating. What else you got?" He leaned his head against the door frame.

"I've got B.L. and Bonnie Dawson without alibis. Ron and Nita, too, I guess. Ron was supposed to be working late, alone. Seems to run in the family. He got home sometime after Nita went to bed about eleven, which leaves him unaccounted for during the time we need to know about. I think the boys could vouch for her. And now that I think of it, I'll bet the boys know what time he got home." I scribbled a note to myself and looked up to see Hen grinning.

"You're really enjoying this, aren't you?" he asked.

"We do have to find whoever did it, don't we?"

"We sho nuff do."

"So why not enjoy the hunt?"

"No reason a-tall. Does it strike you that not very many of the people in this town stay home at night with their families?"

"I noticed that. Hen, do you think one of the Dawsons could have killed Reed?"

"Even being exposed to the seamier side of human nature, as I have in natural consequence of my chosen profession, it's still hard for me to see anybody I've known all my life in the role of a cold-blooded murderer. But in theory, I believe you could drive almost anybody to murder. Theoretically, I could see old B.L. killing for power. If you've seen him in action at a town council meeting you know what I mean. Yep, I could see that. And he'd believe he could get away with it, too. The problem in this case is that I can't see where Reed would fit into any scenario that would be a threat to B.L.'s power."

"Would B.L. kill for Vivi or Mark? That's a connection, anyway."

Hen shook his head slowly.

"Well, then, what about Vivi? How about her as a killer?"

"A temper fit, if somebody crossed her. And Reed sure knew how to cross her."

"So she's a better bet than B.L."

"But from what we hear, Reed wasn't in any shape to thwart her that night, which would mean she'd have had to been planning it ahead of time. I don't know about that."

"Okay, then," I said, moving on down my list. "How about Bonnie?"

"That's hard. I have trouble picturing Bonnie Dawson committing a crime of any kind, much less one calling for physical exertion and brains. And if she had done it, I'd expect to find her standing over the body with a match in one hand and a smoking golf club in the other."

"I'm trying to be serious. What about Ron or Nita?"

"Ron would if B.L. told him to. Nita? She's a big buddy of Teri's. They do the PTA and room-mother stuff. She might kill somebody if she thought they were threatening one of her kids. Lord, she even babies Ron."

What a hypocrite! If Henry Huckabee thinks there's something wrong with women babying their men, I'm Gloria Steinem.

"How about Gordie, or Suzanne, or Billy Watson? They're the only other people we know are involved so far, besides you and me and Phil."

"Unless we get desperate, I'll excuse you and me and Phil. Gordie? Well, I hear business hasn't been good for him lately. Real estate isn't exactly booming, and his peanut crop wasn't good last year, either. Maybe if he had a lot of debts, he'd kill for money. Suzanne? Really?"

"No. She looked like somebody'd pole-axed her. No."

Hen doggedly finished our list. "Billy? Billy's too relaxed to kill except for...let's see...maybe if somebody did something to hurt his business. Or messed with his necktie collection."

"What about you, Hen? What would it take to drive you to murder?"

He grinned. "I might be willing to kill that sorry Sheriff

Rufus Badcock if I thought I could get away with it and was sure I could have his job. What about you?''

''I can't think of anything I want bad enough or care enough about to drive me to murder. Maybe Delcie, but you'd beat me to that. Does that mean I'm shallow?''

''More likely it means you're well-balanced. Or maybe a shade unemotional.''

''Thanks.''

''Now, let's take those golf clubs over to the station and get Dwight on the road with them, and then I guess we better get out and talk to Vivi before she talks to some of her kin and gets to feeling neglected because we haven't interrogated her.''

''We?''

He turned the dark glasses in my direction.

''I think you ought to go back to bed,'' I said. ''Teri and Aunt Lulu would back me up.''

''You buckin' for an official reprimand for insubordination to add to your collection of reprimands?''

''No, I was just showing concern for a pig-headed macho jerk, no disrespect intended. Really, Hen, I can handle it.''

He rested his head again. ''I don't doubt that, but I'll go along and see if I can learn anything from watching your interrogation technique.''

Sure. And he'd voted for Rufus Badcock in the last sheriff's election, too.

On the bright side, he'd be able to help me find Vivi's trailer.

I drove on to the station, where Hen supervised the transfer of the golf bag from my car to Dwight's and lit a fire under Dwight, who obviously suffered from the same affliction Hen did, but seemed to be in much better shape. Phil's photos were already there, too, so Hen told

Dawn to give a copy to everybody and tell them to keep an eye out for the shoes that made those prints as they went about their other business.

Dwight drove off and we climbed back into my car.

"Maybe Dwight's had enough sleep so he can stay awake while he drives over to Statesboro," Hen said after he'd loosened his seatbelt. "Did I ever tell you about the time he fell asleep at a briefing with his eyes wide open? We like to never figured out where the snoring was comin' from—thought it was some kind of varmint that had got stuck in the air-conditioning."

"No," I said. "You'll have to tell me about it sometime; but first, let me tell you what I've done to repel alien invaders."

SIXTEEN

I DROVE OUT of town on a narrow road that angled toward the river. Even with Hen helping, it wasn't easy to find Vivi's place. One wrong turn took us to a neat little cinder-block house with a bright plastic menagerie in the yard; another, to a fire pit littered with Budweiser cans.

On the third try, we turned off the road across from a little white frame church. At one edge of the church's dirt yard was a sign that could have been mistaken for a realtor's sign except that it said A Fire Burneth Up His Enemies Around About. Ps. 97:3. For balance, at the other edge of the property, another proclaimed Whoremongers Shall Have Their Part In The Lake Which Burneth With Fire. Rev. 21:8.

"They're kind of hepped on fire, aren't they?" I observed. "Or am I just noticing it today?"

"Looks like those signs have been there a while. A good detective would be able to tell by the rust." His eyes must have been in better shape than I'd thought.

"You'd think they'd vary the message once in a while, just to get people's attention, put up something about blessed are they who do something or other."

Hen grunted. "This bunch don't want anybody getting the idea life's easy. Wide is the gate, and broad is the way, that leadeth to destruction."

"And many there be which go in there-at." I wasn't about to let him top me at sounding like the King James

Bible. I'd spent at least as much time in Sunday School as he had.

I caught sight of a trailer ahead, sitting twenty-five or thirty yards back from the water, on a lot that was mostly white sand and palmetto. There was no shade anywhere near it. On the river side of the trailer, a wooden frame held up a roof of wavy green Plexiglas over a concrete slab. In the evenings, it would make a good place to sit and look down past the boathouse and wooden dock to watch the river.

"This is the right road, at least," I said. "I wonder how Vivi likes having to pass those signs every time she comes home." I pulled up near the slab and turned the cruiser off. The engine began to tick loudly in the silence.

"Looks like nobody's here," Hen said.

"Oh, shoot." Too much to hope that he'd give up and go on to something else, or back to bed where he obviously belonged, and let me come back by myself. I sighed and tried to sound disappointed. "Well, what next?"

Before Hen could answer, we heard the crunch of tires on gravel and a red Chrysler convertible careened into view. It skittered around my car and squeaked to a stop under the Plexiglas. Vivi was out of the car, slamming the door behind her, before the dust had settled. It took the boy, struggling with a backpack, a little longer. He bore a family resemblance to his cousins, but just as David was a paler version of Danny, Mark was a paler version of David. He didn't even have his mother's eyes.

Vivi glanced at the struggling boy, saw that he was managing, then leaned against the back end of her car and gave her attention to Hen and me.

Phil's phrase, the queen of the world, came to mind. Even in jeans and a T-shirt, Vivi had style and presence. As usual, I felt fat and stodgy beside her.

"Hey, Vivi. Hate to bother you, but we need to talk," Hen said.

"Sure, Hen," Vivi said. "What's the matter with your face? You get left out in the rain too long?"

Mark had stopped by the car, bug-eyed.

"I got poisoned in the line of duty," Hen explained. "What we need to talk about is Reed. About the fire."

"I could tell you a whole lot about Reed. Don't know anything about the fire. But I guess you might as well come on in and read me my rights."

What was it with this family and Miranda?

"It's a little early for that," Hen said. He smiled down at Mark, who edged farther away from the fearsome sight. Vivi led the way into the trailer and Hen held the door for me and Mark, who kept as far as possible from Hen as he sidled in.

"It ain't contagious, son," Hen said. "Sorry about your daddy." Mark showed no sign of having heard.

Inside the trailer, my first impression was of stale smoke; my second, of clutter overlaying the avocado-and-orange prefab decor of the trailer. Maybe Reed had gotten his housekeeping standard from Vivi. Mark dropped his knapsack on the floor just inside the door and went straight to the kitchen. He hadn't spoken a word.

"How're you doing?" I asked, sinking into one of the unappealing green and orange tweed armchairs. Vivi had taken the other one, from which she could keep an eye on the kitchen. She slung a slim leg over one arm of the chair and leaned on an elbow against the other. Hen straddled a chrome-and-plastic kitchen chair, resting his arms on the back.

Vivi smiled faintly. "Fine. I'm doing fine. We were divorced, you know."

Hen jerked his head toward the boy.

Vivi shrugged again and spoke without any shade of hesitation. "Mark'll be okay. He didn't see that much of Reed, anyway. It'll be one less place for him to be jerked around to."

What an epitaph for her ex. She raised her voice as though she thought Mark wouldn't be able to hear her otherwise, hadn't heard the rest of the conversation. "Leave the carton on the counter so I'll remember to get more."

Mark still hadn't spoken, but he left the empty milk carton on the counter.

Vivi spoke again. "Mark's okay. He was just three when we got divorced, so he doesn't remember much about how it was before. All he's ever known is how it is now."

"And how is it now?" I asked.

"Is this girl-talk part of your investigation?"

I gave Vivi my best imitation of her own nonchalant shrug, and smiled.

Hen picked up the thread. "You mean your life—and Mark's—will suit you better now?"

"It will. Mark spends a lot of time over at Ron and Nita's, right next door to mother's. Their two boys are about his age. But you know that. Mark gets bored out here. He stayed with Reed some, but he got bored there, too, and usually wound up back at Ron and Nita's or mother's. So now he's got one less place to be bored."

"Sounds like a pretty informal arrangement," I said.

"It is. Any reason it shouldn't be?"

"No, except that from what I'd heard, you and Reed were on such bad terms that I'd have expected to find all kinds of court orders about who could do what."

"Well, I didn't like him, but I didn't think he was a threat, some criminal I needed to get court protection from. He got the house, I got the trailer. It's a better trailer than it was a house. He kept the sedan, I got the convertible. His car's better, mine's flashier. We took turns with Mark. And I didn't have to give him alimony.'' She laughed at that, knowing we'd know there was no question of him having to pay her.

"Do you like living out here?" Hen asked.

"I wouldn't live here if I didn't."

"No, I reckon you wouldn't."

"I like being on the water and I like being able to lead my own life. Try doing that under B.L.'s eye."

I smiled. "It must have been a hard choice. It looks pretty comfortable over there on Lake Loop."

"Not such a hard choice. Even if I didn't have this place, Lake Loop is the last place on earth I'd want to live. It's not even all that great a place to visit."

"That's a pretty independent attitude for a single mother whose family over on Lake Loop picks up a lot of the slack in child care," Hen suggested. Vivi didn't react. She was watching as Mark put his glass of milk on a pile of papers on a table at one end of the couch and returned to the kitchen for a plate full of cookies. He put the plate on the couch and cautiously sat down beside it. Then he crossed his legs, campfire style, and put the plate in what passed for his lap.

"Aren't you going to offer anybody else a cookie?" Vivi asked.

"Would anybody like a cookie?" Mark asked, looking not at us but at the plate.

"No, thanks," Hen said.

"Maybe later," I said.

"Does he maybe have some homework?" Hen asked Vivi.

"Mark knows what happened. There's no point in hiding anything from him."

It was a point of view, if not a particularly maternal one. I remembered Nita comparing Vivi to a mama lion. Survival of the fittest. Nature in the raw. Et cetera.

Hen sighed. "You know by now that Reed didn't die an accidental death. So we need to reconstruct his activities that night, and we're trying to talk to everybody we know of who saw him."

Vivi folded her legs into a pose much like Mark's, elaborately unconcerned, and smiled. "I sure do hope I have a good alibi. When do I need one for?"

"Let's try to cover from nine o'clock on," Hen said.

"Well, if you know I saw Reed that night, you know it was at Billy Watson's. I work at the animal hospital and I usually go to Billy's to relax a little after work, as soon as I get the dog and cat hairs scraped off and check myself for fleas and ticks. Wednesday night it would have been about seven-thirty, eight, when I got there. Maybe Billy could tell you. I was there when you came in looking for Reed." She looked at me for confirmation.

I nodded, and for the sake of showing some initiative I asked, "Who were the men you were with? I didn't know them."

She gave me a knowing, self-satisfied smile and a half-shake of her head. "Just some fellas I play with once in a while. Cards."

"Don't they have names?"

She flashed a smile, obviously enjoying herself. "Of course they do."

"Why don't you share them with us?"

"The names?"

Well, honestly. "I might want to look them up."

She laughed then. "It's Dan and Stan, or something like that."

"Cut it out, Vivi." Apparently, Hen found Vivi even less amusing than I did.

"Really, we're not all that good of friends. Dan and Stan is right. They said they work out at the sawmill."

Hen started asking her about Reed's enemies, and I found myself watching Mark. Maybe it didn't bother his mother for him to be hearing all this, but it bothered me. I got up and took a seat on the couch with Mark and his cookies, not too close. He looked at me suspiciously.

"Is school out today?" I asked him.

He shook his head.

"Are you playing hookey?"

He shook his head again. "It's not hookey if your mama knows. Anyway, I'm not in real school yet."

"Oh?"

"Just kiddygarter."

"Oh."

"And I didn't go today because of Daddy."

I nodded in sympathy. In spite of what Vivi had said, I said, "You'll miss him a lot, I bet."

Mark nodded and fixed his stare on the cookie plate.

"I'm sorry," I said.

He nodded again.

"I could use one of those cookies now, if you don't mind," Mark held the plate out to me. There were three cookies left on it from the original pile. I took my time choosing one. "It looks like this one has three more chocolate chips in it than the others," I explained. "I really like chocolate chips."

"Me, too."

"Want me to leave this one for you?"

"No. I already had about a hundred. And I can get

some more if I want them. There's a million in there."
He nodded to the kitchenette. "And I know where Vivi
buys 'em."

So Reed was Daddy and Vivi was Vivi.

"You're a pretty sharp cookie." I watched to see if he
got the joke, but he seemed to have inherited the Dawson
sense of humor.

"Yeah. I'm as sharp as David and Danny, no matter
what they think."

"Don't they think you're smart?"

"No. They always think I'm dumb."

"I'll bet you are smart. Tell me something smart you
did." I didn't care what we talked about as long as it
covered up what Hen and Vivi were talking about.

A crafty look came into Mark's eyes and he glanced at
Vivi and lowered his voice. "Danny and David are always
bragging about how they sneak out at night and do all
that gang stuff, but they won't let me sneak with them."
He paused and looked at me to see if I was paying attention. I nodded encouragement.

"I sneaked out the other night by myself, before they
sneaked out."

"Wow! Then they knew you were smart, I'll bet."

He shook his head and crumbled one of the remaining
cookies. "They didn't believe me. I even showed them
my bed buddy."

"What's your bed buddy?"

"I sleep with it. In my bed. Get it? And Danny said I
must have just found it at their house, that it was there all
the time, but I didn't. It wasn't. I had to go get it. I'm a
better sneak than they are. I saw them go out and they
didn't see me. But they don't believe me."

"Well, I believe you. Where did you have to go get
your bed buddy?"

"It was at my daddy's. It was a little scary going in the dark all by myself, but I wasn't much scared. My daddy was asleep, and I got it without waking him up. He didn't know I sneaked good, either. And now he's dead and I can't ever tell him."

As I stared at Mark, I heard Hen saying, "That's an interesting angle. Another traditional angle is 'who stands to benefit?' What do you know about his will?"

"What would I know? We've been divorced for three years. But it would sure surprise me if he had enough to get killed over."

"Vivi says I won't miss him, but I will," Mark whispered. "He said he bought me the biggest Easter Bunny in the world. Danny and David didn't believe that, either."

"Maybe they did believe you and just wanted to tease you."

As Mark pondered this, crumbling the cookie crumbs even smaller, I was delighted to see Hen get to his feet, but he wasn't finished yet.

"One more thing, Vivi. You mind if we look around? There are a couple of things missing from Reed's that we'd like to find."

"Don't you need a search warrant?"

"A search warrant or your permission."

"Would you get a search warrant if I said you couldn't look around?"

"Abso-tively. Might take a while, but I'd get it," Hen said.

"And if I knew what you were looking for and had it, that would give me a chance to put it somewhere else."

"Sure would."

"And then you'd be convinced I *had* had it."

"Not necessarily, but letting us look around now might convince me you don't."

"You want to tell me what you're lookin' for?"

"No."

"Okay," Vivi said. She reached for her cigarettes. "Go ahead. You care if I come and watch?"

"Good idea," Hen said. "You can keep me honest."

"Thanks for sharing your cookies," I said to Mark. Then I had an idea. "Hen, you don't need me to help you look around, do you?"

"Not if you've got a better idea."

"I do. Come on outside with me, Mark. I've got something you can tell Danny and David about."

Mark followed me outside and into the front seat of the police car.

"There," I said. "Push that."

A dozen black birds leapt from a bush down by the river and even Mark jumped as the siren cut harshly through the heavy air.

"Now try that." The steady blast gave way to the oo-wah, oo-wah, then back to the steady blast as Mark manipulated the knobs and switches. Finally, he'd had enough.

Silence fell.

He smiled at me then and my heart melted. He was a beautiful, sad, troubled child, a child with a mama lion he called by her first name, and a surrogate mother hen, but no daddy at all.

We were still sitting in the car when Hen and Vivi came out of the trailer. We watched them go to Vivi's car. Hen looked inside, under the seats. Vivi opened the trunk and Hen poked around in it before he slammed it shut and came to the police car. He spoke through the open window at Mark, who was in the driver's seat.

"You think you've scared the wildlife enough so we could go now, son?"

"Yessir," Mark said.

Hen opened the door and Mark clambered out.

We were all the way back to the hellfire and damnation signs before either one of us spoke.

"You didn't find anything?" I asked.

"No. What would I find? The woman has fifteen pairs of shoes which don't match Phil's picture and a river not a hundred feet from her front door. We won't drag that 'til after we've looked a few more places."

I said, although I hated to, "Mark was there that night. At Reed's." I cleared my throat and continued. "He says his daddy was asleep when he was there."

Hen looked at me. "He say what time that was?"

"No. Hen, he might have just missed the murderer."

"Or he might have set the fire," Hen said, voicing my real fear.

We rode in silence to the edge of town.

"Might as well talk to Billy again, seein' we're so close," Hen said. "Maybe have some pie."

SEVENTEEN

WHEN WE ENTERED Billy Watson's Fish Place, Billy looked up from where he was in conversation with a group of customers at the bar. He broke away from the group to usher us to a table, a service you don't usually get.

"What happened to you?" he asked Hen, but didn't wait for an answer. "You look like you've been marinated and are ready to go on the grill. Come on back here out of sight so you don't ruin anybody's appetite." With the paper he was holding, Billy waved us toward the back of the room and we followed his blue-and-white-striped rugby shirt to a booth.

"I knew you'd be around sooner or later, so we've been working up a report for you," Billy said, holding out the paper. "Thought it would save time."

"What is it?" I asked. I didn't reach for the paper, which was transparent with grease.

Billy glanced proudly back at his cohorts. "It's a time-table for Tuesday night. Seeing as how the murder almost happened right here, me and my regulars feel like we were might near eyewitnesses."

"Too bad one of 'em wasn't," Hen said. "That would make our work easier."

"We're gonna make it easier anyway. We've been getting our stories all in a line for you. No reason for you to have to waste your valuable po-lice time listening to us arguing over whether Luther or Olin got here first that night, or what time it was that Idella dropped the tray with four beers on it.''

"Mighty thoughtful," Hen allowed. "We sure wouldn't want to have to listen to that kind of thing."

Billy looked hurt. "We didn't put all of that down for you, but it helped us keep track of the comin's and goin's."

"I had no idea you were such an organizer," I said to Billy.

"Cain't run a kitchen if you cain't organize," Billy said. "You wouldn't believe the amount of organizin' Idella takes out of me."

"That's the Lord's truth." Idella's baritone came through the door from the kitchen, wafted on a sardonic laugh and the smell of hot grease.

Billy ignored her. "Matter of fact, once upon a time I thought of joining the FB and I, and I fancy myself a keen observer."

"Let's see what you've got." Hen reached for the paper, but Billy held it out of his reach.

"Let's sit down and go over it. Y'all want something? Some hushpuppies?" The host took over from the frustrated FBI man.

"What kind of pie today?" Hen asked.

"Peach and chocolate meringue."

"Chocolate and iced tea," Hen said.

"Make mine peach," I said, peach pie being more like fruit and cereal than chocolate is. I hadn't had breakfast, after all, just Teri's cup of coffee and Mark's cookie.

"Y'all go on and sit down while I get the pie and tea. Booth three, here, is where Reed had his last meal."

"You planning to make a shrine out of it?" Hen asked.

"Reckon not," Billy said, straight-faced. "Reed didn't eat here all that much."

Hen planted himself in the middle of the bench on one side of booth three, facing the door. I slid in far enough on the other side to make room for Billy.

"Idella, I'm off," Billy yelled toward the kitchen as he deposited the tray with the food and drink on the table.

"I've known that for years," Idella yelled back.

Ignoring the resulting laughter from his regulars, Billy spread the paper on the table at an angle so all three of us could see it.

"We got these three columns here—when, what, and who says, in case you want to check it out. See here. We started at five minutes to seven o'clock, when Reed came in. Joe and LuAnn Ditmer signed over here by 'Who says' 'cause they were going out when he came in and they made a joke about how if they didn't get going Joe was gonna miss 'Wheel of Fortune' and wouldn't get rich tonight. See, they had allowed enough time to get home before it started. I signed for that, since I remembered it."

"Reed was by himself?" I asked.

"He came in by hisself. He sat at the bar and started on a Coors and then in a little while—let's see, seven-twelve, we decided—Gordon Albritton came in and I put 'em back here. They said they had some business to talk about and wanted to be out of the way."

"They said?" Hen asked. "Which one of 'em?"

"Gordie," Billy said after a moment's thought. "Gordie said. And Gordie took a look at Reed's Coors and frowned and ordered coffee for hisself and they both ordered the special, four pieces of catfish, slaw, hushpuppies for three ninety-nine. I brought it out at seven twenty-eight. Idella wanted me to put that in to make a public record of how fast our service is."

"Everybody knows it, anyway," I said.

"And they had a piece of pecan pie at eight oh one.

They usually eat faster'n that, but they was talking a lot, which slowed 'em down.''

Billy tapped the chart with a forefinger and continued. ''Not knowin' who your suspects are, we've got everybody down, figurin' an alibi would be the main thing. Now, Johnny—''

Hen interrupted. ''For the time bein', let's skip on down to the more likely suspects. What about Vivi Dawson?''

''Sure,'' Billy says. ''Makes sense.'' He smoothed the paper and ran a finger down the column. ''Vivi. Here. When Vivi came in, she sat at the bar like she always does at first. Gives her a chance to check out who's here before she decides who to settle in with. We had a lot of discussion about when she came in, because they wasn't any reason for anybody to notice particularly. Then Hal Beasley, he clinched it, because she was here when he came in at eight-fifteen, so here's Hal's name in the 'who says' column.''

''Do we get to have that sheet or should Hen be taking notes?'' I asked.

Hen gave me a squint-eyed look, but Billy took the question at face value. ''You can have it. After Reed and Gordie finished eating, they stayed on, Reed drinking beer, and the first thing I knew, Gordie was hollerin' something about 'you have to,' and 'I'm desperate.' Like that. And Reed was hollering back things like 'I don't have to' and 'don't threaten me.''''

''Do tell,'' Hen said to his pie.

''Well, when Reed started yelling, Gordie realized they'd gotten loud. Hadn't heard hisself yelling, I guess. He looked around, kind of embarrassed I thought, and they quieted down some. But the damage was done as far as Reed was concerned. All the hullaballoo had got Vivi's attention. She'd been up at the bar and hadn't noticed them back in the booth 'til then, but once she saw Reed was back there, she got her bunch to move over there to booth five and she sat where Reed couldn't help but see her, but she had her back to him, so she wouldn't have to look at him. She's a case, I tell you." Billy shook his head and sucked a tooth.

"And she set right in to get on his nerves, which she knew how to do all right. And between her making cracks loud enough for him to hear across the room, and Gordie trying to talk loud enough to keep Reed from paying attention to Vivi, it was getting a little uncomfortable for me. This is a family place. I don't have a bouncer. So I was glad when they all left."

"All?" Hen asked. "Who all left?"

Billy blinked at his list and frowned. "Reed, Gordie, and Vivi left."

"Together?"

"No-o-o-o."

"And that was what time?" Hen asked.

"Lessee. Says here they left about nine. You can see that's all we have 'til right at midnight, when Officer Roundtree came in looking for Reed."

Hen turned to me. "Trudy, didn't you say Vivi was here when you came in?"

"She was."

Billy heaved a martyr's sigh and raised his voice so he could address the congregation. "Okay. We got a loose end here. I'm gonna put down that Vivi left about two minutes after Reed and Gordie did, but we don't have what time she came back."

There was no immediate response, then a man in the next booth said, "She couldn'ta been gone long. I saw that red convertible of hers parked out front when I went by between nine-fifteen and nine-thirty."

"That can't be right," another said. "I know it was after nine-thirty. Closer to ten. I didn't get here 'til a quarter to, and she came in after I did."

The first man wasn't shaken. "You can just ask my wife what time I got home. She'll know 'cause it irks her to hold dinner for me like she was doin' Tuesday night, waiting for me to get back from Swainsboro."

"I don't need to talk to your wife to know what I—"

"Hush!" Billy yelled. The men didn't hush completely, but they did lower their voices and watch Billy out of the corner of their eyes.

"I'm sure sorry about that, Hen," Billy apologized. "Thought we had it all ironed out for you." He fumbled under his overalls for a stubby pencil. He made his entry—nine-thirty with a question mark and two sets of initials—then slid the greasy paper back toward Hen and patted himself on the chest. "Anyway, I know Vivi and those two fellas she was playing cards with left at the same time right after Trudy did. I'll sign for that myself, but it's too late to help you any, ain't it? I think that does it. Anything else you need to know?"

"We'll let you know if we find any gaps. Thanks for taking such an interest." Hen slid a bill under the edge of his plate, which Billy pretended not to see, reached across the table to shake Billy's hand, which Billy also ignored, then Hen slid out of the booth and straightened his uniform. Billy took the hint and let me out.

Outside in the late afternoon warmth, Hen frowned at the paper and held it out to me. I still didn't want to touch it. Hen leaned meditatively against the car and frowned at the paper again. "Funny how nobody mentioned before now that Reed and Gordie were fighting, or that Vivi left for a while after Reed and Gordie left."

"They probably didn't think about it. She was back

well before the fire could have started, anyway. How reliable you think all this is?"

"Don't matter how reliable it is. Now that they've collaborated, we have no chance of getting anything different out of any of them."

"Look on the bright side. If they've all thrashed it out, it probably is what really happened. Reckon they've got a pool on who did it?"

"You're not suggesting Billy might be harboring illegal gamblin', are you, Trudy?"

"Oh, no, sir," I said earnestly.

Hen nodded. "Good. Now, you want to go with me to talk to Gordie again?"

EIGHTEEN

GORDIE WAS STANDING at the door to Albritton Realty with his key in the lock when we came to the top of the stairs at the Old Bank Building.

"Talk to you a minute?" Hen asked, gesturing toward the office.

Gordie's expression made it clear that he had been leaving, rather than arriving, but he unlocked the door and led the way inside.

"How'd you get such a bad sunburn?" Gordie asked as he flicked the light switch and took the chair behind the desk.

Hen grunted and settled firmly in the client chair, planting his feet wide apart on the floor. That's how he likes to sit if he can't put his boots on the desk top. That left the uninviting couch with its angular wood frame and scratchy cushions for me. The loose cushion slid away from the sofa's back when I sat on it, leaving me leaning too far back for comfort, my legs thrust too far forward. If this was how Gordie treated potential clients, no wonder his business wasn't booming.

"So what can I do for you?" Gordie asked, "Can't remember when I've had so much police attention."

"Fact is," Hen went on, "The picture has changed some since you and Trudy talked earlier."

"What's changed? Have you found who did it? It's hard to believe—"

Hen interrupted. "You and Trudy already talked about how you were the last one anybody saw with Reed Tuesday night. And now we have witnesses who say y'all had been fighting before you left. And everybody agrees he had been drinking a lot more than usual and wouldn't have been able to put up much of a fight if somebody lit into him. So we thought maybe we ought to hear what you have to say about all that.''

"Who says we were fighting?"

"It seems to be the consensus down at Billy Watson's."

"Well." Gordie considered. "Billy must attract a pretty genteel clientele if they think that was a fight."

"What would you call it?"

"Disagreeing, that's what we were doing."

"Okay, let's say you had a disagreement. Whatever you call it, you left with Reed and that's the last time anybody saw him alive."

There was a delayed reaction as though somebody was translating and Gordie had to wait for it. He shook his head. "Hold on, Hen. I don't much like the way this conversation is going. Why would I kill Reed?"

"I've got to tell you, Gordie, you really wouldn't like the way the conversation was going if I knew the answer to that." He raised a swollen finger. "You were at the scene about the time Reed died. That's opportunity." A second finger joined the first. "There's no question you'd have been able to do it. That's means. That just leaves motive."

"And the idea is that I'm going to provide that by telling you what we were disagreeing about? I think I'd better get hold of my lawyer."

"Who's your lawyer? Ronnie Dawson? What kind of help would he be? I guess he could tell you to quit talking if you were going to incriminate yourself, but all that would do is make it look like you got something to be ashamed of. On the other hand, if you want to tell us what y'all were quarrelling about, it might help you instead of hurting you.''

''How?''

''Well, maybe it wouldn't sound like a reason to kill him.''

''What if it did?''

''Then you'd be smart enough to shut up without having a lawyer tell you to. We aren't charging you with anything, Gordie. We're just trying to find out what happened.''

Gordie thought about that, then asked, cautiously, ''What do you already know?''

''Let's do it the other way around, Gordie. You tell me first and I'll see how it fits with what I already know. That will make it more convincing.''

Gordie didn't look happy. ''It sounds like I don't have much to lose. And I don't think you really believe I could have killed him, anyway. Okay, here's the deal. You know the town's getting ready to buy some land for that big park and sports complex?''

''Right.''

''And B.L. Dawson has enough pull with the town and the county that the development will go just about wherever he says.''

''There is an official process,'' I pointed out, struggling to the edge of the couch so I could sit upright and look dignified. It wasn't much of a point, and I had no interest in protecting B.L.'s name, but I felt like I had to put my two cents in somewhere. This was my investigation and Hen was taking it over just like I wasn't even there, and I'd been sitting there on that booby-trap of a couch letting him do it.

"Yeah," Hen said. "B.L. cain't just pick out the land he wants."

"Maybe there's a little more to it than that," Gordie conceded. "Let's put it this way: There's no way that park will go anywhere B.L. doesn't want it to."

I got in again. "What does this have to do with what you and Reed were fighting—disagreeing—about?"

"It happens that the best piece of land for the purpose belongs to me. And Reed."

"How'd that happen?" Hen asked. "I didn't think Reed had much of anything." I guess I hadn't mentioned to him what I found out about that when he sent me over to the county clerk's office. Careless me.

"He had this piece of land. Half of it, anyway. It was our Grandpa Stone's farm, and he left it to us equally. We were the only grandsons. Our mothers were sisters."

"And the quarrel?" I persisted.

"The land wasn't ever going to be much good to either one of us, with both of us owning it, and couldn't either one of us afford to buy the other one out and do anything with it, even if we'd wanted to. We've been leasing it, but that hasn't been doing much more than pay the taxes. And here was a chance to sell it for a good price."

"Maybe sell it," Hen said.

But Gordie was warming up. "Well, I'm pretty sure B.L. favored it, too. It's east of town, and with the traffic the park would bring past his car lot he was inclined to favor it. I know he didn't want it over near Lake Loop, lowering the tone."

"Regardless, you must be one silver-tongued rascal if you could talk B.L. into favoring something that might have done Reed some good," Hen said.

Gordie nodded. "It's the truth B.L. didn't have much use for Reed. Maybe he figured if Reed had some money, he and Ronnie could figure out some way to take it away from him."

I stuck my oar in again. "Was this the way Reed thought he was going to raise money to leave town?"

Gordie made a face. "No. See, I thought that would make him more inclined to sell. Maybe he'd want the money to help him make the move. But he said he didn't need the money. He said B.L. was going to give him some money."

"B.L.?" Hen asked. "You didn't believe that, did you?"

"Well, it did strike me a little off, so I made him say it again. 'Ol' B.L.'s gonna help me out.' That's what he said, and he grinned when he said it. He was enjoying the idea."

"Sounds kind of farfetched to me," Hen said.

"Yeah, me, too, but that's what he said."

"That's interesting, all right, but we've gotten away from what you and Reed were quarrelling about," I pointed out.

No longer stimulated by his own sales talk, Gordie began to look nervous again. "Reed didn't want to sell. It hadn't occurred to me that he wouldn't, and I'd gone ahead and put all this work into pitching it to B.L. and everything."

"Why didn't he want to sell?" Hen asked.

"He said it was the one thing he had that he could give to Mark—something for Mark that didn't come from the Dawsons."

"Good point."

"I could see his point, too, but that didn't help me any. It left me high and dry. Reed's biggest problem his whole life—not counting marrying Vivi, which was in a class all by itself—was making up his mind. He told me he hadn't even gotten around to changing his will since the divorce. Anyway, that's what our difference of opinion was about. His attitude took me by surprise and I might have reacted stronger than I should have, been a little loud about it, but we weren't fighting.''

"Billy said the word 'desperate' came up. How would that have been?'' I asked. I was determined not to let either one of these men forget I was there.

"I might have told Reed I was desperate for the money. I told you, it took me by surprise, and the truth is, the money would come in handy right now. I've got one young'un wanting to go to college and another one needs work on her teeth.''

"So, tell us, how'd your granddaddy leave that property, anyway?'' Hen, of course.

Gordie opened his mouth to speak, closed while he thought, then took on a glazed look. "Oh, Lord. I knew I shouldn't have tried to talk without a lawyer. I thought I could just tell you what happened and that would be all.''

"Could be.'' Hen waited.

Finally, Gordie said, "It was equal shares. Grandpa Stone naturally wanted to keep it in the family if he could, so it was set up so that we both had to agree to sell. The way it was set up, I couldn't just sell my interest to somebody else, for instance.''

"My, my.'' Hen said, and I could practically see the ideas chasing themselves around in his head. "And if one of you died?''

Gordie looked uncomfortable. "I'm not sure about that.''

"Really now?'' Hen asked.

"Probably the lawyers would have to sort it out,'' Gordie admitted, "But I guess whoever inherits it would be subject to the same rules. Like if I'd died, Joy Lynn would have gotten it and she and Reed would have had to decide what to do with it.''

"Uh-huh," Hen said.

"But you didn't die," I pointed out. "Reed did. My goodness, the questions that do come up! Does Mark get it? And who will be his guardian? And would that person be more inclined to agree to sell?"

Gordie looked shocked.

"How bad does that girl of yours need orthodontia, Gordie?" Hen asked.

We left Gordie in his office. For some reason he didn't seem to be in as much of a hurry to leave as he had been earlier. Maybe he was going to call his lawyer.

"Several interesting ideas came out of that, don't you think?" Hen asked as we headed back to the station.

"Yes, I do think," I responded. "Why do you think Gordie took it for granted that Granddaddy Stone wouldn't consider leaving the land to his granddaughters?"

"No idea. Granddaddy Stone and Gordie are probably both male chauvinist pigs. Besides that.''

"Is this a test?"

"Yes."

"All right, then. Gordie and Reed were joint owners of some land that might be valuable. We might want to find out exactly how that inheritance works. Maybe Gordie inherits Reed's interest in the land, so that could be a motive for Gordie. And he said Reed hadn't changed his will since the divorce. If Vivi knew that, she might also know about the land and think she'd inherit that. Mark getting it would probably be the same thing. No telling what she overheard at Billy's. That could be a motive for her. If the amount we're talking about is enough to murder for.''

"The amount worth murdering for might depend on how desperate you are—for orthodontia or whatever.''

"What beats me is why B.L. Dawson would help Reed leave town. B.L. didn't mention that when I talked to him, and Bonnie said Reed wasn't going to leave, but Suzanne and Gordie both say he was talking about it. Gordie must believe it. It sure didn't do his cause any good to tell us that.''

"Downright confusin', ain't it?''

NINETEEN

ON SATURDAY MORNING I communed with my cats and, inspired by Billy Watson, began to sketch out a timetable for Tuesday night, combining Billy's chart with what I remembered of what Miss Sarah had told me about the comings and goings at Reed's that night and what I had picked up from Mark, Danny, and David about what they'd been up to.

I had gotten as far as deciding, with a shiver, that Reed was probably already dead by the time Mark rescued his bed buddy, when fire sirens and bells cut into my thoughts and scattered the cats. For an awful moment everything that had happened since I last heard those sirens washed over me in a gruesome *déjà vu.*

Then I remembered. This was the signal for the beginning of the Easter egg hunt on the courthouse lawn. Ogeechee being what it is, I rationalized deferring my police puzzle by telling myself all the principals in the case would be there and I might learn something important. I set off along the path from my house to the courthouse square.

There's something wonderful about a community gathering like this. In spite of my years away, and Teri's skepticism about me, I've never found anything to compare with the feeling of belonging I get when I stroll through a crowd and recognize almost everybody I see. It's like being in an extended family; sometimes better.

As I joined the group in the parking lot, waiting for the ropes to come down from around the area where the treats were hidden, I waved at Half Pint, Japonica, and an assortment of other people I took to be Conroys. Pint was missing, probably too mature for an Easter egg hunt. Through the crowd, I caught sight of Brenda Whitson and her daughter—Brenda whose permanent night shift duty made it unusual to see her in the daylight. Either she was sacrificing sleep, or it was her day off.

Judging strictly from attendance, Ogeechee's First Annual Chamber of Commerce and Garden Club Easter Egg Hunt looked like a success.

The courthouse grounds had been roped off after close of business on Friday in preparation for the event. Members of the high school football team, the Panthers, were stationed around the perimeter to repel over-eager young Easter egg hunters.

"Quite a crowd," I said to Bonnie Dawson as I passed her and Nita.

"B.L. will be pleased," Bonnie responded. "This was a project he was especially interested in."

She pointed to where B.L. and Mayor Ozzie Rhodes stood, apparently talking together, but nodding and waving to acquaintances without let-up. It must be a skill politicians are born with.

"Where are those boys of yours?" I asked Nita, who responded by rolling her eyes and gesturing vaguely around. "Oh. There," she pointed.

Danny and David were taking turns trying to distract one of the larger football players so that the other could sneak past. All three—Danny, David, and the older boy—seemed to be enjoying the game, since whenever one of the Dawsons did manage to sneak past, he loitered until the guard pulled him back, kicking and screaming. Nodding goodbye to Bonnie and Nita, I moved on.

"Lord! This is going to set the Garden Club back fifteen years!'' This was Aunt Lulu, who had appeared at my side.

"Weren't you hoping for a big turnout?"

"They were. I wasn't."

"Whose idea was this, Aunt Lulu? I can't believe you went along with a plan to encourage uncontrolled traffic on the sacred ground of Courthouse Park."

Aunt Lulu bristled. "Eula Rhodes had her orders from the Mayor and Bonnie Dawson had hers from B.L., so I was outvoted. I did not 'go along.'"

I remembered what the courthouse square looked like fifteen years ago when the Garden Club took it on. The only vegetation had been two magnolia trees and sparse grass.

The courthouse sits in the center of the block, on the northwest corner where Main Street crosses Court Street. Sidewalks lead to the building from the four corners of the block, but countless additional paths had been worn down by people who considered their business too urgent to be delayed long enough for them to find the paved walks.

Then, during one of Grandma's terms as president, the Garden Club coerced the county into finding funds for some benches. Garden Club members donated labor and plants. The magnolias were joined by shrubs, flowerbeds, benches, and some dogwoods, all arranged with the idea of maximizing the obstruction of the unsanctioned paths. It had grown up into a park the town and the Garden Club were proud of.

"Look on the bright side," I said. "Repairing the damage will give the Garden Club something to do. You were running out of worthwhile civic projects, weren't you?"

Aunt Lulu dealt with this heartless question by attacking her beloved son, who had just joined us. "Has any-body told you you look like something the cat drug in?"

"Thanks to the miracles of modern medicine, I'm feel-ing about that good, too, thank you," Hen said. Actually, he looked much better than when I'd left him the day before.

"Whose idea was it to use the football team as gen-darmes?" I asked. "I hadn't heard about that."

"Delcie was scared plumb silly that somebody would get started hunting eggs ahead of her, and I somehow didn't think the situation called for posting police officers, not to mention the strain on the police officers. Dawn came up with this and worked it out. Her brother's on the team. Looks like they're doing a good job. Might be some raw material out there for another officer or two."

"I thought you had all the help you needed," Aunt Lulu said.

"You hear that from Wonder Woman here? She's got an exalted idea of how much she contributes. But I will allow as how I've got all the help I'm budgeted for."

"There's a good prospect for you," I said, indicating the boy who held a screaming Danny Dawson under one arm without seeming to expend any effort. A line was beginning to form for this attraction.

"Yeah," Hen acknowledged. "That's the Schofield boy, Wim. If he could learn some sense, he'd do."

"He's got the right idea about how to handle those kids, anyway," I said. "Keep a line on him, Chief. You're gonna need him when Danny Dawson gets a little older, even with Wonder Woman on the force." Wonder Woman wasn't the worst thing he'd ever called me.

"Reckon who put up the banner?" Hen asked.

"It looks to me like they had Wim Schofield on the Chamber of Commerce end and little old Alma Wilkes on the Garden Club end,'' Aunt Lulu said. ''Why don't you go straighten it out?''

Hen went off toward the lopsided banner.

''Is Delcie here?'' I asked Aunt Lulu.

''Should be. Yes. Over there.'' She started off in the direction of Delcie and Teri. About to follow, I was way-laid by the former Terror of Ogeechee High School, who was stuffing a folded grocery bag into a bag already bulging with other folded bags.

''Morning, Trudy.''

''Morning, Miss Sarah. Are you turning into a bag lady?''

Miss Sarah considered the bags she was carrying before she answered, seriously, ''I think bag ladies carry bags around with them so they can collect things. I've been emptying these. I was in charge of hiding the eggs and candy, and I personally hid the treasure egg, the one worth a gift certificate. I'm expected to be impartial where children are concerned, and above giving hints to any in particular. Since you don't have any children of your own either, I suppose you're expected to be impartial, too?''

''Oh, not at all. I thought everybody knew I'm disgustingly partial to Delcie. It's a good thing I don't know where the treasure egg is hidden or I'd run right over there and tell her. How could anybody look at that and be impartial?'' I pointed to where Delcie, wearing blue corduroy overalls with pink daisies embroidered up the legs, her hair in a French braid, had joined Wim Schofield's groupies.

''I saw you over at Grinstead's with a ham in your basket. Do you have your Easter dinner all worked out?'' In spite of the reference to the ham, I knew she wasn't asking about the menu.

"Yes, ma'am, we do," I told her. "We'll be eating at my house."

She smiled her approval. "Your house. My, my. Good. Good for you. I'm glad." Then she leaned forward confidentially and patted my arm and moved on to her next agenda item. "Would it be all right for me to ask how you're coming with the business about Reed?"

"Of course you can ask," I said. "But I don't have much to tell you. We're working on it. I'm sure we'll find out who did it. How are you doing? I hope you've stopped feeling bad because you didn't see the fire earlier. Especially now that we know it wasn't the fire that killed him."

Miss Sarah shivered. "I can't say it makes me feel a lot better to know I was so close to a murder."

"No. Of course not. But I'm sure you weren't in any danger. What happened to Reed wasn't random or accidental. It was deliberate and happened to him because he was Reed."

Miss Sarah nodded, her fingers busily pleating an empty paper bag. "I understood that as soon as I heard. But there's another thing. I keep going over that night in my mind. It was just impressions, you know. I had no reason to memorize what was happening at the time, but I've remembered something that might help."

She darted a quick glance at me to make sure I was paying attention, a mannerism I remembered from high school. "Yesterday, when I was out doing a little raking in back, I heard a car go by and it had a squeal in its brakes, and that reminded me. It might not mean anything, but I do remember hearing squeaky brakes over there the night Reed died."

I was disappointed. "That was probably Gordie's car. He took—"

The voice of Mayor Ozzie Rhodes on a portable bullhorn drowned me out. "We want to thank the generous members of the Chamber of Commerce and the good ladies of the Garden Club for their contributions. Children, remember, whoever finds the golden egg must bring it up here to the microphone to receive a very special prize. Parents, please keep your children outside the fence until the signal to begin the hunt. When the clock begins to strike ten, the hunt begins. Have fun."

As soon as "fun" had quit echoing back from the courthouse wall, Miss Sarah said, "Besides Gordie's. I realize now that what I thought was Reed and a date must have been Gordie bringing Reed home."

I frowned. "So you're saying there was another car there that night, besides Reed's car and besides Gordie's car?"

"Yes, that's what I'm saying. I wasn't paying particular attention, but when I heard it again, I remembered."

I rummaged in a pocket for the pad I'm never without and flipped back several pages. "When we talked before, you said they left in Reed's date's car, and Reed came back in his car."

Miss Sarah looked off into the distance. "Yes. That's what I thought, but it doesn't sound right, does it?" She looked troubled.

"Don't worry about it," I said. "We'll make sense of it, but let me make sure I understand what you're saying. Reed's date was with Gordie Albritton, so that accounts for one car. And there's the one you thought was Reed's. But now you're saying there was a third car?"

"Yes. Later. One with a squeak."

"It might not amount to anything, but it's something to check out. Whoever it was hasn't mentioned it so far, and there's probably a reason for that. Can you remember what time it was when you heard that other car at Reed's? Oh, here it is in my notes. You said Reed left when you did. About seven?'' I made a question out of it and waited for Miss Sarah's ''yes'' before I went on. ''He came back, you said, in his date's car about nine.''

''Yes.''

''That was probably Gordie bringing him home.''

''Yes. I think it must have been.''

''Then you said you heard Reed's car a little after that, and another car half an hour later.''

''Yes. That's right. And now I remember that last car had a squeak. I still don't understand about Reed's car. You know, I thought it was Reed's, but his car wasn't there, was it? And he couldn't have been driving it, anyway. This was a different one and it had a distinctive squeak. It's very confusing, isn't it?''

I made a note, trying to control my excitement. Could Miss Sarah have heard the killer?

''Miss Sarah, if you heard it again, would you be sure it was the same car?''

''I imagine I would.''

The courthouse clock began to chime. When it did, the bells and siren from the fire truck, which had been sitting quietly on Milford Street beside the courthouse, waiting for an emergency or ten o'clock, joined in.

The Ogeechee Panthers, with better teamwork than they usually mustered on the field, pulled up the stakes and coiled the ropes that had been the makeshift fence. Small children with Easter baskets surged. Almost at once, shrill birdlike cheeps of excitement and success filled the air.

''I put some of them in easy places,'' Miss Sarah said.

''You're sure you don't want to tell me where you hid the treasure egg?'' I asked.

Miss Sarah shook her head sadly. ''I don't believe I

could trust you, Trudy," she said, and began moving away, stroking her neatly folded bags.

With much of the crowd now dispersed across the park instead of just around the edges, visibility was improved. Across the square, I saw Vivi and Mark Dawson just arriving. Did I imagine a squeak as Vivi's car came to a stop? Mark staggered from the car under a mint green rabbit nearly as large as he was. Vivi carried an Easter basket. Seeing that the hunt had already started, Mark thrust the rabbit at Vivi, grabbed the basket, and hurled himself into the melee.

I was moving toward Aunt Lulu and Teri, who had taken possession of the Jessie Roundtree memorial bench, when I looked up to see Gordie Albritton striding in my direction with a purposeful look on his face.

I changed course and strolled to meet him. "You forgot your Easter basket," I said when he came close enough to hear.

"Where's Hen?" he asked.

"He's around somewhere," I said. "What's the matter?"

He looked around again and lowered his voice. "I was watching all this from my office. Thank the Lord my kids are too old for it. I don't know what it means, but I hope it will get you off my back."

"What? What are you talking about?"

"That Easter bunny. That green monstrosity with the purple polka-dot bow tie that Vivi's holding." I didn't have to look where he pointed to remember the bunny. "There can't be more than one of those in the world," Gordie was saying. "It was at Reed's when I took him home Tuesday night. I knocked it off the chest when I was hauling him in to put him to bed and I picked it up and put it back, so I know it was there. And now Vivi has it. So that means she was there after I was.''

''You're sure it was the same Easter bunny?''

Gordie gave me a look so scathing it reminded me of Danny Dawson when I asked about his bedtime.

''Okay. Okay. You're right. Thanks, Gordie.''

''You'll tell Hen?''

''I'll tell him.''

''Okay, then.''

''Thanks.''

Gordie started weaving his way back across the square toward the safety of his office. I looked around for Hen and instead saw Phil and Molly Pittman, near the fire truck, with their father in his wheelchair. I headed in their direction. Phil looked fresh-scrubbed as always. Molly looked tired, but better than she had the day before. At least her face wasn't splotchy and she wasn't constantly dabbing at her nose.

Even so, looking at her depressed me. Carrying on with some man she was ashamed of? If that was the best Ogeechee had to offer a woman, I'd have to give some serious thought about my future, much as I love the town. Suddenly I was embarrassed to think of the time I'd spent on myself in front of the mirror that morning, putting on a little makeup for a change, choosing a dress with a full swingy skirt that made me feel graceful, in a blue-green color that, thanks to Teri, I knew looked good on me.

''You forget your Easter baskets?'' I asked when I was within earshot of the Pittmans. It seemed to be my standard opening, but I hadn't used it on them before.

''I brought mine,'' Mr. Pittman said, indicating the pouch attached to the back of his chair, ''But they won't let me go. These two spoilsports said I'd have unfair advantage.''

"Knowing how competitive you are, I was afraid you'd run over any children who got in your way, and I didn't think I could stand the shame," Phil said. "I'll buy him a chocolate rabbit later to appease him." Mr. Pittman joined in the laughter.

"It's good to see you out," I said to the old man.

"Good to be out. Something like this is as good as a tonic," he said. "Watching children having a great time, running around and yelling and tearing things up, and knowing they're not mine so I'm not responsible for making them behave. Look at that one! I've been watching him."

"That one" was Danny Dawson. He was adding his own brand of spice to the hunt by waiting until other children found the eggs and then trying to sneak them out of their baskets. As we watched, he and another boy took off running and howling through the crowd.

Mr. Pittman slapped the arm of his wheelchair and grinned.

"I'll bet that's the kind of child you were," I teased.

"You're right. Drove my folks crazy. But I was the last of that breed. These two offspring of mine are stodgy and responsible and reliable. Can't think how it happened. Must have come from their mother's side." Phil grinned at the insult. Molly blushed.

"I was telling Daddy how you've taken charge of this murder investigation," Phil said, and I swear he blushed. "How's the investigation coming?"

"For publication? Clues are falling out of the sky," I said. "Chief Huckabee confidently predicts an early arrest. The usual."

"Oh," said Molly.

"Well," I said. "We do have several lines of investigation going. We'll find out who did it."

"Of course you will." Mr. Pittman and Phil were a duet.

When Phil and his father turned their attention back to the hunt, I said to Molly, "You look like you're feeling better today."

She looked startled. "Oh, yes. Thanks. I'm better now. It's a wonder what a day or two can do."

"Time is a great healer," I said.

Molly looked blank.

"Phil—" I started to explain.

"Let's walk," Molly said. She led the way to the fringes of the crowd, stopping near the edge of an azalea bed. She turned to face me and spoke hesitantly. "I know Phil's been worried about me. He thinks I was interested in Reed. I don't know what gave him that idea, but he was wrong."

"Part of what made him think it was your cold-like symptoms the day after Reed died."

Molly dismissed that with an impatient jerk of her head.

"It's not my business, unless it's involved with Reed's death, but you're right about Phil. He's worried about you and he thought you were involved with Reed."

"Well, I wasn't involved with Reed."

Something about the way she said it made me ask. "Is it someone else? You aren't on the brink of bringing somebody home to meet the family? They'd be happy for you, you know."

A laugh that threatened to turn into a cold symptom escaped Molly. "It's over. It was the stupidest thing I ever did in my life. All he wanted was— Well, it's over. And maybe a few of my tears were for that, as well as for Reed."

"I'm sorry."

"I'll be all right."

Pink daisies danced up. "Look, Trudy! I've found two eggs and a bag of candy corn!"

"Good for you, Delcie! You're—"

But the daisies had already danced away, leaving Molly and me in imminent danger of being run down by two racing boys. We stepped back into the flower bed to let the danger pass.

"I knew what Phil was thinking and I wanted to tell you that so you wouldn't waste your time following up a dead-end lead—Reed and me." She offered me a wry smile. "I'd better go see if Daddy's ready to go. He likes getting out, but his energy runs out in a hurry."

Watching Molly rejoin her family, I had to swallow an inexplicable lump in my throat. As I blinked back a sentimental tear, my glance lit on Molly's footprints and my own, clear in the damp flowerbed. I automatically noted that both were too small to be the mysterious print in the picture. Whatever Molly had really been up to, she hadn't been the one who left a footprint behind in Reed's burnt-out house.

Once again, I went looking for my cousin-in-law. We hadn't had a real conversation since I blackmailed her over the telephone the day before, and I needed to see how we stood. She saw me coming and looked steadily at me until I was close enough to speak. It felt like *High Noon*.

"Trudy, I've got a favor to ask," is what she said.

"Sure. What?" I tried not to sound wary. I was determined not to back down. But I'd misjudged her.

"Delcie's been after me to let her spend the night with you. Said she's the only one who knows how to help you with the ham and you have to get it on r-e-a-l-l-y early. I told her I'd see if it would be okay."

For once in my life, I couldn't even think of anything

smart to say. All I could manage was what must have been a goofy smile. I did trust myself to nod.

"I'll tell her, then."

"Thanks, Teri." I have to hand it to her. When she caved, she did a good job of it. I gave her a hug. "I've got something I need to talk to Hen about right now and I have some things I need to do this afternoon. Tell Delcie I'll come get her later, okay?"

"Okay."

By the time the courthouse clock struck ten-thirty, most of the eggs and candy had found its way into little baskets. What was left was harder to find and only the most determined hunters were still at it. When Ozzie Rhodes' voice assaulted our ears again, this time with the news that little Jonquil Conroy had found the treasure egg and was the winner of the twenty-dollar gift certificate generously donated by Annette's Toyland, even those remaining hunters allowed themselves to be persuaded by bored parents that it was time to go.

I intercepted Vivi and Mark on their way back to their car. "Hey there, Mark. That's the biggest Easter bunny I ever saw. Is it your mother's or is she just holding it for you?"

"It's mine." He put his basket down and took the rabbit from Vivi.

"Oh, yes, now I remember. Is this the one you were telling me about? The one your daddy got you?"

"Yes." Mark stroked his cheek with a rabbit ear.

"I'll bet Danny and David believe you now."

He nodded dreamily.

"When did he give it to you, your daddy?"

Mark looked confused. He darted a glance at Vivi. "He didn't."

"We've got to go," Vivi said, picking up the basket

and opening the car door. "Get in the car, Mark. Leave him alone, Trudy; you're upsetting him."

"Just a minute, Vivi. It's a simple question."

I tried to look as intimidating as possible. If I'd have known I was going to try to face down Vivi Dawson, I definitely would have worn my uniform. "How did you get it then, Mark?"

"Now, Mark! Get in the car!" Vivi said.

Mark hugged the bunny. "He gave it to—"

Vivi threw the boy into the car and slammed the door. She screeched away from me, showing her opinion of the police, I guess, and screeched to a stop when she reached the street. I had to admit the screech was tires, not brakes. I started looking around for Hen.

Under Dwight's supervision, the cleanup crew—three misdemeanants with fines to work off for the city—had already begun picking up foil and cellophane candy wrappers. Hen was on the far side of the square. I beckoned to him and he started toward me, stopping en route to pick up a broken dogwood bough and drop it in a trash bag.

When I finished recounting what Gordie had had to say, he grinned.

"How do you like Vivi as a murderer?" I asked. "She could have killed Reed and taken the Easter bunny to keep from disappointing Mark. She wouldn't let Mark tell me how he got the bunny."

"No doubt in my mind she has it in 'er," he said. "Killing Reed, I mean. I can't see her worrying about disappointing the boy."

"Here's something else: Miss Sarah just told me there was a third car there that night, besides Reed's and Gordie's. She doesn't know whose it was, but she thinks she'd recognize it if she heard it again, from the squeaky brakes. I didn't hear Vivi's brakes squeak, though.''

"Might not mean anything, anyway. Stay on it," he said and went off to supervise Dwight.

I started home. As I went past a damp area near a leaky faucet, in a protected area where two hedges meet near a corner of the courthouse, my attention was arrested by a pattern of footprints. Was I developing a footprint fetish? Intent on self-ridicule, it took me a minute to realize what was arresting about the footprints. I recognized Molly's footprints at once. I had just been looking at them along with mine in the flowerbed. Here, Molly had stood with someone else. The footprints of that other person were even more familiar to me than Molly's or mine, familiar from Phil's photo. Molly had been talking with the murderer.

Vivi? I couldn't remember what kind of shoes Vivi had been wearing. Where was Molly? She'd said she was going to take her father home. Had they already gone? A talk with Molly could clear up the whole thing.

I looked around for Hen and saw him driving away.

What to do first? First I cursed the impulse that had led me to walk to the Easter egg hunt instead of bringing a car. Then I cursed my sandals, which would make it hard to run. Then I sprinted for home.

TWENTY

I BROKE SPEED LAWS getting to the Pittman house a mile or so west of town, only to find nobody home. I was returning to town at a much more leisurely pace, trying to think where else to look for them, when I looked up to see Pint Conroy's old Catalina weaving along ahead of me. Never one to question Providence, I hit my siren. I was more than a little surprised when it traveled not more than half a mile farther (and at less than the speed of sound) and turned onto a side road, pulling to a stop on a relatively isolated stretch between widely-spaced houses.

I got on the radio with Dawn to let her know about the contact, but she seemed to have trouble understanding this routine piece of business.

"You're not at home?" she asked.

"No. I just told you. I'm just off Highway Fifty-Six about a mile west of town."

"And Delcie's not with you?"

"Dawn, have you been smoking something out of the evidence room again?"

"Again!" She squawked in outrage. "Trudy, you know I never!" Dawn is so easy to tease it's almost not even fun.

"Then why are you having trouble understanding me?"

"Well, Teri was here a little while ago looking for Delcie, said she disappeared after the Easter egg hunt. She and the Chief thought maybe she'd gone home with you because she was so excited about spending the night."

Bless her little heart! She'd been missing me just like I'd been missing her. I knew what she'd do if she got there and didn't find me. She'd go looking for where the yellow mama cat was keeping her babies. I'd told Delcie about the kittens and we'd tried to guess where the mama was keeping them. I thought it was a trash heap near the back of the smokehouse, but Delcie was sure it was deeper in the pines. Given the chance, she'd try to find it and surprise me.

"No," I said to Dawn. "I told Teri I'd pick her up later." Hadn't I? Lord, don't let anything upset our shaky truce! "I'll get home as soon as I finish with Pint and see if she's there."

As I was signing off, I was surprised to see Pint climb out of the passenger's side of his car and start toward me. Odd that he'd be letting somebody else drive. Odder still that he seemed so eager to get out in the open and talk, instead of lounging in the protective shell of his own space. I got out to meet him.

"You holdin' a blue light special?" He seemed as friendly as always, but there was a nervous edginess to his usual relaxed posture.

My business was with the driver, but as I moved toward the car, Pint sidled into my path.

"I've got a special on citations for people who can't control their vehicles," I said, taking another step.

Pint moved to block. "Aw. You think he drivin' under the influence? Naw. See, what happen is I drop my cigarette and he scared it gone burn a hole in his new pants and he swerve a little. Yeah, he swerve a little, but no harm done."

Another *pas de deux*. "I need to take a look at his driver's license and give him a little talk about all the young'uns and chickens around here that we don't want run over."

"You don't want to make a bad impression, hurt the tourist trade, givin' a ticket to my cousin."

"Of course not Pint, but you know I can't back off my duty to the young'uns and chickens of Ogeechee."

I feinted on Pint and faked him out. It wasn't enough to get me past him without forcing it, but it was enough to let me get a good look at the driver. He had been fumbling around in the car, but looked up at that instant and met my eyes. I had seen those protruding eyes, full lips and cheeks, just two days before, on the wall of the file room at the Ogeechee Police Department, where Hen had posted it so I could be on the lookout for him. Wouldn't Hen be surprised to learn I had actually succeeded in spotting the villain? If I lived to tell him, of course. I swallowed hard and tried to sound casual.

"I don't think I've met your cousin, Pint. He from around here?"

"He from Mobile, visitin'. He trying out my car, see if he likes it. Thinkin' of gettin' one for hisself."

I was no longer trying to maneuver toward the Catalina to ask for the man's driver's license. My hope now was to maneuver back to my cruiser without alarming either one of them. "It's a classy car, all right, Pint. I can see why he'd want one. They must be hard to find these days."

With Pint between me and his car, I had no way of knowing if the other man was alarmed. From what I could tell, Pint, like me, was trying to act normal. "Yeah, ain't no cars like this anymore. But I cain't tell him nothin'."

Suddenly the man in the car screamed, "Move!" Pint hit the sand. I dove behind the protective door of my

cruiser. A bullet ricocheted off the bumper and went singing off into the field.

I crouched behind the door and reached for my gun.
Pint's "cousin," aka Gilbert Dalrymple, started out of the
Catalina, carrying a gun that looked as big as the courthouse. I brought my own weapon up just in time to change
his mind about coming in closer for the kill. He reversed
direction and scrabbled back for the protection of the Catalina. Pint was still on the ground, crawling toward me.

"Drop that!" I yelled, steadying the barrel of my
weapon against the car door.

"Where you want me to drop it?" Dalrymple's voice
was high-pitched, and he laughed, a screechy sound that
told me what he thought of my suggestion.

"Throw it into the road."

He threw a bullet in my direction instead.

I returned the fire, adding another character mark to the
Catalina's hood, but missing my man. I called out, "Pint,
you haven't ever seen me shoot anybody, but don't make
the mistake of thinking I won't. You slither over to the
back of the Batmobile and stay right there on the
ground."

Pint stopped moving altogether.

I sent a bullet into the ground near his outstretched left
hand. His arm jerked wildly before he tucked it under his
body. "Right now, if you don't want a bullet in your
kneecap."

"You cain't shoot me. I ain't got no gun. You know I
never have no gun."

"Don't cain't me! I can shoot you if I want to. What
do you think this gun's for, anyway? You want to argue
about it?"

My attention, already divided between Gilbert Dalrymple and his gun behind the Catalina and the groveling Pint, who had finally decided to scootch in the indicated direction, needed to be divided further if the last thing I ever saw wasn't going to be two men coming at me from behind a rusty Catalina. I thumbed the switch on the radio. "Dawn, get somebody over here quick." That was all the attention I dared give it. Then I drew a deep steadying breath and determined to go down fighting.

A rangy, brown-and-white spotted dog loped up and took a look at the proceedings before disappearing back into the brush. A squirrel complained about our intruding on his territory. A mockingbird tried to cheer us up.

It couldn't have been as long as it seemed before I heard a siren screaming.

At the sound of the siren announcing help on the way for me, Dalrymple fired again. Using the Catalina for cover, he made a break for the woods.

"Stop, or I'll shoot!" I called after him. He turned to fire again, but I beat him to it, missing him by inches and knocking bark off a pine tree. The squirrel, who was having a bad day, was complaining about that, too, as Dalrymple disappeared into the underbrush.

Hen's cruiser careened into the scene and my heart sank as I realized Pint had also disappeared. That made two suspected drug dealers loose in the woods. I quickly filled Hen in and he radioed for as much backup as Dawn could muster.

"Tell Dwight to get over to those houses behind Trudy's, and you start calling the people over there, tell them to lock up and stay inside 'til further notice. Got that?"

Dawn apparently got that quicker than she'd got what I was trying to tell her earlier, but that reminded me. "Delcie turn up?" I asked Hen.

"Teri was going over to your house to look for her," he said. "Dwight thought he saw her starting off down the path from the courthouse."

"She'll be looking for those kittens," I said.

We looked at each other, both trying to remain professional about it, and neither one of us needing to say out loud that we were suddenly more interested in setting our minds at rest about Delcie, who might be innocently playing in these very piney woods, than in making a drug bust. We headed into the woods toward my house. Hen circled a little to the left of the route I chose and was quickly out of sight.

Not being intent on suicide, I was moving as quietly as possible, trying to glide from tree to tree, pause and listen, then glide again, but there's no way to be quiet in a pine thicket and no chance Gilbert and Pint would take my noise for a squirrel or a 'possum. The best thing I could think to hope for was that my racket would draw their attention and they'd shoot at me and the noise would help Hen pinpoint them.

I had gone about a hundred yards and was trying to find some bearing that would keep me headed for my house another hundred yards or so farther on, when I heard Delcie, ahead and to my right, out of sight.

"No, no, no, no, no!" She was saying. "You're botherin' the cat!"

Then silence. Unlike Delcie, the men had reason to be quiet.

I had gained several yards when I heard Delcie squeal. The thought of her pink daisies anywhere near that armed drug dealer answered for me some of the questions about murder that had until then only been academic. I'd have put a bullet through his heart with a smile on my face. I'd have poured sorghum on him and staked him out for fire ants. I'd have... What I actually did was try to work myself closer.

Soon I was close enough that I could hear thrashing and grunting.

"Put me down!" Delcie said, and I was grateful to hear annoyance in her voice rather than fear. I smiled grimly to myself, knowing firsthand how hard Delcie was to hold if she didn't want to be held. Then I heard a slap and Delcie's sobs.

"Shut up." That was Gilbert's high voice. I couldn't stand it.

"Hen!" I yelled, firing in the air. "Over here. They've got Delcie!"

"Stay back," Dalrymple yelled. "We've got us a little insurance policy here."

I moved closer, the sound of my advance covered by another of Dalrymple's eerie laughs.

I could hear Hen coming from my left, making a lot of noise even before he got close enough to yell. "You hurt that girl, you maggot, and I'll deep-fry your balls and feed 'em to you in their own gravy before I cut your gizzard out." Wow. So that's the kind of talk the boys practice out in the blackberry bushes; I can see why it would cramp their style to have my lady-like ears around.

"Daddy!" Delcie cried.

I was close enough now to hear a low-voiced conversation.

"Oh shit, Gilbert! That's the police chief's girl," Pint said. "You hurt her, we're dead!"

Dalrymple laughed again. I shivered and wondered what he was on that had him so high. I could see movement dimly through the brush ahead.

"Naw, don't make no sense to hurt her," Pint said. "She just a little girl."

Dalrymple grunted. I could see that one of his massive arms had Delcie pinned to his chest. She was struggling so ineffectually he didn't even bother to try to stop her. The other arm, the one attached to the hand holding the gun, was weaving back and forth in search of a target as he peered into the woods in the direction of Hen's approach.

I couldn't let him shoot Hen. I fired in his general direction, wide enough not to endanger Delcie.

When I looked again, Gilbert had tightened his grip on Delcie and his gun had stopped weaving.

"You shoot again, she dies," he said.

"Put me down," Delcie said.

"Shut up," Gilbert said.

"Oh, shit," Pint moaned.

I could no longer hear Hen. I assumed he'd found a strategic place.

It was shaping up for a stand-off, but whatever Gilbert was on drove him too far, past tolerance right into desperation. He laughed again, that nerve-jangling laugh. "We leave her here, it'll slow 'em down, won't it? Give us some getaway time?"

I could see that Pint was nodding yes, but then the movement of Gilbert's gun made it clear that when he said "leave her here," he meant "leave her here, dead." Even Delcie seemed to sense it. All in the same instant, Pint yelled, "No," Delcie bit Dalrymple's arm, and Dalrymple's gun went off.

I'm sure the memory of that next moment will have the power to freeze my blood until the day they lay my dead body in the cold, cold ground. Both Delcie and Pint fell to the ground. I took off at a run and so did Hen, but before either of us could reach them there was another gunshot. It took a few long seconds for my blood to thaw enough for me to realize it was all over.

Pint, who had told the truth when he reminded me he never carried a gun, had apparently gotten hold of Dalrymple's gun and fired that second shot. Now he dropped the gun and clawed at his bleeding right shoulder. Dalrymple lay against the base of a pine, blood pumping steadily from a hole in his throat. Delcie, airborne, hit Hen with such a thump they nearly went over backwards. It was up to me to keep a cool head and put handcuffs on Pint.

Dwight and the others had heard the gunfire. They came through the woods from the direction of my house like a pack of wild pigs, Teri right behind them. By then, Hen had his balance back and was relieving his feelings by ordering people around: "Teri, you get Delcie home. I'll be there directly. Dwight, you and your two sidekicks— Abbott and Costello, is it?—get this piece of... vermin...to Cowart Memorial as fast as you can. Practice some of that expensive training I paid for and and see if you can keep him alive 'til you can turn him over to the emergency room people. Let them worry about him."

His lack of sympathy for the bleeding man was, I thought, understandable. I stayed in the background while he got everybody else sorted out, then he and I took Pint, less seriously wounded, to Doc Cummings.

While we were waiting for Doc to dig the bullet out of Pint's shoulder, we got word from the ER that Dalrymple had passed on to his reward. I'm not proud of the thrill of pleasure it gave me to picture the devil grinning in anticipation as he met Gilbert Dalrymple at the gates of hell.

By the time we got back to the Ogeechee Police Department with Pint, what looked like the entire choir and congregation of the New Jerusalem Baptist Church was standing out in the parking lot holding hands. Who needs broadcast news?

"Just keep your mouth shut and keep movin'," Hen said to Pint. Pint did as he was told. The only sign that he was aware of the congregation was that he bowed his head and avoided looking at his mother.

Once in Hen's cramped office, Pint sat stiffly in the client chair, his clean white bandages in shining contrast to the rest of his ensemble, which told the tale of his pinewoods experience. "How much trouble I in?"

"You're running drugs and you just killed a man," Hen reminded him. "What do you think?"

"Does the fact that your mama's whole church is out there having a prayer meeting for you give you a hint?" I asked.

Pint screwed his face up and touched his bandage. "Self-defense," he said pitifully. "I self-defensed me and the little girl. Reminded me of Jonquil, her pigtail."

"His sister," I said, answering the question in Hen's eyes. He nodded.

"You think we ought to give you a medal?" Hen asked, "When we found enough illicit pharmaceuticals in your car to stock three or four drugstores and have enough left over to keep Cowart Memorial running for a year?"

"It's not my stuff," Pint said. "It's Gilbert's. All I know is he say he want to use my car."

"And he said he was using it to take some hymnals to the church house, and he was such a good ol' buddy that you said 'sho nuff.' That right?"

Pint wasn't as bright as his sister Japonica, but he could recognize sarcasm. "Uh…"

Hen relented, a little. "Now, I don't want to give you

the idea it's hopeless," he said. "On the one hand, Trudy tells me you did what you could to protect a little girl. You know she's my little girl, and I appreciate that, but that's beside the point. We got to be objective about this."

Beside the point? Objective? Sure. And I'm built like Dolly Parton.

"On the other hand, you're mixed up in some pretty nasty business." Hen's fingers twitched as though he'd thought about scratching, but decided against it. I wondered if he was going to hold Pint personally responsible for the Poison Whatever.

"Can we make a deal?" Pint asked.

Hen looked amazed. "A deal? Son, haven't you been paying attention? The entire DEA lined up and sang the Hallelujah Chorus in four-part harmony when I told 'em what we had here." He paused and seemed to be considering. "But you think you got something to deal with, I'd purely love to hear it."

"I could tell you something."

"What makes you think you know something we want to know?" Hen looked around at me and I looked as scornful as I could on short notice like that.

"You interested in somebody over by that house that burned Tuesday night?"

The switch in topics threw me, but Hen didn't miss a beat. "Won't do you any harm to try us."

I tried to look like I wasn't particularly interested.

"Saw a big ol' car, shiny new Chrysler, not like the piece of junk usually there."

"You're desperate, Pint. You're making this up."

"I ain't makin' up nothin'. What made me notice, there was something coming outta the house, big spooky green booger. That's why I remember. It scare me, I can tell you! So I just kept on goin' by, just goin' by on the way out to the rib place. I ain't making up nothin'.''

"And you saw the president of the United States buildin' a fire in the carport?"

Pint looked at Hen suspiciously. "I never said that. Just saw the booger, that's all. Just saw him."

"Got any idea what time it was?" I asked.

Pint seemed to be relieved to be able to look at me instead of Hen for a change. He gave me a ghost of his usual grin and said, "Nine-thirty, ten o'clock. Mama don't get home 'til late Tuesdays and she was hungry for ribs. That help you? You go easy on me?"

Nine-thirty? Ten o'clock? What good was that? He'd been using some of Gilbert's stock and was seeing boogers. I was so disappointed I lashed out. "Listen, you nineteen-year-old feeble-minded poor excuse for a Conroy! Go easy on you? You come from a nice family, got a mama who cares about you, and you go and mess around with drugs and people like Gilbert Dalrymple! Go easy on you! If I were you I'd take this close call as a message straight from the hand of God Almighty, and straighten up before I did something I couldn't recover from. If it isn't already too late."

Pint seemed fascinated. He blinked when Hen intervened and I sputtered to a stop. "We'll let you rest down at the jail while we think about it, Pint. You'll be safe from Officer Roundtree down there, but we are gonna let your mama get at you." Pint did not look relieved.

As soon as Pint was gone, Hen turned on me. "Who you think you are? Miss Sarah? You looking to be promoted to Terror of the Ogeechee Police Department?"

"You want to make something of it?" I challenged.

"No, m'am. Not today, anyway." He grinned. "I told you you'd help the DEA by memorizing those faces."

It was only the ringing of the telephone that saved me from committing battery against the person of Ogeechee's beloved chief of police.

TWENTY-ONE

WHAT I OVERHEARD of that phone call put me in Hen's debt, dadgumit.

"Yes, she's here." Pause. "No, I don't think I'll give her that message." Pause. "You don't think she's particularly upset? No? Good." Different she? "Uh-huh. Well, then, it sounds to me like the best thing from everybody's point of view is for you just to leave things alone." Pause. "You don't want to make her think there's something to be upset about, do you? Just let it go. Okay. What's for supper?"

He hung up and studied the door to the evidence room for a minute before he looked at me. Possibly inspired by my look of puzzlement, he said, too casually, as though it had just occured to him, "Still okay with you if Delcie sleeps at your house tonight?"

I nodded, casually, and Hen nodded back. "Good," he said.

"What next?" I asked to keep myself from kissing his boots.

Hen flexed his arms over his head. "Tell the truth, I'm enjoying sitting here basking in the thought of us getting Gilbert Dalrymple when Dillard and his boys are out there looking for him under rocks and behind cypress trees."

"I've got to hand it to you, Your Reverence, you and the other big boys did a lot of fine police work there." I no longer had an impulse to kiss his boots.

Hen merely smiled. "You tryin' to deprive me of the rare experience of baskin' in reflected glory? But I can

see it's making you uncomfortable, and the Lord knows
I don't want that. Maybe you're right, maybe we better
get a few more things done before that adrenaline surge
runs out on us. Especially you.''

"Especially me what?"

"Especially your adrenaline. Never been shot at in my
life that I didn't get a rush of the stuff and I doubt if
you're much different. So what loose ends do we have?"

I resented the implication that I was subject to my
glands, even the adrenal, so I called on my cerebrum.
"One good-sized loose end is that we don't know who
killed Reed, and to tell you the truth, I'm having a hard
time separating questions from answers, useful information from odds and ends."

"What have we got?" He closed his eyes in a listening
pose.

"Okay. We've got Pint's nine-thirty. That's about when
Miss Sarah heard a car with squeaky brakes. If B.L.'s car
has squeaky brakes, maybe we have something. And
we've got photographs of a footprint, and at the Easter
egg hunt Molly was talking to whoever was wearing the
shoes that made that footprint. That's something, isn't it?
She can tell us who that is."

"That's something."

"And Miss Sarah says Reed's car was over there that
night, after Gordie brought him home. It would help to
know who drove it there and why. Of course, if the tires
were flat before then, we can assume she was wrong,
which would be a relief in a way."

"Why don't you see if one of Billy's witnesses can
help you pin that down. What else?" His eyes were still
closed, but he was obviously keeping up.

"About that Easter bunny. It could be the bed buddy
Mark was so concerned about at Nita's, the thing he

couldn't sleep without that turned up there the next morning after all. Maybe he brought it back from Reed's. Or
maybe Vivi did and decided to kill Reed while she was
at it.''

"Nita could settle that real easy, about the bed buddy.''

"Right. And maybe Danny and David could tell me
what time they flattened Reed's tires." I got to my feet.
"Can't get finished if I don't start, and I want to get out
of here in time to get Delcie and spend some time with
her before her bedtime.''

Hen slowly brought his feet to the floor. "Well, you
get on with your murder case and I'll see if anything else
needs to be done on your drug bust.''

He grinned at me and that time I grinned back.

I settled down by the phone in the file room.

"Nita? Trudy Roundtree. Yeah, it looked like the
young'uns all had a good time. Probably turn into a yearly
event if the Garden Club doesn't have too much of a fit
about it. Your two get plenty of loot? Um-hmm... Um-
hmm... Nita, I've got a question that's gonna sound pretty
silly to you, but it might help clear something up for me.
You remember telling me Mark was upset because he
didn't have his bed buddy, and then next morning you
found it there after all? What does his bed buddy look
like? Oh? Really? A one-eared elephant. Thanks.'' Okay,
if Mark did get the bed buddy from Reed's, that still left
the Easter bunny. Was it Vivi after all?

"Oh, Nita, there's something else, something your boys
could help me with. Either one of them there? Well, if
you could pry one of 'em away from the television, I'd
like to ask him a question. Doesn't matter which one. Um-
hmm... I can hold on.''

"Hello?'' It was a boy's voice, tentative.

"Hello. Who's this?''

"David."

"And Danny. I'm upstairs."

"Okay, good. Danny and David, this is Officer Round-tree. There's something I need to know. Remember when we were talking the other day, y'all told me you let the air out of the tires on Reed's car? Right?"

"Are we gonna get in trouble?" That was Danny.

"Not about that. Not if I have anything to do with it. But it would be a lot of help to me, and might put you in good with the police, if you could tell me what time it was when you did it."

Silence.

"Is there some way you could narrow down the time? Was it after your dinner?" I prompted.

"Oh, yeah. It was after Mama put us to bed," David volunteered. Both boys snorted.

"Okay, good. What time was that?"

"Bedtime is eight-thirty on school nights," David said.

"Does that mean you go to bed at eight-thirty?"

Giggle giggle.

"So it was some time after eight-thirty and before you heard the fire siren?"

"You could ask Mama what time she slammed our door and said she'd skin whoever belonged to the next voice she heard," Danny said. Both boys giggled some more before Danny volunteered, "We knew she wouldn't come in and check on us after that, so it was safe to cut out."

"Okay, good. Now we're getting somewhere. And boys?"

"Yeah?"

"Yeah?"

"This could turn out to be really important. Thanks for your help." At the grocery store that day, Nita had pinned that final bedtime down at about nine-thirty. Give them a few minutes to get over to Billy Watson's to do the deed. Say, nine forty-five. So somebody could have driven to Reed's in his car after he and Gordie left Billy Watson's and before the boys flattened the tires. What was I learning from all this?

Billy Watson wasn't simple, either.

"Let me ask around," he said after I explained what I was after.

There was a clunk that sounded like Billy dropping the receiver onto the bar, then I could hear Billy's voice off in the distance, rising and falling. I couldn't make out words. While I waited, I amused myself trying to identify the assorted clatters and clunks that reached me over the telephone. I had about decided Billy had forgotten me when I was proven wrong.

"Hello?" It was a whiny male voice, not Billy's.

"Hello, who's this?"

"Is this the police?"

"Yes, Officer Trudy Roundtree. Who's this?"

"Do I have to tell?"

"No, I guess not, but why wouldn't you want to?"

"Well, see, it's like I think I may know what you were asking Billy about, but I told my wife I was somewhere else."

"Let's don't worry about that, then. Just tell me what you know."

"What did you need to know?"

"Whatever you can tell me." This had better be worth waiting for.

"Billy said you was interested in knowing if anybody saw Reed Ritter's car somewhere besides Billy's parking lot after about nine o'clock Tuesday night."

"That's right. Or even if you didn't see it somewhere else, but can be sure it wasn't in Billy's lot."

"Well, I went by about nine-thirty and there wasn't any cars parked behind Billy's then. I'd seen Reed's car there before, but it wasn't there then."

"Okay. Good. Now—"

"Just hold your horses!"

"What?" But the whiny voice wasn't talking to me. I could hear several voices talking all at once, then Billy's voice above them all, then a different voice came on.

"Hi, honey, this is Luther Spivak. You're talking about a red Chrysler, right? 'Ninety-three? I saw one over by the animal hospital about nine o'clock Wednesday. That the one you're interested in?"

"It sure could be, Luther. Thanks. And, listen, Luther, thank Billy and Junior for me, too, will you?"

I hung up while Luther Spivak's laughter was still ringing. It felt very Hen-like, needling Junior Oglesby like that. I'd recognized that whine from his first word. Maybe I was getting to be a good ol' girl, in spite of everything. Heaven forbid.

I put the phone down and the light went off. I was gazing mindlessly at the blinking light on another line when Dawn came to the door and said, "I put the lab on hold."

"What? Great!" I grabbed it. "Trudy Roundtree here," I said to the lab. "What have you got for us?"

"This is Sonny Moseley, from the police lab in Statesboro," he said. "Thought you'd want to know we didn't raise any prints off that golf bag or any of the clubs."

"Oh. Well, thanks for the call." Until then, I hadn't realized how much I'd been counting on one cold, hard fact to organize all my information around. "I know if there'd been anything to find, you'd have found it. We appreciate y'all getting on it so quick. Have a nice Easter."

"Don't you want to hear about the other stuff?"

"The other stuff?" What was he talking about? It dawned on me that the official voice of the police lab was teasing me.

"Y'all naturally didn't mess with it any more than you had to, so you probably didn't know there was one of those little fire resistant boxes in the bottom of the golf bag."

I cleared my throat and tried to sound casual. "Oh? And what was in it?"

Sonny Moseley laughed. "Well, I won't say it was porn, exactly, but there's lots and lots of pictures of the same good-lookin' woman, and not all of them are the kind of thing you'd want your sister to pose for. Or you yourself, if you know what I mean."

The excitement I'd felt when he'd told me there was something else in the golf bag drained away. I tried to find some significance for this discovery. Had Reed been seeing Suzanne and maybe Molly and still needed dirty pictures to give him his jollies? What could this possibly have to do with anything?

"Well, thanks, Sonny. We appreciate your getting right on this. We'll send Dwight to pick it up, but don't you tell him what it is, now, or he might not turn it in."

"Yeah, I know Dwight," Sonny said, still laughing when we disconnected.

Another loose end I could try to tie up was Molly Pittman. She could tell me who she'd been talking to in the bushes at the Easter egg hunt—the same person who had left those footprints in the house. I told Dawn to send Dwight back to Statesboro for the stuff from the lab, and

I drove over to *The Beacon* office. I was in luck. Molly's car was parked outside.

The door was locked, Saturday not being a business day, so I rattled and knocked and called until Molly emerged from the back room, a pair of scissors in her hand, and opened the door for me.

"I need to talk to you a minute," I said, stepping inside.

"Sure. Come on back and sit down. I haven't been much good the last couple of days, so I thought I'd try to make up for it this afternoon."

"This'll just take a minute."

Molly looked only mildly interested. She obviously wanted to get back to work.

"Molly, I need to know who it was you stood and talked to behind the hedge at the courthouse this morning."

Molly dropped her scissors. She bent to retrieve them, and when she stood again, her eyes were bright with welling tears. "I talked to a lot of people this morning. I don't know where I talked to all of them."

I persevered. "But you do know who I mean."

She studied the scissors' blades, and with the day I'd been having, I tensed, just in case she decided to come at me with them. That's the kind of thing that'll happen to you when you start considering all your friends and acquaintances as murder suspects.

But Molly was considering baring her soul, not baring my bones. "Do I have to tell you?" she asked. "It's over and I'm so ashamed of myself I could die."

Oh. For some reason, it hadn't occurred to me that this mysterious person was also her lover. Egad. She'd said it was over and she was ashamed, so I took the risk that the news he was a murder suspect would incline her to name him rather than otherwise. "Molly, whoever it was you were talking to may be the one who killed Reed."

A little fire came into Molly's eye. "You know, I could believe that. I'd even *like* to believe that. At least then the way he used me wouldn't seem so bad, in context. He wanted *The Beacon*'s endorsement."

"B.L. Dawson?" Of course! Wonderful! Whatever those pictures turned out to be, they'd provide a motive for him.

Molly interrupted my thoughts. "But I really don't think he could have killed Reed."

"Why not?"

"Because he was with me from before ten 'til after we heard the fire sirens."

"Are you sure? Absolutely sure?" I hated to give up on the significance of the footprints.

"Oh, yes. Believe me, we never met that I wasn't watching the time. I don't know what got into me. I'll have to leave town; I'll never be able to hold my head up again."

"Don't put yourself down. Everybody needs to hear some sweet talking once in a while, and needs to be able to believe it. Don't be so hard on yourself." I tried to lighten things up. "See? Now I know, and I'm not appalled or disgusted. Except about that alibi. You're sure he was with you from ten o'clock on?"

"Absolutely." Molly gave a lopsided smile. "Want me to lie? I'd be glad to." A little humor. A good sign.

"It's tempting. But then whoever really did it would get off."

"Let me know if you change your mind."

"You'll be okay, Molly. You are okay."

This must be how manic depressives feel, I told myself as I drove to Hen's to pick up Delcie. One minute depressed that what Sonny Moseley told me didn't prove anything; then elated because I was sure Molly could ID the killer. In the pits again based on Molly's ID and reluctant alibi for B.L.

While Teri and Delcie finished gathering up Delcie's Easter Sunday get-up, I re-capped for Hen, holding up a finger as I made each point. "One: Nita says Mark's bed buddy is a one-eared elephant, not a big green rabbit. Two: Junior Oglesby says Reed's car wasn't at Billy's at nine-fifteen; Luther Spivak says one like it was at the animal hospital about then or a little later. So, three: Vivi must have driven Reed's car to the animal hospital and then over to Reed's where she got the bunny. That all jibes because, four: it couldn't have been earlier than a few minutes before ten when Danny and David let the air out of the tires. And five: the mysterious footprints of the person who was in the house after the fire belong to B.L. Dawson."

I unfolded my remaining fingers one by one, slowly, and shook my head. "But I don't know where it takes us. I'd really like for it to be B.L. but, six: He has an alibi for the time the fire started, and no reason to kill Reed that I know of."

Hen frowned. "Can we be wrong about when the fire started?"

"Phil seems pretty sure."

"Fits with what I'd think, too." He frowned some more.

I yawned.

"Well, it's been a long day. Maybe it'll make more sense after a good night's sleep."

Teri appeared with a hanger which held the Delcie-sized ribbon and lace concoction she'd been working on for weeks. While Delcie said goodnight to her daddy, Teri said in a low voice, "I never want to let her out of my sight again after today, but Hen said there's no point in us scaring her if she wasn't already scared, and Delcie said a promise is a promise and I had promised."

I didn't have to say anything to that, because Delcie appeared with a smart-alecky grin on her face.

"I know where the mama cat is," she said.

TWENTY-TWO

DELCIE WAS ASLEEP and I was sitting at the dining table with a few of the cats, mulling over all my lists and time-tables, when I heard a car in the drive.

Before I could do more than feel a pang of regret that I'd never gotten around to learning to keep my doors locked, I heard heavy steps on the porch and the next thing I knew Hen was settling himself in the chair across the table from me.

He got right to business. With an unfathomable look on his face he slipped a manila envelope onto the table and said, "Dwight just brought these by. Thought you'd want to see 'em."

"I've never been a big porn fan," I said.

"Take a look, anyway, in the line of duty," he told me. "I'll go get myself a cup of coffee. Got any pie?"

He always assumes people want to feed him. "There's a jar of instant coffee next to the microwave," I said inhospitably, and turned my attention to the envelope. As Hen ambled off to rummage through my pantry, I began to look at the pictures.

After a glance at the first one, my interest no longer had to be faked. Whatever I'd expected, it wasn't this. Sonny Moseley was right about you not wanting your mama to see them, especially if you were one of the subjects. But Sonny didn't know the woman.

I took my time going through them, trying to be objective and analytical about what they might mean to our investigation. Most naked bodies aren't all that gorgeous.

Granted, these weren't supposed to be glamour shots, and the grainy photography didn't enhance the natural beauty of the subjects. Phil would have sneered at the quality of the prints and the composition, but there was no ambiguity about the content. There was a joyless, mechanical feel to them, as there is in a lot of pornography, that I find more sad than erotic.

I could smell real coffee making in the kitchen. The hum of the microwave told me Hen had found the peach cobbler in the back of the refrigerator and was helping himself. He didn't ask if I wanted any, which was just as well. I was beginning to feel a little sick.

There were eighteen photos. At first glance, it looked like Vivi was with a different man in each of the photos, but, to be fair, some of them might have been repeaters. It was hard to tell. Strictly speaking, they probably weren't all pornographic, either, but even in the ones where it mattered which end was up it was clear that the setting was not a tea party. I remembered Phil saying that if anybody in the Ritter-Dawson marriage had been running around it was more likely to be Vivi than Reed. She always thought she could get away with anything. Uh-huh.

From this evidence—there was a report from a private investigator in Savannah as well as the photos—she'd been having lots of fun and Reed had known all about it. Befuddled by this turn of events as well as the long, long day, I was slow to work my way through it all. When I looked up, Hen was standing in the doorway with a bowl of steaming cobbler in one hand and a coffee mug in the other. "Want some coffee?" he asked.

"No." But I didn't want him to see me off balance. "How do you suppose he got this picture?" I asked, holding up one of the more confusing ones.

"You shouldn't bother your pretty little head about such sordid things," he said. "He was a trained professional. Let it go at that."

I batted my eyelashes at him and let the photo drift back into the pile with the others.

"Any ideas?" he asked.

Taking it slowly, I said, "From the date on the detective's report, I'd say this could explain why Reed divorced Vivi and how he was able to get away with it."

"But that's old stuff," Hen said. "Why was he keeping it so handy?"

"Handy but hidden," I pointed out. "Obviously, he still had some use for it," I continued. "It had gotten him the divorce he wanted. Leverage. For? Hen, I've got it. Suzanne. He'd fallen in love and wanted a fresh start. He wanted to leave Ogeechee—maybe wanted to take Mark with him. But the Dawson's wouldn't want that, and B.L. certainly wouldn't help. Except for leverage again."

Hen nodded and slurped at the hot coffee. "Vivi?" he asked between slurps.

But I was tired of acting like an eager student. I went to the kitchen for a cup of my own coffee so I could slurp back. "What do you think?" I asked, back at the dining table.

"Reed blackmailing Vivi? Hard to picture."

We slurped some more.

"It fits B.L. better," I said. "Just like everything else."

"How?"

Oh, well. "Say it was B.L. who didn't want this publicized in the first place, not Vivi. Vivi's style would have been to tell Reed to publish it all in the *Beacon*. B.L. is more concerned with reputation. So, three years ago, Reed used this to get B.L. to help expedite the divorce."

"If Vivi married Reed in the first place to rile her

daddy, Reed probably didn't need all this ammunition to get away from her," Hen opined.

"But he might have needed it to help his position with Mark," I suggested. "And now it would matter to B.L. even more since he's thinking of running for a state office."

"That would account for why B.L. kept Reed on as his accountant and also be one more reason Vivi won't cut B.L. any slack. She'd probably have enjoyed the notoriety. It fits right in with her image," Hen said.

"Okay. So it's B.L. And he decided to put an end to the blackmail, so he killed Reed, but then he couldn't find the pictures, so he set fire to the place, hoping to burn them up."

"But thanks to Miss Sarah, Phil and his boys got there too soon."

"And he had to go back later and look for it again."

"And he left footprints."

"But no fingerprints."

"Because he was smart enough to know a missing golf club might call attention to itself."

Was it just because I was so tired that we reminded me of a comedy routine? "But, Hen, B.L. has an alibi for when the fire started."

"I think we've had this conversation before," Hen said. "Maybe what we need is a good night's sleep."

"That won't help me. I'm sleeping with Delcie, remember?" But he knew I wasn't complaining.

TWENTY-THREE

ON SUNDAY MORNING, I got up early enough to put my raspberry jello salad together so it would have plenty of time to set up by mealtime. The kettle was just beginning to sing when a rumpled Delcie appeared in her pajamas, clutching a cellophane-wrapped Easter basket.

"Look! Look what the Easter bunny brought me!"

"Well, what is that?" I asked, just as though I'd never seen it before.

"It's an Easter basket," Delcie explained. "And it has candy in it." She began tearing at the cellophane.

"Hold it there, dumpling. Your mama would never let you spend the night with me again if she found out I let you have candy for breakfast."

"How would she find out?"

"One of us would be sure to tell her, wouldn't we? So you'd better leave that covered up 'til after you've had a bowl of cereal. Okay?"

She made a face but obediently climbed into a chair and waited while I set a bowl and spoon and the orange juice on the table in front of her. Then I stepped into the pantry and we played the cereal game.

"We've got All Bran," I called.

"I don't like bran," Delcie called back.

"We've got Raisin Bran."

"I don't like bran."

"We've got Oat Bran."

"I don't like bran."

"We've got Bran Flakes."

"I don't like bran."

We settled, as always, on Rice Krispies, which is all I stock and which Delcie likes doused in orange juice instead of milk and sugar.

"What're you doing?" Delcie asked between spoonfuls.

"Making the salad for later."

"Can I help?"

"Finish your cereal and I'll let you fancy up the ham."

"Why are you putting ice cubes in it?"

"To cool off the Jell-O before I add the fruit."

"Why do you boil it if you want it cool?"

"Why do you have so many questions?"

"I don't know. Why?"

"I don't know why. It just doesn't work if you don't start with boiling water. You go ahead and eat now."

Delcie finished the cereal and drank the leftover orange juice from the bowl while I made criss-cross slices all over the ham and smeared it with a paste of brown sugar and mustard.

"I'm ready to help."

"Here you go." I handed her the box of cloves. "Stick one of these everywhere you see an x."

We worked in contented silence for a bit, Delcie intent on getting a clove exactly where the knife strokes crossed; I equally intent on not splashing red Jell-O when I put raspberries into it.

"All done," she announced.

I studied the ham. "Good work, Delcie. Now, if you'll wipe off the counter, we'll be finished." I watched while she followed my instructions, as carefully as though the fate of the world depended on it.

"Great. Now stick the spoon in the dishwasher. Oh, oh! That won't do! Hang the dishrag there on the rod."

Delcie had dropped the cloth onto the top of the stove when she finished wiping the cabinet.

"Delcie, honey, it's a real bad idea to leave things on the stove like this. The burner might be on and set it on fire."

"It wasn't on. It's red when it's on."

"It could be on just a little, not enough for you to see. Or somebody might turn it on later."

"Then it would be their fault, if they turned on the stove when there was something on it to catch fire."

"No, it would be your fault for being careless, and I'd come after you, and get you, and—"

"Get all my sugar?" Delcie lowered her chin to make her throat disappear.

"Oh, I would definitely get all your sugar and I wouldn't leave any for your daddy or your mama and they'd be so mad they'd—"

"Turn into Jell-O?"

"They'd turn into Jell-O! And all because you left an old rag on the stove! So hang it up where it belongs and then run and start getting dressed. I'll come braid your hair as soon as I tend to this."

Delcie hung the cloth on the rack and skipped off, leaving me to finish the preparations. Thank God she was still so innocent that the idea of a fire was remote and purely theoretical and didn't have anything to do with the murder of somebody she knew.

I calculated the baking time for the ham, and concentrated on setting the timer. I don't do so much cooking that it's automatic with me, and one time I had it all set, but forgot to push the button that actually starts it, so I came home to an uncooked roast. As I was making sure I had everything right, an idea struck me. I started over, re-set the timer just a few minutes ahead, pushed the "do it!'' button, and opened the oven door. Would it come on? Would it come on with the oven door open?

I was gazing at the heating element when Delcie spoke from the doorway. ''You're dawdling,'' she said accusingly.

''No, I'm working.''

''It looks like dawdling to me,'' she said in her mother's voice. ''We're going to be late. I'm ready for you to help me.''

''Come here. I'll do your braids in here.'' I brushed her hair and began sectioning it off to braid, keeping one eye on the oven.

The heating coil began to glow. Would it work like that on all stoves, or just some stoves? I wondered. My fingers were busy in Delcie's golden hair, my brain, unfortunately, was in Reed's blackened kitchen. Where had I been lately that I saw a stove just like the one in Reed's house?

I gave Delcie's finished braids a tug and said, ''I won't be able to go to church with you, Sweetie. I'll have to drop you off. I've got to go to work.''

Being Hen's daughter, this is something Delcie's used to hearing. Except for making a face very much at odds with her charmingly feminine little dress, she didn't complain.

TWENTY-FOUR

THE TOWN WAS QUIET, like it is on most Sunday mornings. With nothing going on even at the post office, anybody who doesn't get up to go to church stays in bed. There's nothing else to get up for.

This Easter morning, with the sun shining and the azaleas blooming in every shade of pink all over town, was prettier than most Sundays, but I was having a hard time appreciating it. Peace and beauty don't offer protection against ashes and violent death and if my hunch panned out I was on my way to confront a murderer.

I dropped Delcie at the church in the middle of a bunch of other ribbon and lace concoctions. As I drove away I could hear the piano and organ starting up for Sunday School, then the congregation's voices singing, "Up from the grave he arose (he arose!) with a mighty triumph o'er his foes!" I felt a pang when I realized I was trying to pick Grandma's distinctive wavery alto out of the voices. Well, she was gone, and Zach was gone, and Reed was gone. I guess there's more than one way to triumph over the grave—making peace with Teri and getting on with living was one; arresting Reed's killer would be another.

I made my way to Cabana Place hoping Mrs. Edmunds was either a heathen or a tardy churchgoer, and I was in luck.

For once, she didn't seem to be keeping an eye on the street. When I tapped on her front door it took a minute for it to open and when it did it was to reveal a totally unexpected scene.

Mrs. Edmunds was more animated than I'd ever seen her. Without so much as a "good morning, how are you" she motioned me inside and hurried to close the door and rush back to her kitchen.

"I'm fixin' the agents some breakfast," she said. The agents were doing better than I had for breakfast. It looked like scrambled eggs with cheese mixed in.

"Are they working out okay?" I asked.

"My goodness yes! They roam—or maybe you'd say they're on patrol—all night long, when they aren't right in bed with me, and I haven't had any more trouble! They're amazing!"

I didn't want to think about what kind of trouble she might have if her landlord had a rule about pets, but I figured we'd cross one bridge at a time.

One of the agents, A.D. if I remembered what I'd called them, was swishing back and forth against Mrs. Edmunds' legs as she stirred the eggs. Those two stray cats probably thought they'd died and gone to heaven.

"I came to ask a favor, Miz Edmunds," I said.

Her face fell and she put a hand on her heart. "You aren't going to take them away just because I haven't had any more trouble are you? The aliens might come back if they weren't here!"

"Oh, no." Even if that had been my plan, I could never have kept to it after seeing the stricken look on her face. "They're yours for as long as you want them. Permanent assignment."

Tears of relief came into her eyes and I judged it a good time to ask my favor.

"Could you do without the control knob from your oven for a little while?" I asked. Understandably, she looked puzzled. I didn't see any point in trying to explain to her, and I couldn't bring myself to tell her I thought aliens might be using it. "Just something I need to check out," I explained feebly. "I'll get it back to you later today. All right?"

Without a word she smiled and stood aside so I could pull it off. I think I could have taken anything else she had, as long as I left those cats.

Three minutes later, I was in Reed's burnt-out kitchen holding my breath while I tried to slide Mrs. Edmunds' oven knob onto the protruding spike on his stove, where the original plastic knob had melted away. Yes! The position where it fit said "Time Bake." All our careful time tables didn't mean a thing. B.L. could have set the timer to come on whenever he wanted it to.

That's when I called Hen. "Don't bother putting on your Easter bonnet," I said. "I know how B.L. did it."

Hen was waiting for me at the intersection of the highway and Lake Loop. We pulled into the Dawson driveway together just as B.L.'s shiny black Chrysler was trying to pull out. B.L. glided to a stop. He didn't seem alarmed at the sight of us, only mildly irritated.

"What can I do for y'all this morning? I hope it'll be quick; I'm supposed to usher this mornin'." He was spiffed up for Easter, with a white carnation in his buttonhole. Bonnie, in what I assumed was a new beige suit, didn't even look interested, merely vaguely polite.

"We won't be quick enough to suit you, I'm afraid." Hen said. "B.L., it is my duty to inform you..." He stopped and nodded at me, giving me the chance at last to Mirandize a Dawson and mean it.

"B.L. Dawson, I charge you with the murder of Reed Ritter. You have the right to remain silent. If you make a statement it can be used against you in a court of law. You have the right to consult an attorney and to have the attorney present. If you cannot afford an attorney, one will be appointed for you by the state."

B.L. looked from me to Hen and back in a very convincing show of amazement. "I hear you, but I don't understand you. You're accusing me of killing Reed? You hear that Bonnie?" I imagine Bonnie was supposed to register sympathetic outrage, but her look of vague politeness merely gave way to one of vague confusion.

"I don't know what you think you're up to, but you're both putting your jobs on the line here," B.L. said conversationally. "Everybody knows I didn't particularly like Reed, but I didn't kill him. Didn't have any reason to."

"Tell him, Trudy," Hen said.

I nodded and swallowed. "Here's the way it is, Mr. Dawson: Reed was blackmailing you. We don't have to go into the details about that," I added, in case Bonnie was more alert than she seemed. "You killed him, but you couldn't find what you were looking for, so you set fire to the house and hoped everything would burn up and the whole thing would pass for an accident."

B.L. smiled and ran his palms down the front of his spiffy new Easter jacket. Never buy a car from a man who does that. "Trudy, honey, what makes you think I'd pay anybody blackmail? He could do whatever he wanted to with those pictures and it wouldn't hurt me. You've got a real good imagination, though, I'll give you that. That's what comes of goin' off to the big city, I guess. Not that it doesn't make an interesting story."

"Story? I'll admit I come from a line of storytellers, but this isn't one of Hen's tall tales. And you're going to have to come up with a pretty good story of your own to explain all that."

"I don't have to explain anything. Innocent until proven guilty. And you can't prove anything. You say

Reed was trying to blackmail me? He showed me some pictures, but I didn't want to buy 'em. You say somebody killed Reed and set his house on fire? I say I was somewhere else when that fire started—about eleven o'clock Tuesday night, wasn't it?''

As though he didn't know. "I've already spoken to your alibi, Sir Galahad, and you're right. She verifies that you were with her. But you didn't have to be anywhere near Reed's place when the fire started. You could have killed him any time after nine-thirty and set the oven to come on and ignite those boxes and rags whenever you wanted it to. You set it up for when you knew you'd be somewhere else. Alibi doesn't come into it.''

"And you're purely gonna love this part," Hen told him. "We might never have found the pictures that give you a motive if you hadn't gone back to look for them when the place didn't burn plumb to the ground. You left footprints. We know you were in the house after the fire. That'll take some explainin'.''

If I hadn't been sure before, the fleeting look on B.L.'s face at that news would have convinced me. But he hadn't been a car salesman for all those years without learning how to sound sincere. "I don't know what you're talking about. This is all circumstantial and could fit anybody in town as well as it fits me.''

That was bluster and he had to know it. "I do believe we'll make it stick," Hen said.

"I want to talk to my lawyer. Huckabee, you better have some job skills I don't know about, 'cause you are flat on the verge of losing the job you've been holding down.''

Hen wasn't worried. "Your lawyer? You mean Ron? Nothing against Ron, but it's gonna take somebody a sight smarter than he is to do you any good on this. Why don't we go on down to my office and get started on all the paperwork and he can meet us there.''

Hen handcuffed B.L., which was probably unnecessary, but I'm sure gave him a great deal of pleasure, and left for the station. I stayed with Bonnie. It was harder to know what to do with her. She said she'd just sit there and wait for Ron and Nita to come home from church, but I didn't want to leave her alone. Finally, I called Vivi, figuring it was a safe bet she wouldn't be up and at church. I think it woke her up. When I told her it was an emergency and made it clear that it was her mother and not her father who needed her, she said she'd be right there.

It seemed like a long wait, since Bonnie, never sparkling company, was more listless than usual. I convinced her we'd be more comfortable in the house and she led the way between the white columns into a marble-floored entry hall and on into the living room.

Reed had definitely married up. This room was so spacious two loveseats, four wing-back chairs and an assortment of smaller chairs and several tables cluttered with hand-painted china, seemed to be adrift in a sea of pile. The room was practically colorless except for the glowing cherrywood tables and wood accents on the upholstered furniture. The walls, carpet, and draperies were of a shade that might have been called sand. The velvet of the loveseats and side chairs was a shade or two darker, maybe ecru. The china and a half dozen petit-point pillows, all delicate and pale, provided the only break in the monochrome. Sheer curtains (cream) were pulled across the front windows, diffusing and softening the outlines and colors of the pines outside. It could have been a page from a Homestead House catalog or a feature in *Southern Liv-*

ing. It was clearly Bonnie Dawson's room, and she was practically invisible in it.

"What's going to happen to B.L.?" she asked, her eyes focused on something on the other side of the sheer, cream-colored curtains. Not "Do you really think he did it?" or "I don't think he could have killed Reed" or even "You'll never convict B.L. Dawson of anything in this county."

"It's a little early to say," I told her. Sure as I was that he had murdered a helpless drunk in cold blood, it didn't seem necessary or tactful right then to hammer on the thought.

Bonnie picked up a petit-point pillow and hugged it. "Maybe Vivi will come back, with Mark," she said.

"Maybe," I said and that was the extent of our conversation.

Vivi was there within fifteen minutes, with Mark. She sped past the circle drive in front and came in through the kitchen at the back, calling, "Mama? Mama? What is it?"

Bonnie didn't seem eager to explain things, so I did, trying to speak in language Mark might not understand. "Hen's got B.L. over at headquarters."

"What?"

"Reed."

Nothing slow about Vivi. She turned without another word, yanking Mark with her, and in a minute I heard the TV from a back room. She returned without Mark, but with an attitude, exactly the attitude I'd have expected—cynical denial.

"You're out of your mind," she said. "Why in the world would B.L. kill Reed?"

I could have said something like, "It will all come out at the trial," but I said, "It looks like Reed was blackmailing him. Reed wanted to get married again and leave town and he wanted B.L. to finance him.''

"He must have thought he had something good.''

"I guess he did.''

"But B.L. would have either paid him or, more likely, told him to take a hike. Why would he kill him?''

"Maybe Reed wouldn't give up the pictures.''

"Pictures? They must have been some pictures.'' She looked amused.

"Pictures of you.''

"Pictures of me? I don't get it.'' She looked puzzled. "If it had something to do with me, how do you know I didn't do it?''

"You could have,'' I admitted. "You were there. Don't look so surprised, we've checked up on everybody. You were there, between nine and ten, probably on your way to the animal hospital, and you drove Reed's car.''

"I was there, I admit that. I wanted to ream him out for promising Mark he'd pick him up and then not doing it, but he was out when I got there. Like a light. Dead drunk. Or maybe already dead, for all I know.''

"Is that when you got Mark's Easter bunny, for him?''

"I never saw that hideous thing 'til I picked Mark up for the Easter egg hunt. And I didn't kill Reed.''

"No, B.L. killed him, and when he found out the house didn't burn all the way down, he went back, trying to find the photos because he knew they'd give him a motive for the murder.''

"Looking for photos in a dead man's house doesn't mean he committed murder.''

"No, but—''

Suddenly, Mark was in the doorway, dragging that green bunny. We all fell silent and watched as he climbed up in the chair with Bonnie, dragging the bunny with him.

He whispered something in his ear, and she whispered back, smiling fondly at him, "Shh, it's a secret."

I couldn't help noticing it was Mark's grandmother, not his mother, he went to.

"It was those same pictures, Vivi. From the divorce," Bonnie said, indicating she'd been following the conversation, startling me. She's so easy to overlook.

"Oh. Well, that was old news. B.L. certainly wouldn't have paid him for them."

"He said he'd use them to get custody of Mark if B.L. didn't give him money." She patted her grandson's arm.

"Mark's not going anywhere, Mama. It'll be okay."

Vivi glared at me as though this was all my fault.

DISMISSED, I WENT to the station to see how Hen and B.L. were coming along.

It was hours later, after B.L. had been well and truly—but not quietly—remanded to the custody of the common jail, when Hen looked at me and smiled. "What're we having for dinner and do you reckon they saved us some?"

"I called and they waited," I said, feeling a deep, warm satisfaction at the thought of Aunt Lulu, Teri, Delcie, and the cats keeping the home fires burning for us—at my house.

"I don't know about the whole menu," I told Hen. "I was just responsible for ham and Jell-O. I'm sure the Jell-O is okay, and if the oven timer came on, the ham's ready, too."

I didn't want to think about the Easter dinner some of Ogeechee's other families—the Dawsons, the Conroys, or even the Pittmans—were having.

TWENTY-FIVE

WHEN HEN AND I finally got to my house, it was obvious that Teri, Aunt Lulu, and Delcie had been picking at the ham, which must have been done on time, and Teri'd had so much pent-up bustling to deal with that she'd rummaged in one of the closets and come up with silver candlesticks and serving dishes, so they'd whiled away the time polishing the tarnish off and—I'm guessing here—casting lady-like aspersions on the quality of my, and maybe even Grandma's, housekeeping. That's what family's for, isn't it?

Anyway, we had a delicious and beautifully presented dinner. Every dish—the ham, raspberry Jell-O, cheese grits, green beans, green salad, and onion pie, on the way to banana pudding and pecan pie—was well-spiced with "Well, I never" and "I declare" as we tried to digest everything that had happened in less than a week—the murder, Delcie's close call, the resolution of the murder case, and the drug bust.

"I just can't get over it," Aunt Lulu said, "B.L. Dawson! Is there any doubt that he did it?"

"None in my mind," Hen said. "No telling what story he'll tell in court, but we're satisfied. But Wonder Woman isn't the only one's been busy around here this week. Let me tell you about the holdup we had over at the Quik Stop."

"Henry, you're not trying to tell us there was time for anything else!" Aunt Lulu said, her face shining with pride and anticipation—and triumph, as she beat Teri out at spooning up more banana pudding for Hen.

From the tone of his voice—that deep, sing-songy, once-upon-a-time quality he could put on—we all knew we were in for one of Hen's tales. Hen would tell outrageous tales about people we didn't know, but wouldn't gossip about people we did. The photos of Vivi might or might not figure in B.L.'s trial, but they wouldn't figure in our dinner table conversation. I, for one, was ready for a tale, tall or short, as long as it didn't have anything to do with Reed Ritter or Gilbert Dalrymple.

"Yessir, we had us a robbery, and I think we did the poor feller a favor, lockin' him up. It's a pure kindness to put him away where he don't have to bump up against the slings and arrows of outrageous Ogeechee."

"Who was it?" Delcie asked. She's a good straight man.

"His name's William or Kenneth or something, but we call him Tiny," Hen said, "Because he's about six foot seven. A feller as conspicuous as he is shoulda found another line of work."

"What's conspicuous?" Delcie asked.

"Means he's real easy to recognize," Hen told her, indicating with his arms how conspicuous six foot seven would be. "Now, the first we knew about this robbery was when Cindy Moore, who's a clerk over there, called us up and told us Tiny had come in with a bag over his head and waving a big gun and robbed her. Naturally, being the finely trained investigators we are, our first question was how she knew it was Tiny if he had a bag over his head."

Hen interruped himself here to enjoy a guffaw before he let us in on the joke.

"Cindy knew it was Tiny because..." Hen went off in gales of laughter again.

"Because he's conspicuous," Delcie offered.

"Yes, darlin', that's exactly right. He's conspicuous. Besides being six foot nine inches tall—"

"You said six foot seven," Delcie insisted.

"Did I? That was a mistake. He's six foot nine. Anyway, a week or so back Tiny broke his arm and he was so proud of the cast he'd had all his friends sign it."

"Don't tell me he was wearing a cast?" Teri said.

"Yes, ma'am. Not only was he still wearing that cast, but Cindy's autograph was still on it."

We went off into gales of laughter at that, but Hen, waving his fork, tried to quiet us. "Wait! That's not the best part!"

When we finally subsided, he told us the best part. "About the mask, now. I told you he'd pulled a paper bag down over his face?"

We all nodded.

"Well, I didn't tell you this. Tiny can't see out of but one eye."

"Oh, no!" I could guess what was coming.

"Oh, yes! He'd only poked one hole in that bag!"

When we'd more or less recovered from that and were down to wiping our eyes and wheezing stage, Aunt Lulu turned to me.

"Trudy, you haven't told us how you knew to stop those drug dealers."

"Yes, indeed, our modest officer, Trudy Roundtree, here, has scored her first big drug bust. What am I doing talking instead of having another helpin' of banana puddin' while she tells you about it?" Hen shot me a warning glance, but I knew very well what was called for. As Teri politely elbowed her mother-in-law out of the way of the banana pudding, I took up the challenge.

"They were tooling along in a black stretch limo with bulletproof tinted windows. And it was the dark glass that got my attention. And there were four of 'em, all scar-faced and mean-looking enough to curdle milk. They shot through town at a hundred and twenty-five miles an hour and it was all I could do to get a roadblock set up to pull 'em up. They skidded the length of the football field when they stopped, tires screaming all the way."

Tires screaming. Something was wrong. My audience waited expectantly. I re-focused and went on with my story. "Did I say there were four? Actually, there were five. I was forgetting the one in the trunk, who popped out with an automatic rifle when we got 'em stopped."

Delcie still doesn't understand hyperbole. "No, Trudy! It was only two, the big mean one and the other one, the one that made him quit hurtin' me."

Bless her heart. She hadn't yet realized how Pint got Dalrymple to quit hurting her, or how much hurt Dalrymple had intended. "You're right, Sugar, there were really only two, but this makes a better story."

"Oh." That made sense to her and she went back to arranging the pecans she had pulled out of her pie into intricate patterns on her plate. She likes her pecan pie without pecans.

Tires screaming. Brakes squealing. Grinstead's parking lot.

"What's going to happen to Pint?" Teri asked, for once not fussing at Delcie's table manners.

"We'll have to see," Hen said. "Naturally, I put in a word for him."

"Asked for the Purple Heart, didn't you?" I suggested absentmindedly, trying to do my part.

"And the Victoria Cross," Hen confirmed.

Aunt Lulu sighed.

"Could we get the truth for once?" Teri asked.

"That's the truth," Hen told her, looking as innocent as possible for an overweight middle-aged man with banana pudding on his upper lip and the fading blotches of poison something-or-other on the rest of his face.

"But we want the real truth."

Suddenly the image of Dalrimple holding Delcie blended with the image of Mark holding his green Easter bunny and of Mark and Bonnie whispering together in Bonnie's colorless living room. Squeaky brakes. I knew what their secret was.

It all came together for me. "Hen, finish your dessert and wipe your face. We've got to go. It wasn't B.L."

I HAVE TO GIVE Hen credit for giving me credit. He didn't argue at all, just took one more bite of banana pudding and pushed away from the table. He doesn't know it, but that marked a milestone in our relationship, as far as I'm concerned.

As he drove out to Lake Loop, I explained. Even though, as it had turned out, the alibi times didn't make any difference, there were a couple of significant points we'd overlooked in the clutter of all the circumstantial evidence.

"Makes sense to me," he said, "but I'm easy. I'm gonna enjoy watching you explain it to the Dawsons."

He might have been giving me enough rope to hang myself, but I prefer to think he was giving me a chance to prove my mettle. We both needed mettle—like a steel rod, for instance—in our spines when we knocked on the back door at Ron Dawson's house, having had no response at B.L.'s. Fleetingly, thinking of my own family's habits, I wondered if Ron and Nita's had been the family gathering place before now, or if maybe today's events had brought about a shift in the family center. More shifts to come.

Nita answered the door and led us into the kitchen, a big, warm, modern interpretation of an old-fashioned country kitchen, with brick walls around built-in stove top, ovens, and refrigerator, and a braided rug under a big round oak table. Through the door to the dining room, we could see crystal and china gleaming under the dimmed lights from the chandelier overhead, all set and ready for a family feast. That answered my question about where the family tended to gather. Good ol' Nita—it couldn't have been good ol' Bonny or good ol' Vivi—had gone to some trouble to make things nice, but instead of a Norman Rockwell Easter dinner around that beautiful table, the food and the people were in the kitchen, Ron and Vivi trying to out-shout each other, and Danny and David flicking peas at Mark.

All sound and motion came to a stop when they caught sight of Hen and me. They weren't glad to see us, but at least we had their attention.

"Tell 'em," Hen said.

"We've come to tell you we're letting B.L. go," I said, pausing only briefly to give Hen a dirty look.

"I knew you couldn't hold him, you—" from Vivi, about the same time we got "False arrest. We'll sue you for—" from Ron, and a sorrowful sigh from Nita and a look, I swear, of disappointment from Bonnie. We ignored everything except Nita's, "Ya'll want some tea?"

"Just got up from dinner," Hen said, waving the suggestion away.

"I hope you enjoyed it," Vivi said.

"Thank you, we did. Nobody makes banana puddin'

like my mama," Hen told her complacently. I made a mental note of that, the first time to my knowledge Hen had ever gone on record on the subject, but I had more important considerations at the moment.

"We—I—did make a mistake in arresting B.L.," I said, and waited until they simmered down again. "I had forgotten a crucial point: There was a car at Reed's that night that hadn't been accounted for, a car with squeaky brakes. When I realized that, I knew there was someone I had overlooked, someone with all the motive B.L. had to kill Reed, someone who isn't tough enough to bluff like B.L. might have, someone who couldn't stand the idea that Reed might be able to take Mark away from her. Someone who didn't mind killing a man and burning his house down, but who wouldn't let a child's Easter bunny burn with it."

"Grandma saved my Easter bunny, but it's a secret," Mark said.

For once, Bonnie understood what was going on before anybody else did. Of course, she had a head start.

"Yes, precious," she said to Mark, before she turned to the rest of us. "It was so easy," she said quietly and dreamily. "So easy. I knew it was wrong, knew it even when I was doing it, but what he was doing was wrong, too. I just wanted to tell him that, but he was drunk when I got there, drunk and unconscious, and I saw how I could solve everything. So I picked up that golf club and hit him with it."

By now Ron had recovered his power of speech. "Hush, Mama. Don't say another—"

But Bonnie was so used to tuning out the rest of the world she might not even have heard. "It's not as though it hurt Reed. He was unconscious. It doesn't hurt if you're unconscious."

It doesn't hurt if you're unconscious. It might have been her philosophy of life.

Ron jumped back in. "That's enough, Mama." This time she obeyed, but I don't think it's because she heard him. I think she was through.

I won't pretend the next couple of hours were pleasant. Even if B.L. had been nice about it, which he wasn't, I hated letting him out and arresting Bonnie. A policeman's lot is not always an 'appy one.

TWENTY-SIX

I WAS FINALLY getting my day off.

I was stretched out in the sun, dozing in one webbed lawn chair with my feet in another one. A cat purred in my lap, another dozed in the shady patch under the chair.

In spite of all that had happened in the last few days—only days!—I felt good, better than I had in a long time. And sleepy.

My peaceful doze was brutally destroyed when a shadow fell across me, startling the lap cat, who dug his claws into my thigh as he leapt away. The under-the-chair cat joined him in a loud yeowl and a run for safety.

"Ow!" I jerked, unbalancing my chair. Struggling to recover my balance, I only succeeded in tangling my feet through the arms of the chair where they'd been resting. I landed on the grass with a thump that took my breath away.

"Oh, Lord." The voice was Phil Pittman's, and when I got myself right-side up, I was looking into Phil's troubled face. "I'm sorry, Trudy, are you okay? What's the matter with those cats, anyway? Let me help you up."

On my hands and knees by now, I waved off his help. I rolled to my feet and dusted at my slacks, massaging my thigh where the cat's claw had gone. "Nice to see you, Phil. What brings you around?"

His freckles blended into his blush. "I came to bring you something."

"That sounds interesting. You got time to sit a while? Have a glass of tea? I had two chairs here a minute ago."

"Sure," he said.

I went into the house for the tea and he straightened up the chairs, pulling one into the shade of the towering pecan tree. "Is this okay?" he asked when I returned with the tea. "You want yours in the sun? I burn easily, so I like the shade."

I handed him his tea. "It's fine. Thanks."

He picked up an envelope he'd dropped on the ground and turned it over and over in his hands.

"This is for you."

"Extra copies of the *Beacon* with my picture in it? You shouldn't have." He had given me a lot of career-enhancing publicity for my drug bust. "Phil, I don't know if I told you how much I appreciate your not making a lot of fuss in the paper about my part in the murder investigation."

"I figured a sensitive case like that, you might rather keep a low profile."

"Worse than that. I really wanted it to be B.L."

"Why were you so sure it wasn't?" He leaned forward, the picture of the entranced listener.

"Well, everything we'd thought pointed to B.L. also pointed to Bonnie, and once I thought about it, some of it fit her better. We'd assumed Reed had been black-mailing B.L., but B.L. would either have laughed at him or paid up, if it was only money Reed wanted, just for the sake of being rid of him. What Reed wanted was money and Mark. If he'd gone to court with those pictures, even in this county, he might have gotten sole custody of Mark. Bonnie wouldn't have been able to stand that."

"So all the business with the cars and the time tables didn't mean anything?"

"Yes, but not what we thought. It was Bonnie's brakes

that squealed, not B.L.'s. And she's the one who would know about an oven timer, not B.L. He was never home, and everybody assumed she'd be in bed—with a bottle— early every evening, so we all sort of overlooked the fact that she didn't really have an alibi.''

Phil was shaking his head.

"Don't you think it holds together?" I asked.

"It's all circumstantial."

"Yes, but very strongly circumstantial. Actually, it was that awful Easter bunny that pinned it down. Pint said he saw a booger at Reed's place about ten o'clock, a booger and a big new Chrysler. Well, B.L. had an alibi about ten o'clock. That booger was Bonnie, carrying that huge rabbit. Mark said his daddy gave it to his Gramma for him. Poor little thing, it's a good thing he's got Dr. Whittaker. This has got to be rough for him, losing his daddy, now his grandmother, the two people in the world who really seemed to care about him.''

"Maybe Vivi will settle down."

"And maybe the sports complex field will go in on Lake Loop, but I'll believe it when I see it."

"Do you think you could have proved your case if Bonnie hadn't admitted it?"

"Not for publication?"

"Between friends," he said.

"I don't know. I wish I could say yes, but I just don't know. I do know the whole thing made me appreciate how straightforward most crime is around here." Our near-miss with B.L. still rankled. Even though Hen didn't seem to be holding it against me, it rankled. B.L., naturally enough, did not turn into a paragon of sweetness and light when we released him. He took the line that we were wrong about him and we were wrong about Bonnie and we'd live to regret it. It couldn't have made him any sweeter-tempered to realize that she'd have been willing to let him take the rap. If it hadn't been for Bonnie's squeaky brakes, and that bunny, I'd still be trying to tag him for it. I didn't enjoy thinking about it. "Did you say you brought me something? Would that be it you're holding?"

"Oh, yes." Phil leaned back, no longer the avid listener but the nervous newsman I'd come to know. He thrust the envelope at me.

From the envelope I drew a photograph. It was a framed enlargement of the telltale footprints in the ashes of Reed Ritter's kitchen, mine and Phil's and Hen's and B.L.'s. I looked at Phil and raised my eyebrows in question.

"I thought you might like a souvenir of a major clue in your first murder case. Even if it turned out not to be the major clue we thought it was."

"It's a great photograph," I said.

"That sounded sincere, but qualified," he said with a frown.

"Oh, the photograph is great. That's sincere. I guess it will keep me humble to have this reminder that what I thought was a major clue wasn't one after all."

"It was an important part of the whole puzzle, Trudy. And you did solve that mystery. It isn't any reflection on you that it didn't happen to solve the murder."

"I'll try to look at it that way. Okay, where do you think I should hang it? Not at the station. It would just get swallowed up. Maybe in the pantry. Or the hall. Yes, the hall. Someplace where I'll see it every day and it will keep me humble. I'll find a place."

Phil shifted in his chair and re-settled his glasses. "I have something else to ask you."

"Okay. What?" I closed my eyes and waited, turning

my face toward the sun, basking. "I've thought about this case so much I know all the answers."

"It isn't about the case. I just got a notice from a gallery in Atlanta that they're having a reception for the artist for their new show, an artist who does cats. I'm planning to go and since you seem to appreciate cats, I thought— I hoped—I wanted to ask if you'd like to go with me."

My eyes were wide open by the time he finished. I never knew Phil was partial to cats. Was this what Hen had warned me about? Sure sounded like it. So what?

Phil's face was frozen in a look of boyish expectation. "Of course, not everybody likes that kind of thing," he said.

"Sounds like fun to me," I said. "Atlanta, eh? Atlanta's a nice place to visit, even if I don't want to live there. When is it?" I decided not to torture him by asking, then, whether he had in mind to drive up and back in the same day. It's possible, but it makes a long day.

Phil blushed. "I thought we'd work out the details later. We've got a couple of weeks."

I was feeling so good I laughed out loud, and Phil joined in. By the time Phil left, the shade had moved enough that I had to move my chair again to put it in the sun. I stretched out again so I could bask better. I fell asleep wondering what we'd find to talk about on the way to Atlanta, but I didn't dream about anything.

FATAL FLAW

FRANK SMITH

AN INSPECTOR PAGET MYSTERY

What drove seventeen-year-old Monica Shaw to take her life with an overdose of insulin? The pain of being alone and unwanted for the holidays at Thornton Hill Girls' School— or something else? It's a Christmas murder for Detective Chief Inspector Neil Paget.

Neither the village of Shropshire nor Thornton Hill School can fully mask the secrets making the winter landscape icy and treacherous for Paget as he navigates the fear, desperation and dark deeds that hide the twisted motives of the innocent…to find the fatal flaw of a killer.

Available December 1999 at your favorite retail outlet.

Denise Dietz

**AN ELLIE BERNSTEIN/
LIEUTENANT
PETER MILLER
MYSTERY**

Throw Darts at a Cheesecake

Fat Free Murder

At the weekly meeting of Weight Winners, losing is everything. Group leader Ellie Bernstein herself has shed fifty-five pounds, along with a cheating husband and an unfulfilling life. But she quickly discovers losing weight is not only murder, it's downright lethal.

One by one, the group's Big Losers are being murdered. Is some jealous member of the Friday meeting a secret killer? Motive aside, Ellie's got to watch her back as well as her calories before she finds herself on the most permanent diet of all…death.

Available December 1999 at your favorite retail outlet.

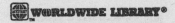